A STUDY IN RED (THE SECRET JOURNAL OF JACK THE RIPPER)

THE STUDY IN RED TRILOGY BOOK 1

BRIAN L PORTER

Dedicated to the memory of Enid and Leslie Porter,
to Juliet, and...to Sasha!

ACKNOWLEDGEMENTS 2020 UPDATED

2020

A Study in Red, The Secret Journal of Jack the Ripper was originally published in 2008, by the recently defunct Double Dragon Publishing. I was therefore extremely grateful to Miika Hanilla at Next Chapter Publishing, the publisher of over twenty of my more recent works, who agreed to publish new, updated versions of the three book in my Ripper trilogy, *A Study in Red, Legacy of the Ripper* and *Requiem for the Ripper* in addition to my novel *Pestilence*. Without Miika's help and confidence in my work, the four books would have been consigned to the annals of history and been unavailable to readers any longer.

I must also say a big thankyou to my researcher/proof-reader, Debbie Poole who has painstakingly helped to check and update the original manuscript.

And now, the original acknowledgements, which remain as relevant today as they were at the time of the original publication.

2008

In the course of writing 'A Study in Red' I was amazed at how many people became involved along the way. It is with them in mind that I take this brief opportunity to say thank you, for without their help and co-operation the story would never have been completed.

Much of the source material used as reference notes by the character of Robert in the following pages was derived from my own references to the most comprehensive website on the Jack the Ripper case I could find. I thus convey my thanks to Stephen P Ryder for his generous permission to use the www.casebook.org name in the text of the novel, and as a source of reference. Equally, thanks are due to Edward McMillan of the Police Information Centre of the now defunct Lothian and Borders Police, (Now Police Scotland), for his invaluable help in tracing the history of the historical City of Edinburgh Police force. His knowledge of the subject was invaluable in putting together an important section of the story.

I would never have reached the final page of the book without the inestimable patience and hard work of my own team of volunteer proof readers, who took it upon themselves to read, critique, and suggest changes to word or plot where they felt it necessary. So again, a big thank you to Graeme S Houston, editor of Capture Weekly Literary Journal, and to the late Malcolm Davies and Ken Copley, both sadly no longer with us, and to Sheila Noakes, your help was invaluable. The final reader of the raw proof of the book was my dear wife Juliet who has spent many lonely hours as I sat at work on the novel, then reading and correcting my errors, and has kept me going on the many occasions when I thought I'd never complete the work.

There have been others who have encouraged or given small 'sound bites' of help and advice along the way, and to all of them I also extend my gratitude. I hope the book does them all justice.

INTRODUCTION

The London of the 1880s differed greatly from the city of today. Poverty and wealth existed side by side, the defining line between the two often marked only by the turning of a corner, from the well-lit suburban streets of the middle-classes and the wealthy to the seedy, crime and rat infested slums, where poverty, homelessness, desperation and deprivation walked hand in hand with drunkenness, immorality, and crime most foul. In the teeming slums of the city by night the most commonly heard cry in the darkness was thought to be that of 'Murder!' So inured were the people who lived amongst such squalor and amidst the fever of criminal intimidation that it is said that, in time no-one took any notice of such cries.

It was into this swirling maelstrom of vice and human degradation, London's East End, that there appeared a malevolent force, a merciless killer who stalked the mean streets by night in search of his prey and gave the great metropolis that was London its first taste of that now increasingly common phenomenon, the serial killer! The streets of Whitechapel were to become the stalking ground of that mysterious and as yet still unidentified slayer known to history as *'Jack the Ripper!'*

AN EXTRACT FROM THE JOURNAL

Blood, beautiful, thick, rich, red, venous blood.

Its' colour fills my eyes, its' scent assaults my nostrils,

Its taste hangs sweetly on my lips.

Last night once more the voices called to me,

And I did venture forth, their bidding, their unholy quest to undertake.

Through mean, gas lit, fog shrouded streets, I wandered in the night, selected, struck, with flashing blade,

And oh, how the blood did run, pouring out upon the street, soaking through the cobbled cracks, spurting, like a fountain of pure red.

Viscera leaking from ripped red gut, my clothes assumed the smell of freshly butchered meat. The squalid, dark, street shadows beckoned, and under leaning darkened eaves, like a wraith I disappeared once more into the cheerless night,

The bloodlust of the voices again fulfilled, for a while...

They will call again, and I once more will prowl the streets upon the night,

The blood will flow like a river once again.

Beware all those who would stand against the call,
I shall not be stopped or taken, no, not I.

Sleep fair city, while you can, while the voices within are still,

I am resting, but my time shall come again. I shall rise in a glorious bloodfest,

I shall taste again the fear as the blade slices sharply through yielding flesh,

when the voices raise the clarion call, and my time shall come again.

So I say again, good citizens, sleep, for there will be a next time...

To my dearest nephew, Jack,

This testament, the journal, and all the papers that accompany it are yours upon my death, as they became mine upon my father's death. You Aunt Sarah and I were never fortunate enough to have children of our own, so it is with a heavy heart that I write this note to accompany these pages. Had I any alternative, I would spare you the curse of our family's deepest secret, or perhaps I should say, secrets! Having read what you are about to read, I had neither the courage to destroy it, nor to reveal the secrets contained within these pages. I beg you, as my father begged me, to read the journal and the notes that go with it and be guided by your conscience and your intelligence in deciding what course of action to take when you have done so. Whatever you decide to do dear nephew, I beg you, do not judge those who have gone before you too harshly, for the curse of the journal you are about to read is as real as these words I now write to you.

Be safe, Jack, but be warned.

Your loving uncle,

Robert

ONE
A REVELATION

MY GREAT GRANDFATHER WAS A PHYSICIAN, with a penchant for psychiatry, as were my grandfather and my father and it was always a given thing that I would follow in the family tradition, as, from childhood, I wanted nothing more than to follow in my forebears footsteps, to alleviate the suffering of the afflicted, to help ease the mental pain experienced by those poor unfortunates so often castigated and so badly misunderstood by our society. My name? Well, for now let's just call me Robert.

My father, whom I admit to idolizing for as long as I could remember, died just over four months ago, a sad waste, his life snuffed out in the few seconds it took for a drunk driver to career across the central reservation of the dual-carriageway he was driving along, and to collide head-on with Dad's BMW. By the time the ambulance reached the scene of the crash, it was too late, there were no survivors!

Dad was buried in our local churchyard, beside my mother, who passed way ten years ago, and the private psychiatric practice I had shared with him for so long became my sole domain. As a mark of respect, I took the decision to leave Dad's name on the brass plaque that adorns the pillar beside the front door. I saw no reason to remove it. A week after the funeral, I was surprised to receive a phone call from Dad's solicitor, saying that he was in possession of a collection of papers my father had bequeathed to me. This was strange, as I thought that the will had been straight forward, everything shared equally between my brother Mark and myself. I had received Dad's share of the practice, Mark a substantial and equivalent cash sum. As I drove to the solicitor's office I wondered what could be of such importance that Dad had left it to me in such a mysterious fashion.

As I drove away from the solicitor's office, I stared at the tightly bound sheaf of papers, wrapped in brown paper, and tied up with substantial string, that now resided on the passenger seat of the car. All that David, the solicitor could tell me was that Dad had lodged the papers with him many years earlier, together with instructions that they were to be passed to me alone, one week after his funeral. He told me that Dad had placed a letter in a sealed envelope that would be on top of the package when I opened it. He knew nothing more. Knowing there was little I could do until I got home, I tried to put the package out of my mind, but my eyes kept straying towards the mysterious bundle, as if drawn inexorably by some unseen power. I was in a ferment of expectation as I drew up on the gravel drive of my neat detached suburban home, I felt as if Dad had something important to relate to me, from beyond the grave, something he obviously hadn't been able to share with me during his lifetime.

My wife, Sarah, was away for the week, staying with her sister Jennifer, who had given birth to a son four days after Dad's funeral. Jennifer had been married for three years to my cousin Tom, a brilliant if somewhat erratically minded computer engineer, who she had met at a dinner party at our house. Sarah had been reluctant to leave me so soon after Dad's passing, and the funeral, but I insisted that she go and be with Jennifer at such an important and emotional time. I'd assured her that I'd be fine, and, as I locked the car and made my way to the front door of our home, I actually felt relieved that I was alone. Somehow, I felt that the papers I now carried under my arm were reserved for my eyes only, and I was grateful to have the time to explore their contents in private. I still had the rest of the week off, having paid a locum to baby-sit the practice during my official period of mourning, so the next few days were mine to do with as I chose.

Little did I know that, as I closed the heavy front door behind me, I was about to enter a world far removed from my cosy suburban existence, a world I had barely perceived from my history lessons at school. I was about to be shocked, all my conceptions of truth and respectability were to be rocked to the very core, though I didn't know it yet.

I quickly changed into casual clothes, poured myself a large scotch, and retired to my study, eager to begin my investigation into Dad's strange bequest. After seating myself comfortably in front of my desk, I took a sip of the warming, golden liquid in my glass, then, taking a pair of scissors from the desk, I tentatively cut the string from around the bundle of papers. Sure enough, as the solicitor had indicated, there on top of a very thick loosely bound stack of papers was a sealed brown envelope, addressed to me, in the unmistakable handwriting of my father. I held it in my hand for a good minute or so, then, as I looked down and saw that my hand was trembling with anticipation, I reached out with my left hand for the solid silver paper-knife in the shape of a sword that Sarah had bought me for my last birthday. In one swift movement I slit the top of the envelope, reached inside and removed the letter within. The letter, handwritten by my father and dated almost twenty years earlier was a revelation to me, even though, as I read, I was still unaware of the true significance of the loosely bound papers that accompanied it. The letter read as follows:

To my dearest son, Robert,

As my eldest son, and also my most trusted friend, I leave to you the enclosed journal, with its accompanying notes. This journal has been passed from generation to generation of our family, always to the eldest son, and now, as I must so obviously be dead, it has passed to you.

Be very careful, my son, with the knowledge that this journal contains. Within its pages you will find the solution (at least, a solution of sorts) to one of the great mysteries in the annals of British crime, but with that solution comes a dire responsibility. You may be tempted my son, to make public that which you are about to discover; you may feel that the public deserves to know the solution to the burning mystery, but, and I caution you most carefully, Robert, should you go public with the knowledge, you will risk destroying not only everything that our family has stood for through over a hundred years of medical research and progression in the field of psychiatric medicine, but you may also destroy the very credibility of our most cherished profession. Murder most foul Robert! It is of that most heinous crime that you will read, as I read following the death of your grandfather, and he also before me. But are there worse things than murder in this world? Do we have the right as doctors to make the judgments that the courts should rightly dole out? My son, I hope you are ready for what you are about to learn, though I doubt I was at the time I read the journal. Read it well my son, and the notes that go with it, and judge for yourself. If, as I did, you feel suitably disposed, you will do also as our family have always done, and keep the knowledge of its contents a closely guarded secret, until the time is right to pass it on to your own offspring. The knowledge is I fear the cross the family must bear, until one day, perhaps, one of us feels so ridden by conscience or some form of need for absolution, to reveal what the pages contain.

Be strong my son, or, if you feel you cannot turn the first page, go no further, reseal the journal in its wrappings, and consign it to a deep vault somewhere, let it lie forever in darkness, where perhaps it rightly belongs, but, if you do read the contents, be prepared to carry the knowledge with you for ever, in your heart, in your soul, but worst of all, in your mind, a burden of guilt that can never be erased.

You are my eldest son, and I have always loved you dearly. Forgive me for placing this burden upon you,

Yours with love
Dad

As I finished reading the letter, I suddenly realized that I'd been holding my breath, such was the tension I felt inside, and I took a deep breath and then sighed. The trembling in my hands had increased, and I reached for the bottle of amber liquid at the side of the desk and poured myself another large one. Suddenly, I felt as if whatever was contained within these papers lying unopened before me was about to irrevocably change my life, not outwardly perhaps, but I knew before I even looked at the documents that whatever was contained within these pages was obviously of grave significance. If not, why had my family gone to such pains to protect the secret contained within them? I gulped the scotch down, too fast, the liquid burned my throat, and I coughed involuntarily.

At this point of course, I had no idea what the papers contained, though my father's words had given me a sneaking suspicion that I knew where this was leading. Unable to wait any longer, I broke the tapes around the journal, and there it was, the family secret, about to be unveiled! The first sheet of paper, resting on top of the rest, was definitely old, and written in the typical copperplate handwriting of the nineteenth century. There was no date or address at the top of the paper, it seemed to be little more than a series of notes, there was no signature, nothing at all to identify the writer.

I read as follows: *How do I begin to relate all that has happened? Would anyone believe the incredible story? Is it the truth? Is he really the man? The journal could be the work of a clever man, an attempt to deceive those who read it, but no, I knew him too well, spoke with him too often. He was telling the truth! As for me, what of my part in all this? Am I guilty of complicity, or have I done the world a favour by my actions? That he will trouble the people of London no more is now certain. That he was deranged I could testify to myself, but what of proof? What of evidence? Apart from the ravings of the lunatic, all I have is the journal, and I had it too long, knew too much too soon, to bear the disgrace of admitting that I could have stopped it all if I had spoken sooner. Now I cannot speak at all for to do so would destroy me, my work, and my family. Who would understand that I held silent because I thought him mad, too mad to believe, and yet his madness was the very thing that drove him, and I should have believed? And when I did believe, what then? It was too late, I could do no more, God help me, I should have stopped him, stopped him right at the beginning when he told me, when he laughed and laughed and told me that no-one would ever catch him, why, oh why didn't I believe him then?*

After the most hideous death of that poor girl, Mary Kelly, I had to do something, and I did, but, knowing what I know, what I knew already, I should have acted sooner. May God forgive me; I could have stopped Jack the Ripper!

I was holding my breath again, and, as I exhaled, my eyes moved to the final note at the bottom of the page, seemingly written some time later than the rest of the notes, the writer's hand less bold, as though he were shaking as he wrote these final words.

Jack the Ripper is no more, he's gone, forever, and yet, I feel I am I no better than the monster himself? I swore an oath to save life, to preserve, not to destroy, I am naught but a wretched, squalid soul, as squalid as the streets he stalked in life, and will forever, I am sure haunt in death. I bequeath this legacy to those who follow me; judge me not too harshly, for justice may be blind, and I have acted for the best as I saw it at the time. I have despoiled my oath, his blood is mine, and that of those poor unfortunates, and I must bear what I have done within my heavy conscience and my aching heart for the rest of my days!

Jack the Ripper! I knew it, it had to be, just as surely as the page I'd just read had to have been written by my great-grandfather. I knew from our family history that my great-grandfather had spent some time as a consulting psychiatric physician at the Colney Hatch Lunatic Asylum during the 1880s, and it now seemed that he'd been privy to knowledge that the rest of the world had been seeking for over a century, or, at least, he believed himself to have been. Yet, what did he mean by the references to his complicity, what *action* had he taken?

Another sip of scotch, more fire in my throat, and I was ready to take the next step. I had to see the journal; had to know what my great-grandfather knew. If he'd solved the mystery of the ripper murders, why hadn't he revealed the truth? What could possibly have enticed him to keep silent about the most celebrated series of murders ever to strike at the heart of the great metropolis that was nineteenth century London? What part did he play in the tragedy, how could he, a respected physician and member of society have been complicit in the foul deeds perpetrated by Jack the Ripper? He was my great-grandfather after all, I refused at that point to believe that he could be in any way connected with the murders of those poor unfortunate women, and yet, in his own words, he'd stated that he could have stopped the Ripper. Again I asked myself, what could he have known, what could he have done? Looking at the loosely bound journal on the desk in front of me, I knew there was only one way I was going to find out!

TWO
THE JOURNAL BEGINS

FOREGOING the temptation to top up my by now half empty glass of whisky, (I'd decided a clear head would be imperative as I read the journal), I paused only long enough to ensure that both the front and back doors of the house were securely locked. Though not expecting any visitors this late in the afternoon, I wanted to ensure that no-one could walk in unannounced, and there was always Mrs Armitage from next door. She'd promised to 'keep an eye' on me for Sarah while she was away, and had developed the habit of knocking and entering before descending upon me with a plate of home-made scones or cakes or some other 'treat' she was sure I'd enjoy whilst on my own. Slightly overweight, a widow with more money than she could cheerfully spend, she appeared to want to alleviate her own personal boredom by 'cheering me up', as she put it. Not today thank you, Mrs Armitage!

Though I was sorely tempted, I resisted the urge to take the telephone off the hook, or to switch off my mobile. Sarah might try to call me, and, if she didn't get a reply, I was sure she'd call

Mrs Armitage and send her scurrying round to check on poor lonely little me! No, leave the phones on, safer by far.

I settled myself down once again in my chair and turned to the journal. I've referred to it as such because that's the way my father, and my great-grandfather referred to it, but, in truth, it wasn't so much a journal, as a collection of papers, punctured with a crude hole punch over a hundred years ago, and then bound together with tightly drawn tapes, or, perhaps, very stiff ribbons. After the passage of years it was hard to be sure what they were originally, and, after all, I'm a doctor, not an expert on antique book bindings.

There was no cover as such and no identifying title or name on the first page, but there were other sheets of paper protruding at various parts of the journal, (my great-grandfather's additional notes, I surmised, I'd read them as I got to them). "Jack the Ripper", I thought to myself, surely there was no-one in the civilized world who hadn't heard of the famed Whitechapel murderer, and here I was, about to be taken, perhaps too closely, into that dark world of shadows and brutality inhabited by that most infamous of serial killers, and yet, as I began to read that first, aged and wrinkled page I was convinced that my father and those before him had fallen for the literary rantings of a madman.

The journal began:

6ᵗʰ August 1888,

Ate a fine dinner, red wine, (blood), the tenderest veal, rare, (more blood), and the voices hissing at me through the gas mantle, the lights flickering, screaming, and ringing in my head. Blood! Let the streets run red with the harlots blood; avenge the pitiful wrecks brought to foul disease by the tainted blood. Spill the blood, the streets are mine, the blood shall be mine, they will know me, fear me, I am justice, I am death! What foul pestilence they spread, and I shall cause to die such evil that men shall raise my name on high! I hear the voices, they sing to me, ah, such sweet melodies, and always red, they sing of red, of whores and their foul-smelling wicked entrails, that I shall put aside forever.

The cheese was a little over-ripe, though the cigar my friend left on his last visit went admirably well with the after-dinner port. Very relaxed as I sat enjoying faint warmth of the evening.

I hear the voices, and I must reply, but the only reply they want to hear is the sound of death, the drenching of blood on stone, yes, they need me, I am the instrument of fear, red, red blood, running like a river, I see it, I can almost taste it, I must go, the night will be upon me soon, and the cigar smoke hangs like a fog in the room. My, but the port is good, I swill it round the glass, and it is the blood, the blood that will flow as I begin my work, such fine port, such a good night for killing.

***

7^{*th*} *August* 1888

'Twas a fine clear night for the job to be done. Had no real good tools to work with, kitchen and carving knives, very poor show. The whore was waiting, eager, needing me. So gullible as to invite me indoors, did her on the first-floor landing, started and couldn't stop. She was so surprised, oh yes, her face, that look, pure terror as the

knife slashed into her softly yielding flesh. First one
straight to the heart, she staggered, fell, and we set about
the work. I say we, for the voices were there with me,
guiding, watching, slashing and cutting with me. Lost
count of the number of times I cut the whore, she didn't
even scream, just a low gurgling as she expired in the
dark. Took care to purify the whore's breasts, her gut, her
vital parts. She'll spread no pestilence no more, the river
ran red, as they promised it would. I must take care the
next time; there was too much blood upon my self.
Lucky man, to have thought to remove my coat before I
began, had to burn a perfectly good jacket and fine
trousers this morning. Though no-one saw me when I
left, it was a messy job, I'll get good tools the next time,
better clothes for the job.

It was a good start though, of that I'm sure, and there'll
be more, so many more!

I had to stop and take a breath. Surely these were the
ravings of a total lunatic! There was a clarity of thought evident
in certain parts of the text, an almost urbane banality in the
references to relaxing with a cigar, the warmth of the evening,
and the casual references to getting 'better tools next time'.
Then the almost unbelievable savagery of expression in the
description of the death of that poor woman. Though short, it
was terrifying, chilling, the work surely of a man devoid of
reason or conscience. Even though these crimes had taken
place over a century ago, the first pages of the journal filled me
with a fear and dread as real as if I'd been there in London in
1888.

Though not a phrase we like to use in these enlightened
times, I had to think in terms of the times in which these crimes

took place, and I thought that this couldn't be right. Jack the Ripper, from what little I knew, had been clever, a master of concealment and bravado, these words couldn't be those of the Ripper, surely not! These were the words of a seriously disturbed individual, which, though the Ripper also had to have been similarly deranged, seemed to belong more in the realms of fantasy than reality. Could the writer have written this journal after the event, and, as many deluded souls have done through the years, imagined himself to be the notorious murderer. In other words, could this have been written by a seriously ill, delusional individual seeking to gain attention?

My own knowledge of the Jack the Ripper murders was scant at best, so, before continuing, I fired up my computer, and accessed the internet. There, I found a welter of sites offering information and speculation on the Ripper murders, and, I quickly printed off a couple of informative pieces, in the hope that they would be able to give me some useful points of reference as I progressed through what I thought of as the madman's journal lying on the desk before me.

Sure enough, there it was. In the early hours of the morning of the 7th August 1888, the body of Martha Tabram had been discovered on a first-floor landing of a tenement building at 37 George Yard. In total 39 stab wounds were discovered on her body, the majority of the damage having been caused to her breasts, belly, and private parts. It seems that, as the Ripper murders progressed, the killing of Martha Tabram was discounted by some as having been committed by the same man who killed the other, later victims. If my lunatic, (as I thought of him at the moment) had indeed been Jack the Ripper, then it was plain to see that Martha Tabram had perhaps been his first, tentative venture into the world of bloody murder. At this time however, the police and the public had no inkling of the carnage that was waiting in the wings, preparing to unleash itself upon the streets of Whitechapel. Of course, in 1888 forensic science was non-existent, the use of fingerprints for identification was still many years in the future, and the police were, in the case of poor Martha Tabram, virtually clueless. At the time of her death Martha was 39 years old, the estranged wife of Henry Tabram, and had spent the last nine years living on and off with a William Turner, who last saw her alive on the 4th of August, when he gave her the sum of 1/6d (71/2p). On the night of her death various witnesses stated that she's been seen in the company of one of more soldiers, and the original police theory was that she may have been murdered by a soldier 'client'.

Unfortunately, the murder of one 'shilling whore' raised scant headlines in the press or in the public conscience at the time. All that was soon to change!

I decided at that point that I needed a strategy, a means of working through the journal, whilst ensuring that I maintained a grip on the realities of the case. How easy it would have been to skip straight to the end, to read my great-grandfather's final notes, to see if the Ripper was identified, either by his own words, if true, or by great-grandfather. I'd never known him, he'd died before I was born, but I'd learned enough about him to know that he was a highly respected physician in his day, and I was sure that his conclusions would be a revelation in themselves. No, I couldn't do it. I had to read each page in order, had to assimilate the information in chronological order in order to understand what this was all about. It wasn't just the Ripper, no, my great-grandfather was also nursing some other secret, and, before I read what it was, I needed to understand what had happened to lead to his final solution, whatever that had been.

I presumed that the journal would take me on a journey, a journey through the terrible events that took place back in

1888, so I decided that the best course of action would be to read the journal, referring to any notes made by my great-grandfather, and then to refer to the texts I had printed from the internet, checking the facts as I went. In fact, I took the time to find more websites, and printed out reams of information on the murders, and it was quite some time before, having collated them all into a working chronology, I settled myself once more into my chair, took another sip of whisky, and slowly reached out to take up the journal once more.

THREE
A CRY FOR HELP?

12th August 1888

*After breakfast suffered a violent headache. Came from
nowhere. So sudden, it almost knocked me from my feet.
Forced to lie down, remained prone for some time. It's
them, the voices, they're shouting in my head, even when
I can't hear them, they must be! They'd been silent since
I finished the whore, and yet, they're in there all the time,
sleeping. They must wake inside my head and talk, and
I don't always hear them. I don't like the headache.*

THE DIAGNOSIS and treatment of mental illness in the 1880s
was, like the science of criminology, extremely basic compared
to today's standards. My great-grandfather would have been
astounded to see the massive advances that medical science has
achieved in the last hundred years. Nowadays we understand
so much more, we treat with care and compassion, yet, back in
the days of the Ripper saga, we built huge Gothic asylums,
where we incarcerated and tortured those poor afflicted souls in

the name of medicine. We were, I'm afraid, as a profession, in the stone ages.

The few words I'd just read had convinced me that the writer was indeed a sufferer from some form of mental disease. The hearing of voices is of course the classic mark of the psychopath, or possibly the sign of some form of mania. This man however, seemed to feel that the voices were speaking to him even when he couldn't hear them. He was indeed a sick man, but, with the limited knowledge and resources available in the nineteenth century, it was unlikely that he would ever have received effective or curative care. The comment 'I don't like the headache' showed an almost childlike desire for someone to take away his pain. I could almost feel his hurt, his anguish, though I wasn't yet convinced that these were truly the words of the man known as Jack the Ripper!

Now, you may be wondering why I was doubting the veracity of the journal. It was obvious that, for whatever reasons, my great-grandfather, my grandfather and father all believed in the truth of the documents now in my possession, and yet, I felt that with the benefits of modern-day technology at my disposal, and with the additional knowledge that now existed relating to the ripper murders, it might be possible for me to arrive at a different conclusion to my forebears. Only by reading the journal, the notes, and comparing them with the facts I had accessed from the net could I hope to come to an objective conclusion in the matter. Psychiatry has also moved on to such an extent that I felt I may be able to perhaps throw a different light on anything my great-grandfather had surmised from the journal. I was, of course, still to discover what his part in the whole affair had been, and that gave me cause for concern. It wouldn't be fair however, to jump the gun and rush to the end of the journal or the notes. I had to go slowly, had to take one step at a time.

13th August 1888

*Couldn't leave the house today, so much pain and
confusion in my head. I have to go out sometime, there's
so much I need to do. My work must go on, but the tools,
I must have the tools. Now I know the way to find safe
retreat. I never realized how much blood the whore
would spill upon me. There's no way to hide the blood,
and I can't risk being taken, not when there's so much to
do! The voices told me how to hide the blood. Hide
myself, and the blood will be hidden too. Be invisible.
That's the answer. THE SEWERS. Use the sewers, get a
map, a plan, they run under every street, every house,
and no-one shall see me, they'll never find me, never
beat me. I'm invisible, invisible and invincible.*

***

14th August 1888

*Feeling so much better, had work to do. Not the whores,
they'll have to wait, the office, boring, but necessary.
Everything normal, that's the way, let no-one suspect.
My neighbour called today, brought a copy of The Star.
Seems someone killed a whore called Tabram. Didn't
know whores had names, how shocking! Left work early,
got all I needed on Whitechapel High Street. Surgeons'
knives, so sharp, so bright, and maps, all the maps I need
to complete the task. Be careful little whores, I'm
coming.*

This was truly chilling. I was beginning to believe at last
that this could indeed be the journal of The Ripper. There was

a manic yet highly intelligent brain behind these words, of that I was becoming sure, one minute coherent and methodical, the next, almost ludicrously psychotic in his train of thought. Was he shocked that whores had names, or that someone had killed Martha Tabram? Had he at that point detached himself from the actual act of cold-blooded murder, becoming, for a short time, just another citizen indignant at the repugnance of the wicked crime? Apart from anything else, I had to admit to myself that as a case study, this was becoming totally engrossing. I could feel the tension building with almost every word I read in this strange, crumpled journal. The very age of the paper gave it a decrepit, tomblike feel, and added to the chill that was beginning to surround me as I sat in my comfortable chair, at my familiar desk, where, suddenly, nothing felt quite the same as it did just a short time ago. I felt as if I was being slowly and inexorably dragged back in time, so tangibly that I could almost envisage the sights and sounds of Victorian London being just outside my comfortable suburban home. Does that sound ridiculous? Maybe it does, but it's true. That's just how it felt. The more I read, the more I was being transported to another era, I could almost taste the fear of those uncertain times in that great, yet partially squalid city, I was beginning to realise why my family had kept this secret so close. The journal, though quite indistinct in many ways, and while not providing much in the way of the minutiae of the story up to this point was still like a time machine. Once you began you couldn't release yourself from its hold. I had to continue.

17th August 1888

Visited a few of the drinking establishments in
Spitalfields and Whitechapel. Drank beer in The
Britannia, the Princess Alice, and The Alma in Spelman

*Street. Got quite drunk. So many whores wanted me.
Me! Used the drink to avoid their dirty pestilence.
Played the well-heeled but drunken punter. Couldn't do
it, ha! That's what they thought! Couldn't do it? I'll do
them all, filthy, rotten bitches, whores; I'll send them all
to hell! TO HELL, DAMN THEIR FILTHY HIDES!*

He was getting angrier by the day, and it was clear that he
was plotting, reconnoitering the area, he was putting his plan
together, and would strike when he was ready. This was
premeditation on a grand scale, he was getting ready to unleash
the fire and brimstone of his own brand of hell upon the poor
unfortunate women of that sadly deprived and neglected area
of the great metropolis. What felt even worse was the fact that I
felt as though I was about to be given a ringside seat at the
proceedings. The words were so graphic, so real, so terrifying.

20ᵗʰ August 1888

*They're back, the voices, calling louder than ever. They
fill my head, they want me, need me; I'm so glad they
came, but they hurt me when they all scream at once.
Why don't they speak one at a time? Sometimes they're
so loud I can't hear them properly. My, but that's a
grand piece of lamb upon my plate tonight. I knew it
was good before I tasted it. Not too rare, we're not ready
to go out again, not just yet. When they say so, I'll be
ready, ready for the blood, the river, the river of red that
will flow through the streets as surely as the Thames
splits the city in two. The whores will pay, and pay in
full, I'll have no more of their wicked pestilence, their
evil bitch heat fouling the air, filling innocent beds with
their filth, I'll have them all, whores, nothing but whores.*

They're gone again, for a while at least, but I wish my head wouldn't hurt so much. Why do they leave me like this? I don't want my head to hurt, not like this. I wish it would stop.

So, one minute he was the avenging angel, the next, a frightened little boy, that's how I saw this tortured soul. I could almost imagine him lying alone in his bed at night, weeping silently into his pillow, willing the pain to leave him, and, when it didn't, crying out aloud for help. I wondered, did this man, this murderer, Jack the Ripper, did he cry in despair for his mother?

I turned to the texts I'd printed on the facts of the case. I wanted to check the chronology of the case. The writer of the journal hadn't made entries for every day, as one would in a diary, and I wondered how many more pages I would have to read before reaching the entry for August 31st. I knew there'd be one that day, especially for that night. It was the night the true terror of Jack the Ripper began!

FOUR
TENSION

My mouth was dry, very dry, and I felt the need for refreshment. Though I was sorely tempted to refill the glass on my desk, I needed to keep a clear head, and so reluctantly rose from my chair and headed for the kitchen. Coffee was the order of the day, and while waiting for the kettle to boil, I continued to scan through the loose pages of script I'd printed from the computer, trying to glean whatever I could from them before returning to the more intense work of studying the journal. I rubbed the back of my neck; it felt stiff, the tension was gripping me tightly in its grasp. Just a short time ago, I'd been a pretty ordinary fellow, mourning the loss of my poor dear Dad, (I suppose I'd been feeling a little sorry for myself), and, despite my reassurances to her, I was missing Sarah. Now, here I was, alone in the house, which suddenly seemed a much larger and lonelier place, apparently surrounded by the unknown ghosts of the past, which had reared up and taken me totally by surprise. How could my father have kept this a secret for so long?

My grandfather had died many years ago when I was just a

young boy, so that meant that Dad had kept this to himself virtually all my life. Why couldn't he have told me? He'd never dropped the slightest hint of the journal's existence. Whatever it had yet to reveal, it was obvious that it was of such profound importance, and at the same time, connected with some dark family involvement in the terrible events to which it related, that he'd kept his own counsel on the subject for all these years, as, quite obviously had his father before him.

Ten minutes later, armed with a pot of steaming, freshly percolated coffee and a mug, I returned to the study. The light of the day was growing weaker, and as I settled myself back into my chair, I reached across the desk and switched on my desk lamp. The sudden illumination cast an eerie glow across the slightly faded, yellowed manuscript of the journal, and I shivered involuntarily. Was I being foolish? Was I becoming spooked by the whole thing? Somehow, I felt as if the day itself was closing in around me. I felt a sense of oppression in the air, a malevolence, as though the spirit of evil that had laid bare the words on the paper before me could somehow transcend the years, crossing the vast ocean of time to reach out and touch me, the reader, with the sheer force of it's power. "Come on, Robert," I spoke aloud to myself, "Don't be so bloody stupid. Get a grip! It's just words on paper, nothing more."

I took a large gulp from my coffee cup, and instantly topped it up from the cafetierre, black, no sugar, just as I like it, though Sarah could never understand how I could take it like that. That settled my nerves a little, and I turned back to the journal.

"Hellfire!" I exclaimed, as the telephone on the desk began to ring. I admit I nearly jumped out of my chair, and for a moment could do no more than stare at the irritatingly ringing piece of plastic on my desk. The jangling tone of the ringer seemed fit to burst my eardrums; I'd never before realized how loud the damned thing was. Should I answer it? I realized that if I didn't, whoever was calling would probably keep trying until I did pick up, and I wished I'd brought the cordless phone from the lounge into the study with me, that way I'd have been able to see who was calling via the caller id system. I'd insisted on having an old-fashioned corded phone on my desk, because I though it matched the room's ambience better!

"Hello?" I almost shouted down the line.

"Robert, darling, what's wrong? You sound angry."

It was Sarah.

"Oh, hello darling, no, sorry, I'm not angry with you, it's just that I'm in the middle of reading through some particularly important papers, and to be honest, I was miles away when you rang. The phone ringing just sort of took me by surprise, that's all."

"Oh Robert, I'm so sorry to disturb you darling. I've just called to see if you're ok, I hope you're missing me."

"Of course I'm missing you, you gorgeous lady," I replied, "How're Jennifer and the baby, and Tom of course?"

"Everyone's fine Robert, Jennifer and Tom have picked a name for the baby. Do you want to try and guess?"

"Aw come on, Sarah, my love, there must only be about ten thousand possibilities when it comes to boys names. Just tell me, there's a darling."

"You're a spoilsport Robert, you really are. Well, OK then. I must admit I was a bit surprised at their choice, but he's their baby. They're going to call him Jack!"

I was stunned. I must have gone deathly quiet and didn't reply to Sarah for a few seconds.

"Robert, are you there darling? Did you hear what I said?"

"Yes, of course Sarah, Sorry, I was just mulling it over in my mind, you know, how it sounds, that sort of thing. Jack Reid.

Yes, sure, sounds ok to me my love. I'm glad he's well. I'm sorry if I sound a bit distant. Don't worry about me; I'm fine, just a bit preoccupied with these papers that's all."

"Yes, I know, I'm sorry I've disturbed you when you're busy. Listen, I'll get off and give you a ring later, when you're not so busy. Is Mrs Armitage calling to check on you from time to time?"

"Yes darling, she is, silly old busybody."

"Now don't be cruel Robert. You know she only means well."

"Yes, I know, bit I'm sure she thinks I'm a little boy who's been left home alone and needs constantly looking after."

"Don't worry darling, it won't be long until I'm home. You just look after yourself. As I said, I'm sorry for disturbing your work. I'll ring back later."

"Alright my love, give my love to Jennifer and Tom, and to little Jack of course."

"Right then, I'll say 'bye my darling, take care, I love you."

"Love you too, 'bye Sarah."

The room felt deathly quiet after I'd hung up the phone. Jack! What on earth had inspired Jennifer and her husband, my cousin, to decide to call their new-born boy Jack? It was almost too much of a coincidence, and why had Sarah chosen this very moment to telephone me and inform me of it? It was almost too spooky for words. I needed more coffee, it was cold, I'd have to go back to the kitchen and make some more before I carried on.

As I made the refill, I reflected on my conversation with Sarah. I'd not been entirely truthful with my wife, though not through any intentional desire to lie to her. It was just that I didn't think I should mention the journal to her, not at this time anyway. I didn't even know the truth of it yet anyway, or how it would end, so I thought it best to keep the whole thing to myself for now. As for Jennifer, it might not be the best time to reveal that I was reading the purported journal of Jack the Ripper, and that my family might have been involved in the affair just when she'd just decided to call her first son Jack!

It was almost dark outside by the time I returned to the study. The desk lamp still cast its eerie glow over the desk, but I needed more light, so switched on the wall lights. Their warm glow seemed to take some of the gloom and chill from the air, and I felt a little more relaxed as I sat down once again. My wife's telephone call, inconvenient as it might have seemed at the time, had in fact helped to release some of the tension that had been building up inside me, and I felt lovingly grateful to her for that.

I looked down at the journal, and the words on the paper seemed to virtually rise upwards from the page to meet my eyes as I refocused my attention on those long-ago dark days of the year 1888.

FIVE
COUNTDOWN TO MAYHEM

23rd August 1888

I've felt quite well for the last few days. Even the voices have been silent, they've been resting I think, as have I. Only a couple of jobs, nothing taxing, and no-one suspects a thing. I'm ready now, I could start the job tomorrow if they call, but they're silent. Never mind, the blades are sharp, my mind is clear, and everything's in place ready to begin. so call me, call me, talk to me, my friends, my voices, lead me on the path of destruction, and I'll eradicate the whores, the filth, the harlots of the filthy streets, I'll put them all to sleep, for ever

It's so quiet tonight, tried reading for a while, but my eyes grew heavy, so tired, I need sleep, the one thing that evades me, a fair night of slumber. Why do the headaches come so hard at night? I wish the headaches would go away. Perhaps they will when I've done for the whores!

HE WAS CALM NOW, or so I thought; calmer than in some of the previous entries in the journal. He seemed to be almost at peace with himself, as if he were adrift in the eye of a hurricane, alone and in the midst of calm, but with the threat of a violent raging storm waiting just around the corner. In light of my own experiences with certain disturbed patients over the years, I could sense that this man was a highly strung individual, almost driven to breaking point by the incessant clamour of the 'voices' in his head, and yet, there again, was the plea for the pain to stop, for the headaches to go away. Within the darkest recesses of his mind there remained a small, tenuous link with reality, a spark of humanity remained within him, but, as was proved by the events to follow, that spark was soon to be extinguished.

24th August 1888

Results of the inquest on Whore Tabram. As expected, 'Murder by person or persons unknown'. A long report made by an Inspector Reid, who knows nothing at all. Ha! Stupid, bungling fools. They'll never know, never find me, never find US! I was invisible at the back of the room, unseen and unnoticed by anyone. I'll be even more invisible when I go back to work, to do the job. Oh, the sport that awaits, better than all the trophies in the cabinet. I'll be top of the league, best in show, holder of the blue riband. They'll know my work if not my name, and I'll wash the streets clean with the blood of harlots. The darkness shall be my friend, the night my close companion, the sewers my safe refuge from prying eyes. Let them all be damned, let them weep and cry for their own bloody souls, while I cut the whores in droves.

In referring to my printed reference notes, I found that an Inspector Reid did in fact submit a report on that very date to Scotland Yard detailing the results of the Tabram inquest, though how our man came to glean such knowledge so quickly I couldn't fathom. Of course, until the Ripper struck again, the police had no idea who or what they were dealing with. Martha Tabram was consigned to history at this point as one of the many unsolved and unsolvable murders which were all too frequent in the great city in those murky, far away days. Things were soon to change; however, tragedy was lurking in the dark, dank, mist enshrouded streets of Whitechapel.

My thoughts turned for a moment to the days on which our man had made no journal entries. What was he doing? Where was he? Was he still sufficiently sane and lucid that he was holding down a good job, or some job at least, and that no-one of his acquaintance had noticed anything unusual in his recent behaviour? Was he so in control of himself in public that he could appear totally normal in every respect? The writer of this journal was indeed a phenomenon; I suspected that he may have been so disturbed that the man who wrote the journal would have been unrecognisable, (even to himself) from the man who went about his daily business in the most normal and orderly fashion. This would explain the gaps in the journal. The writer would see no anomalies in the missing dates. Those days belonged to someone else, someone apparently sane. For him, they simply hadn't existed! I had to admit that, as a case study, most psychiatrists would give their eye teeth for a chance to work with such a patient, to study at close quarters the gradual decline from sanity into the abyss of the psychosis that was about to envelope the tortured soul of the hapless victim. Yes, it's true I used the word victim, for to be afflicted with such an illness, and an illness it most surely is, must be one of the most frightening and disorientating experiences for the human mind to endure. The writer of the journal, if indeed he was Jack the Ripper, was himself a severely tortured individual, as much a casualty as those poor wretched women who were to achieve lasting and tragic fame as his victims. Added to that, the diagnosis of such a psychosis would have been almost impossible in those early days of psychiatric science, and any treatment, if attempted at all, would have been arbitrarily punitive and painful: the administration of electric shocks and the use of water hoses the probable and wholly unsatisfactory methods of approach. We have to remember that there were no specific drugs available to those physicians who did their best to help the mentally ill in the nineteenth century. There were no anti-depressants, no tranquilisers, and no comforting specialist nurses trained to help the afflicted. The asylums of Victorian England were little more than places of unhappy incarceration for those interned in them, hell holes by modern standards, where the sick and infirm of mind could be locked away out of the sight and mind of the public conscience, where they could do no harm, and be 'protected' from self harm; in other words, detained in chains and kept confined in solitary confinement. Such was the civilised treatment of our mentally ill in the age of Victoria.

I wasn't prepared to criticise my great-grandfather at that point of course, he could only work within the confines of his profession at the time, and I'm sure he always thought he was doing his best for his patients, as did all doctors of the time. No-one was deliberately cruel or unfeeling. They were simply ignorant of things which we in these enlightened times are only too aware. I was relatively sure that the journal was the work of someone suffering from a form of paranoid schizophrenia, though that would have meant little to the physicians of my great-grandfather's day. I should add that at that point of course, such a theory was based purely on what I'd read so far and could at best be seen as little more than hypothetical guesswork. I supposed it could never be more than that, as I'd obviously never have the opportunity to talk to the writer in order to arrive at an informed diagnosis.

Schizophrenia, an awful illness, perhaps needs a little explaining at this point. At certain times in history, sufferers of this dreadful ailment were thought to be possessed by demons, and many unfortunates were locked away in terrible institutions, tormented, often exiled, reviled and at times, hunted down and killed like wild animals. Even today, despite tremendous advances in our understanding of the disease, and many effective treatments being available, the public conception of it is still clouded by fear and suspicion.

The sufferer will in general appear outwardly 'normal' to most people he or she encounters in daily life. Should the disease take a firm hold however, the individual may begin to display unusual behaviour caused by their radically altered thought processes. They may suffer from hallucinations and become delusional. Many hear imagined voices, normally as a precursor to some form of self-harm, or in some case leading to highly intense false beliefs, (delusions). Violence is not always a by-product of schizophrenia, and, when it is evident, it is usually self-directed by the individual into attempts to end his or her own life. Only in exceptional cases, (one of which I felt I was examining in the journal), will the violence be directed outwards towards strangers or groups of individuals as in this case. In our enlightened modern society the sufferer, once diagnosed, has the options of psychotherapy, group therapy, and drug therapy at his disposal in the search for a means to control and alleviate his suffering. A combination of antipsychotic, antidepressant and anti-anxiety medications can go a long way towards relieving many of the day to day symptoms of the illness. The disorganised speech pattern displayed in the wording of the journal also provided me with a clue, this, together with the equally disorganised thought processes revealed in the writing, being a classic symptom of the disease.

None of these medical corrective therapies were available to our Victorian counterparts however, and the chances of effective diagnosis and, more importantly, any form of controlling or curative treatment were virtually non-existent. If, indeed, the writer of the journal was a sufferer of this dread illness, then his chances of obtaining help or of even managing to control his illness were almost non-existent. The only prognosis for this poor individual, had he sought help, or, worse still been committed due to his actions, would have been dreadful incarceration and inhumane treatment in one of the aforementioned gothic asylums of the day. Understanding and compassion were not the bywords of the Victoria era when dealing with the mentally ill, but I think I've already made that point!

25th August 1888

Visited The Alma again tonight. Whores everywhere! What a vile house of ill-repute that is. Smelled of stale beer, cheap tobacco, and whores! Cracked music from a cracked piano. Such false jollity, and voices, voices everywhere. Singing, shouting, making merry as though there were no tomorrow, and there won't be soon for some of them whores. No tomorrows at all. I'll see to that! So loud in there, I could hardly hear my voices when they spoke to me. They made me retreat, it's not time yet, not the time to start the work, but, it won't be long, I've seen them, watched them, I know where they are, where to find the pestilence, where to go to rid the world of their smell, their sickness.

My headache got so bad I had to leave, why won't it go away?

So, the next bloody rampage was getting closer, and the headache was getting worse. I found it strange that my great-grandfather hadn't added any notes to the journal so far, the first inserted page of notes was still quite some pages further into the journal. Then I realised that, at this time, he obviously hadn't met the writer! His own notes, when they came, would evidently appear after some form of meeting or communication between them In other words, he didn't know the writer before the murders began or, if he did, he had no inkling of his illness, and this I couldn't believe. My great-grandfather was a physician after all, and though not equipped with the knowledge and science of today, I'm sure he would have recognised the delusional state of the writer had he been a personal acquaintance of the man. His notes, stuffed into the later pages of the journal, were therefore of importance in respect of the aftermath of the killings, I would wait and bide my time. They were arranged in that way for a purpose, and I decided to stick with the original plan, and read every page chronologically.

A look at the printed texts I'd obtained showed me that the writer was now only six days away from the next murder, that of Mary Ann Nichols. The last entry I'd read showed that the writer was indeed becoming angrier and angrier with each passing day, his headaches were getting no better, and the voices were speaking to him at what appeared to be ever decreasing intervals. As his anger continued to build I knew that the pain in his head and the delusions in his brain would increase exponentially until something gave way. The next few entries would be crucial in helping to determine his state of mind at the time immediately before the night of the ghastly slaughter of the poor unfortunate Mary Ann.

SIX
A LAST SEMBLANCE OF CALM

I WAS GROWING QUITE stiff and weary. I'd been sitting in my office chair for so long, apart from the breaks for coffee, and become so engrossed in the journal, that I hadn't realised that I'd been holding myself almost in a state of suspended animation. I'm sure you know what I mean, when you're so tense and intense that every muscle in your body seems to tighten, and you seem incapable of fluid movement. I had to get up and move around for a few minutes, I needed to relax a little.

I rose from my chair, stretching to relieve the stiffness in my neck and back, I felt so taut, every sinew ached. I realised that I was quite hungry, I hadn't eaten for hours. Mrs Armitage would have been horrified! It was now quite dark outside, and, though the day had been quite fine and warm for the time of year, quite a strong breeze was blowing. The branches of the tree outside the study were beginning to sway in the breeze, casting the shadows of eerie fingers across the darkened glass of the window. I shivered again, stupid really, but I felt as though I wasn't alone in the room.

Shaking such childish thoughts from my mind I made my way to the kitchen once more. I removed a large microwave meal for two from the freezer and set the microwave to work preparing it. With the machine whirring in the background I sat at the kitchen table with a glass of water and flicked through the research documents I'd brought with me from the study. Almost everything about the Jack the Ripper murders was shrouded in mystery and a distinct lack of credible information or facts. Over the years, so many suspects had been suggested that it seemed as if almost the entire population of London could have had a case built against them if one worked hard enough at compiling a circumstantial case! There were doctors, lawyers, butchers, peers of the realm, even a member of the Royal family, yet none of them had ever been proven to have had any direct connection with the murders. Inquests on the victims had been perfunctory at best, information withheld on occasions, for no apparent good reason, and the police seemed to have approached the whole series of killings without any real sense of leadership or direction. While those 'on the ground', the officers most directly involved with the individual murders appeared to have done their level best, they appeared to have been hampered by the attitudes and lack of foresight displayed by their commanders. Evidence which may have been helpful was either suppressed or, in the case of a section of graffiti left on a wall supposedly in the Ripper's hand, the senior officer in charge had actually ordered the words to be removed, so as not to offend certain sections of the community!

I was appalled and astounded at some of the things I was reading. Despite the lack of forensic or technical assistance, it seemed that there were clues available at the time, but the police were either unable or unwilling to investigate them fully. Perhaps the low station in life of the victims played a part in this, for surely, had the victims been high born ladies of society, the public outcry and the need for justice would have galvanised the police into a flurry of activity and the case would have been investigated far more vigorously, with the killer more likely to have been apprehended.

The microwave pinged; dinner was ready! As I sat at the table eating the extremely large lasagne, (made for two remember), I tried to think my way through what I'd read so far.

My great-grandfather, a Victorian physician dealing with diseases of the mind, had obviously come into contact with the writer of the journal. The writer, obviously male, had presented himself in some way as to convince my great-grandfather that he was Jack the Ripper. Great-grandfather had felt that he could have done something to stop the murders. Did he know of the writer's intent before, or at some time during the killing spree? He certainly believed in the man's story, enough to take some form of as yet unknown precipitate action eventually. What that action was, was as yet unknown to me. Whatever had taken place, he had thought it important, (and scandalous) enough to pass on to his son, and those who came after him, as a macabre legacy, with a request to continue to keep the secret within the family.

Though I knew that I could find some quick answers by turning to the back of the journal and reading my great-grandfathers final notes, I felt compelled to continue as I'd started, to take one page at a time, in the order in which they were written. It was as if the journal had a life of its own, as if it was intent on not revealing its darkest secrets until it was ready to do so.

There I went again, being foolish, so I thought. How could a collection of papers over one hundred years old have such power? They had no hold over me whatsoever; I knew that, I was a rational man, so why didn't I just turn to the end? I don't know. I just knew that I had to go on with my strange quest for the truth, and I felt that the journal would lead me to the answers if I was patient and thorough. I needed to understand more, and the only way was to read each and every page, to study every word.

My meal finished, I put my solitary plate, knife and fork in the dishwasher, with the plates and cutlery from my last four meals, tomorrow would do for the washing-up! As I wandered from the kitchen, down the hall, and back to the study, I heard the sound of the wind outside. It had gathered in strength and sound whilst I'd been eating and had become almost a gale. I was glad to be indoors. As I opened the door to the study, I could have sworn that I saw a fleeting shadow dart across the room, from left to right, disappearing behind the bookcase to my right. Once again, I chided myself for my own childish stupidity. It must have been the shadow caused by the door opening into the room, and cutting across the light, nothing more. Nevertheless, I couldn't resist a quick peek behind the bookcase, like a nervous schoolboy, before sitting down in the chair once more. There was nothing there, of course.

I decided one more whisky wouldn't impair my thought processes unduly, so poured myself a small one. On returning to the journal, I saw that two days had been omitted by the writer, his next entry being three days after the previous one.

28ᵗʰ August 1888

Feeling fine, just waiting. Soon, the time to begin will arrive, and the world will hear my voice, see my work, and the whores will tremble. Earned some money, have to keep body and soul intact. Evening at the club. A gentleman is a gentleman after all. Shared a meal and a bottle of fine port with Cavendish. He's a head doctor, haha!

At last! Cavendish! My great-grandfather. So he did meet him before the murders, well, before the majority of them took place anyway. Remember that most people later dismissed Martha Tabram's murder as not being the work of the Ripper. The journal however, places that death alongside the others, so as far as my story is concerned, Tabram was the first. He mentions the club, obviously some all-male preserve, many of which existed in those days. He must have been a member of my great-grandfathers club, or at least been a guest there, I understand that they were very snobbish, quite exclusive places, where non-members would have been decidedly unwelcome, and he must also have been a gentleman, or at least purported to be one; and there's yet another clue. He mentions earning money, doing what? What kind of job did he do, this strange and deadly 'gentleman'? Was he a doctor himself, or a lawyer, a solicitor perhaps? In one short paragraph, the journal had taken me so much deeper into the strange happenings of so long ago. I was beginning to feel even more drawn into the web surrounding my great-grandfather and the mysterious writer of the aged, crumpled pages of yellowed foolscap.

The journal continued....

He was most sympathetic when I told him about my headaches. Just the headaches of course, nothing more. He wouldn't understand the voices, not yet. They wouldn't speak to him anyway. He suggested a small daily dose of laudanum. Thought it might help the headaches and calm my nerves. He thinks I've been overworking! Poor Cavendish, poor fools, all of them, they just can't see, they just don't know, only the voices

*know, they're with me all the time, even when they're
quiet, they're still there, sleeping, resting. I've got the
laudanum, from the grocers shop on the corner, enough
to last a while, just in case it doesn't work straight away.
Must admit, the headaches weren't so bad last night.
Good old Cavendish. Got that one right. Still hurts a bit
though, my forehead throbs. So tired tonight. No little
trips to take. Sleep, sleep, sleep.*

Laudanum! My great-grandfather had suggested he take
laudanum. Popular as a cure-all in Victorian times, laudanum
was an opium derivative that could, and frequently did become
highly addictive. It would certainly have had the effect of
calming the writer down to some extent, but its hallucinogenic
properties would probably have served to further inflame his
delusions and perhaps to amplify the severity of the voices in
his head. It seemed to me that my great-grandfather may have
unwittingly helped to pour fuel onto the already smouldering
fire that was about to explode into life from within the tortured
mind of the writer of the journal. The journal moved on to the
next day.

29th August 1888

*The laudanum is working. The more I take, the better
I feel. Hearing the voices much clearer now, less
clutter, less babble. Headache still there, but bearable.
Another visit to the taverns, the cess-pits of iniquity,
foul beer in dirty tankards. Too many whores to count.
I shan't forget the whore who lay with me, and caused
my suffering, the dirty, filthy, diseased bitch whore! I
hope she died in agony, I haven't seen her, she must be
gone by now, but the others will do, the wretched*

whores, they're all the same, foul pestilence upon the
world.

I was almost breathless with the task of reading the page
before me. It was now like a roller-coaster ride. He was getting
closer to the moment when his illness would push him over the
edge, when the voices would give the word, and he'd lose his
final tenuous hold on reality, and plunge into the pit of
damnation from which he would never escape. His reference to
his dalliance with a whore that led to 'his suffering' led me to
believe without a shadow of a doubt that, this man was infected
with syphilis, and that he was quite likely in the later or
Tertiary stages of the disease, when the body itself can start to
exhibit lesions known as gummas, which slowly eat away at the
skin, bones and soft tissues. The most awful part of this phase
of the disease is the progressive brain damage which takes
place, once known as general paralysis of the insane. Though
antibiotics and effective testing have all but eradicated the
disease from the developed countries of the modern world, in
my great-grandfather's time syphilis was rampant, and our
unfortunate writer would have been described by the
physicians of the time as being 'sexually deranged'. So, I now
felt that the writer of the journal was infected with syphilis,
suffered from paranoid schizophrenia, either as a result of his
syphilis or in tandem with it, and I now knew, deep down
inside that this was indeed the journal of the man known to
history as Jack the Ripper!

30ᵗʰ August 1888

All the preparations are in place. Maps, clothes, the
tools, most importantly, the tools. I've never felt so good,
so calm, no pain, the headaches have gone, the voices

singing quietly to me, soothing me, telling me where to go, what to do, to be invisible. I'll always be invisible. The dark streets will be my home; my heart will beat in time to the rhythm of the night. It's a warm night, so quiet outside, so calm, and I also am calm, and at rest. Yes, I must rest tonight. Tomorrow my work begins!

I must admit to you that, on reading that entry in the journal, I could feel my heart rate increase. Although the writer may have been calm, I was anything but; I was physically and visibly shaking as I put the page down on the desk. Although I was reading about events that took place over a century before, I confess that I was afraid, afraid of what I was going to see in the following pages. Poor Martha Tabram had been a trial run. Now the conflagration of fear and death that went by the name of Jack the Ripper was about to be fully unleashed!

SEVEN
THE REAL WORK BEGINS

In a move intended to calm my own nerves slightly, and to compose myself for what I was about to read, I gently laid the journal down on the desk, and took up the printed fact sheets I'd printed out earlier. I wanted to acquaint myself with more of the facts of the case before returning to the words of 'The Ripper'.

History records that on the night of the 30th August 1888, Mary Ann Nichols, (known to all as Polly), was seen walking alone in Whitechapel Road at about 11.30 p.m. At 12.30 a.m. she was witnessed leaving a public house in Brick Lane and was last seen alive by her friend and sometimes living partner Ellen Holland at 2.30 a.m. at the corner of Whitechapel Road and Osborn Street. She was drunk, and steadfastly refused to return with Holland to their shared room in Thrawl Street.

Her lifeless body was found in Buck's Row, a dark and lonely street known today as Durward Street, with her skirt pulled up, at about 3.40 a.m. by two passers-by, Charles Cross and Robert Paul. Three policemen were soon in attendance, and one of them, police constable Neil noted that her throat had been cut. She was pronounced dead at the scene by Doctor Rees Llewellyn, the duty police surgeon, and her body removed to the mortuary shed at the Old Montague Street Workhouse Infirmary. It was during a subsequent examination of the body in the mortuary that the horrific abdominal mutilations, soon to become the trademark of the Ripper were discovered.

At the hastily convened inquest into her death, (that very day), it was revealed that the poor woman had suffered two cuts to the throat, so deep as to reach the vertebrae, her abdomen had been slashed, and her left side had received a gash that ran from the base of her ribs almost to her pelvis. There were numerous cuts to her right abdomen, and, horrifically, two stab wounds directly in her genitals. Though initially it was thought that she'd been killed elsewhere, and the body dumped in Buck's Row, due to the small amount of blood found on the street, it was later deduced that her clothing had absorbed much of the blood and that Buck's Row, was, in fact, the scene of her murder. One important attendee at the inquest was Detective Inspector Frederick Abberline, who had been brought in to co-ordinate the investigation. At this time however, the police had nothing to go on, no witnesses, no suspects, and no evidence.

Had The Ripper ended his killing with the death of Polly Nichols it is likely that the crime would have remained unsolved and forgotten, and the killing would have been no more than a footnote in the dark criminal history of the East End of London, and the name of Jack the Ripper would have never been known to the world.

I returned to the journal. Strangely, there was no entry for the night of the 30th August, when he so obviously must have left his home and prowled the dark streets in search of his victim. Had he been too excited to write? Had he been so preoccupied by his task that he'd forgotten the very existence of his journal? In light of my theories on the state of mind of the writer, I presumed that to be the most likely conclusion. He was so wrapped up, so totally absorbed by his cause, his 'work', that the journal would have been an insignificance to him, barely worth a thought, as indeed I believed to be the case. He had, however, returned to his literary account the next day, and the entry, though short, was as chilling to me as if he'd written a five-page dissertation on the killing of that poor unfortunate woman.

1st September 1888

Am well. Continued the work last night. After the first whore this was easy, like gutting a fish! Slash, slash, slash, so easy, so quick. The whore never saw me coming, lying drunk in the filthy doorway of the hovel. This is the real thing, now I can't stop, for the whores are ripe for plucking, and I'll reap a bloody harvest. Her blood was sticky warm upon my fingers, but the whore is cold, cold as the grave, good job.

I even walked back to look, but they'd shifted the whore. No-one saw, I was invisible. Solved the blood problem. The apron will wash, and the sewers keep me safe. Door to door, hahaha.

So, here it was, probably for the first time. A confession (of sorts), to the murders of both Martha Tabram and Polly Nichols, by one individual. If this journal was indeed the real thing, (and this was becoming more self-evident to me with each page I read), then all the past conjecture as to whether

Martha Tabram was a victim of The Ripper was ended, (for me at least).

Poor Polly Nichols! Left to bleed into the street in the depths of night, probably without even knowing what was happening to her. That, I supposed, was a blessing of sorts. She hadn't been dragged screaming to her horrific death. If the writer was to be believed, he'd come across his victim lying virtually helpless in a doorway, probably too stupefied through drink to realize that her throat was being cut, until it was too late. Though the subsequent mutilations were horrific in their extent and ferocity, they were at least inflicted post-mortem, she wouldn't have felt the blade slicing into her flesh, cutting her open, despoiling and defiling her most intimate, private parts. The depths of the cuts to the woman's throat would have ensured that she'd died almost instantly. I sat and shivered again, and, even though the act had occurred so long ago, I said a silent prayer for the soul of Mary Ann (Polly) Nichols.

That he could be so sparse in his words on the killing, and so matter of fact about the acts of depravity he'd committed was frightening, and I shuddered inwardly as the wind again howled at the window, and I felt the strange feeling once again, the feeling of being not alone, though I knew I was. I was getting jumpy, and little wonder.

2nd September 1888

The voices called to me today. They're celebrating, elated, telling me to rest now. The work won't go away, but it will wait, until the time comes again when I shall rise in answer to the call. The headache came again, far worse, but the laudanum helped.

***

3rd September 1888

Saw 'T' today. Also Cavendish paid a courtesy call. I listened but spoke little. Thanked him for previous advice. He asked how I was. Fine I replied. Fine. Fine. Fine. He was on his way to the asylum, so many unhappy souls in there, would that they could enjoy the sunshine, the freedom to walk, to talk, to be human again. I know such is not their destiny, my own self would treat them if I could, help them find the release they need. But I cannot, I must bide within my own confines, and take solace in the work, I'll wait for the voices, let them rest, they too are tired, soon enough I'll feel the blood of the whores on my skin again, I'll watch the next wretched strumpet bleed as I slice her good and well. Won't be long my lovely, won't be long, I promise.

There was my great-grandfather once again and mention of someone referred to only as 'T'. Why didn't the writer name him, as he had my ancestor? Would naming him have given too much away, made it too easy for the writer to be identified if his journal had fallen into the wrong hands? It was obvious to me that my great-grandfather had no inkling of the writer's connection to the murders at that time, or I was sure he'd have added something to his notes. There was nothing, and yes, the man 'T', if it was a man, must have been too close to home for the writer to identify. There was also the vague reference to his wanting to do something to help cure the inmates of the asylum. Was that just the rambling of an insane mind, or did this man, as many have suspected of the Ripper, have some medical connections? Could he indeed have been a doctor himself? That would certainly explain his presence at the same club as great-grandfather. Were they professional colleagues I

47

wondered, or just passing acquaintances? I knew that I could probably solve the mystery instantly by turning a few pages, looking at the final entries, perhaps seeing a name in my ancestors' hand, but, no, I couldn't. I felt compelled to see this through to the end, to read each and every page as it opened before me, to follow the trail of the journal to whatever conclusion it arrived at. Only by fully understanding what had happened in those far-off days would I discover my family's own dark secret, and perhaps, at the same time, discover the identity of Jack the Ripper.

4ᵗʰ September 1888

I must go away for a couple of days. The whores can wait, but I'll be back, by all that's true, I'll return in time to cut the next one hard.

So, he was going away. To work? To visit a friend, or family perhaps? I referred to my research papers, looking for any reference to any of the many suspects having been absent from London between the 4ᵗʰ September and the date of the next murder, which would take place on the 8ᵗʰ. There was little information, the only information relating to any of the alleged suspects referred to Prince Albert Victor, Duke of Clarence and Avondale, the grandson of Queen Victoria. The prince was recorded as having been staying with Viscount Downe at Danby Lodge in Yorkshire fro the 29ᵗʰ August to the 7ᵗʰ September, and thence at the Cavalry Barracks at York until the 10ᵗʰ. Unless he could have been in two places at once, that let the prince off the hook as far as I was concerned. I felt that to be a preposterous theory at any rate, though perhaps others may have acted on his behalf? I felt it more likely that the writer was fulfilling some pre-arranged appointment, perhaps, as I'd already thought, to visit a relative, or, if he was a medical man himself, to attend to some pressing out of town business, perhaps he was himself treating patients at a hospital, or God forbid the thought, at an asylum!

Try as I might, I couldn't shake the thought that I was being inextricably drawn into a web so vast, so deep, that I might never be the same again. Would the knowledge I was about to learn over the next few hours leave me unscathed, or was I cursed to carry some vile and bitter secret with me to the grave? Was that what my poor father had done, and his father before him? The yellowed, crinkled, aged paper in my hand seemed almost warm to the touch, as if the warmth of the blood of that poor hapless victim of the Ripper was seeping through the very pages of the journal, reaching across the vastness of time to touch me here in the warm safe confines of my study. Something about the writing on the page made it assume an almost three-dimensional appearance in my mind, the page was moving upwards in my hand as I looked ever closer at the words, searching for some hidden clue, some sign of whatever it was that was causing me to suffer such an illogical reaction to the old, worn manuscript. I saw nothing unusual, nothing at all, and yet, there was something about the journal, something dark and malevolent, though I'd no idea what it was. Was it him? Was it The Ripper, his words themselves were chilling enough, but could it be that something of the evil lurked within the fabric of the parchment, could he have somehow burned his own brand of evil into the pages? Rubbish! How foolish I felt for even thinking such a thought. Even so, I hurriedly placed the journal down on the desk, ashamed of my own irrational fear and stupidity. It *was* just a collection of old papers after all, wasn't it?

EIGHT
A QUIET EVENING

THE ICY CHILL of the journal's words had taken a grip on my thoughts and emotions. I had fully expected the Ripper (if this was indeed the Ripper), to describe his work in far more graphic detail than he had done. It seemed as if the actual act of killing Polly Nichols, the barbarity of his vicious assault on her lifeless body, had been no more than an adjunct to his day, a casual act, committed with no more emotion than he would have displayed if he'd been swatting a fly, or eating a meal. The 'sticky warm blood' upon his fingers, 'was nothing more than a passing remark, a short statement of fact. He wasn't in any way repelled by the act of murder, as most murderers are after they realize the magnitude of what they've done. This man was incapable of remorse, more than that, he enjoyed the acts he was perpetrating, and dismissed them as nothing more than an everyday occurrence. I confess that at that point in time, I was actually afraid, though of what I couldn't be sure. I wasn't one normally prone to irrational or illogical fears, but something about this journal, this night, was deeply unnerving to my soul. For reasons I can't explain, (it was after all just an old journal), I felt as though I were staring into the jaws of Hell itself, with only a small portion of that terrible destination having been revealed to me. Knowing that there was yet more to come, descriptions of even more horrific events, that the bloodletting was only just beginning, sent paroxysms of shivers down my spine. Despite the intoxicating, addictive pull of the journal, I had to tear myself from it, I needed to rest, to gain a few minutes of respite from the horrific Victorian melodrama being played out in words before me. It took courage, I know you won't understand that, but it's true, and I summoned that courage to place the pages of the journal on the desk, rise from my chair, and walk out of the study, into the kitchen, where I made yet more coffee, and then sank into Sarah's fireside chair with my head in my hands. Without my realising it, the coffee grew cold, my eyes grew heavy, and in minutes I fell into a fitful, shallow sleep.

I dreamed, an awful dream, of blood, and bright, silver blades, cutting and slashing at my flesh. The blood was everywhere, flowing from my arms, my legs, and when I looked down, a gaping wound in my abdomen was opened from side to side across my body, my entrails were hanging out, and the kitchen floor was stained red with the river of blood that stemmed from my wounds. I tried to scream, I couldn't, and I saw the shadow of the man as he raised his blade once more, ready to strike the final blow, to end my torment, and then......

I woke, trembling, sweating, the kitchen was quiet, the floor was clean, dry, not a drop of blood in sight. Almost unconsciously I felt my body, checking for wounds, there were none of course, and I cursed my own stupidity, my weakness in being deceived by a dream. I was definitely becoming spooked. That much was certain. I tried to clear my head, to think rationally. After all, I was, by profession a logical and rational man. I spent my working life attempting to help the sufferers of mental illnesses of all genres and depths, even the rare case of some poor individual exhibiting symptoms similar to those of the writer of the journal. Why I should now be so affected by the revelations contained in this nineteenth century text was beyond me.

I concluded that tiredness must be a major contributory factor to my current malaise. I'd not had much rest since Dad's death, and, today in particular had been a tense and fraught affair, beginning with the visit to the solicitors office, followed by my almost obsessive fascination with the journal. Allied to that were the disturbing words it contained, and the veiled threat of some long-hidden family involvement in one of the great crime mysteries in history. I'd fallen asleep in a chair, after all, something I'd never normally do, and of course, I'd drunk a few small whiskies along the way.

I decided to put the journal away for the night, to get some sleep, and begin again in the morning, when I'd be refreshed, have a clear head, and yet, I knew I couldn't. I just couldn't do that! I needed to know more, and the thirst for that knowledge just couldn't wait until the morning in order to be quenched.

Feeling as though I was being driven by some unseen force, a power that wouldn't let me go, I rose from the comfort of the fireside chair, and let myself be drawn once again into the study, drawn deeper, ever deeper, into the dark and blood-stained world of Jack the Ripper!

As I settled myself down once more in my chair, I decided to forego reading any more of the journal for the time being. I wanted more factual information, more background to the case. I accessed the internet once more and found and printed another collection of facts on the case. Although the case is over a hundred years old, there exists a vast network of websites devoted to the crimes of The Ripper, and there is no shortage of information to be gleaned if one wants it. I say I was searching for facts, though of course many of the so-called facts attached to the Ripper murders were themselves open to conjecture. It seemed to me as I read much of the information before me that what had been accepted by the police and public as the truth one day, had, on many occasions been condemned to the realms of fantasy the next! Wading through the mixture of truth, half-truth, and downright falsehood was like trying to wade through a sea of mud whilst hampered by wearing a full deep-sea diver's suit.

I'd never realized that there were so many suspects, or at least alleged suspects, many of whom hadn't even been considered at the time of the murders. It seemed that, even today, new names were being added to the list with unerring regularity. Rather than the case drawing nearer to a conclusion as time went on, it appeared to me that a solution grew less likely with every passing day. There had been murders before, and there continued to be murders after the five canonical murders attributed to The Ripper. Martha Tabram of course, had not been one of these, though the journal now placed her firmly within the list of Ripper killings. I'd read the alleged Ripper's account of Tabram's murder, followed by his short chilling description of the death of Polly Nichols. Still to come, if the journal listed them all, were the murders of Annie Chapman, Elizabeth Stride, Catherine Eddowes, and Mary Jane Kelly, her murder taking place on the 9th November. Further murders over the next three months were at one time or another attributed to The Ripper but were soon discounted as being the work of others. It has even been suggested that one or more of the above victims may not have been actual Ripper victims, but I hadn't the time to try to follow up on that hypothesis. If the journal ran true to form, any questions about the number of his victims would be resolved by reading its pages, by following the words of the writer, (The Ripper?), to its conclusion.

I looked again at the list of alleged suspects. From what little knowledge I'd gleaned so far, even I found some of them to be too fanciful for words. I'd already discounted the Prince of the Realm from my thoughts and looked at those I thought to be the main suspects *at the time of the murders*.

There was 'Leather Apron' a name attributed to the Ripper before his later appendage, thought by many at the time to be a Polish cobbler by the name of John Pizer. A resident of Mulberry Street, Pizer, like some of the other suspects was Jewish, (strange how many times the Jews have been the scapegoats for heinous crimes). Pizer was cleared of involvement by the police.

Another Pole, also Jewish, this time a hairdresser also fell under suspicion. Aaron Kosminski was to be revealed in later papers as having come under suspicion at the time, and he was at one time incarcerated in the Colney Hatch Asylum, where my great-grandfather attended patients from time to time. (A connection?).

The boyfriend and at one time live-in lover of Mary Jane Kelly was Joseph Barnett. Barnett was interviewed at length by the police, and later released. It is thought that Barnett may have committed the murders as a means of trying to get Mary Kelly to give up the world of prostitution, hoping the murders would scare her off the streets. When this failed, he killed her in a most brutal and sustained attack, only to retire from his murderous deeds thereafter. I admitted to myself that he would be a reasonable possibility.

Michael Ostrog, a man of many aliases, and of uncertain nationality, possibly Russian, maybe Polish, and surprise, surprise, described as Jewish, had a long criminal record by the time of the murders, and a history of mental illness. Said by police at the time to be 'a dangerous man', he was one of the three chief suspects of Sir Melville Macnaghten, Assistant Chief Constable, Scotland Yard, from 1889-1890, later becoming Chief Constable.

Together with Ostrog and Kosminski, Macnaghten's third chief suspect appeared to be a respectable, but slightly unstable barrister by the name of Montague John Druitt. A first-class sportsman and one-time schoolmaster at Mr Valentine's school, Blackheath, Druitt appeared to have been regularly though not lucratively employed as a barrister while having at some time taken to teaching either to supplement his meagre legal earnings, or for some other, unknown reason. That side of his life seems shrouded in mystery, as is much to do with all of those suspected of being the notorious killer.

There were others, many others, too many to warrant including them here. That is not after all the purpose of my words. I thought as I read and re-read those notes that perhaps in a few hours I would have the answer that had eluded the police of Victorian London, and all the scholars and historians since who had tried to put a name to The Ripper. I still believed that it was a simple as that. Turn to the back page, and it'll be there, I told myself. See for yourself, if not in his own hand, then surely great-grandfather would reveal the truth, if he really knew him, and if the journal were genuine. I didn't do it of course, I couldn't, I've already explained that haven't I? Whatever was waiting for me at the end of my strange journey into the past that was being generated by the journal would have to wait until I'd read every word along the way, felt the pain of the victims as the writer described his horrendous and heinous descent into what I now saw as inevitable madness, finally to discover, I hoped, the fate of Jack the Ripper.

It was now pitch dark outside, and the wind had become a

howling gale, so much stronger than before. The dark shadow fingers of the tree continued to dance their twisted ballet across the window panes, and occasionally one would brush against the glass, sounding as though someone were gently rapping on the window, pleading to be allowed in, to escape the wind, the dark, the raging storm that was gathering by the minute.

Knowing that I couldn't put it off any longer, I reached out once more to take up the journal, and, making a great effort to steady my hands, and my nerves, I turned the last page I'd read, and watched the words of the next page float up to meet my eyes, as I left behind the raging storm outside the window, and found myself once more caught up in a storm of a very different kind!

NINE
METAMORPHOSIS?

MY FIRST REACTION on turning to the next page of the journal
was one of shock. It took less than a second for me to realize
that the handwriting had changed. Whereas the previous pages
had been written in a firm hand, almost displaying the rage in
the words with the obvious pressure applied to the nib of the
pen, and the expansive strokes displayed in certain letters, now
suddenly, the writing appeared smaller, upright, and very
ordered in its application to the page. Was this a different hand
at work? I looked closely at the page and attempted a
comparison with the one I'd recently finished reading.

Close examination revealed that many of the letters,
although smaller and seemingly more ordered in construction,
displayed the same characteristics. The construction of the
letter 'f' for example, and also the flourish applied to the 'y'
were quite distinct in their commonality. There were other
matches present, all of which confirmed to me that the writer of
the two pages was one and the same individual. Of course, it
would take a handwriting expert to confirm such a conclusion,
but I had no doubts at all.

What had changed? Why had the Ripper's (I know; alleged Ripper's), handwriting suddenly undergone this strange metamorphosis? I guessed I might discover the answer to my question in the words I was about to read.

5th September 1888

The silence of the world sits heavy upon my weary shoulders. It's so quiet in here, so very quiet. I'm not sure where I am any more, or indeed who I am. This place is dark and cold, life is bright and warm, but I am not. The loneliness that steals me from the comfort of the day lies as a pall upon my heart. I am entombed in sadness. There's hopelessness in every breath I take, I want to be alive, I hate this place, I need to breathe fresh air, to taste just once the breath of goodness. These things are not me!

He was different, that was certain, at least for now. The rage displayed in every previous page was absent from this melancholy extract. These were the words of an unhappy, extremely depressed individual, who appeared to fear loneliness above all else. He saw himself as cut off from the world, as though living in it, but not really being a part of it. At the time of writing these words, I doubt he even knew or realized what he'd done in the last few weeks. There was a lucid calm, though his thoughts were still distorted by anxieties and repression. In addition to those other psychoses I suspected he suffered from; this individual could have also been afflicted by what today would be referred to as a multiple personality disorder. The change in handwriting, the alteration to his sentence construction, and the sudden switch from rage to depression could have been symptomatic of this, though I couldn't be sure of course.

Why had no-one noticed this man's problems, I wondered? Surely, he must have had some day to day contact with friends, family or colleagues. From what I'd read so far, he was a deeply disturbed individual who must have had some difficulty in masking all of his symptoms from those around him. Why had no-one suspected his dark secret, or had someone tried and failed to get help for this man, maybe attempted to obtain treatment for him? Perhaps though, if one analysed his words a little further, he was indeed a lonely man and therefore in all probability a loner, living, working, and killing alone. I'd read that there'd been theories about the murders being some sort of conspiracy, that were two or more killers involved, but, if the journal were the real thing, then there had been just one man, but that one man may have had many different faces. As of now, I'd just met number two!

I paused to make a referral to my printed fact sheets. I'd heard in the past, and it was now confirmed for me, that throughout the course of the Ripper investigations a number of letters had been sent to the police and other agencies concerned with the case purporting to be from The Ripper. Many, if not all of these had at some time been dismissed as hoaxes, in no small part due to the differences in handwriting between them. It had been concluded that no one man could have been responsible for so many varying styles of handwriting, and that therefore they couldn't all be the work of the murderer. Could it have been, I wondered, that one or more of those letters *could* have been from the killer, written whilst in the form of one of a number of distinctly different personalities? As I hadn't even got to the point in the case where the first of those letters had appeared, I decided to reserve judgment for the time being.

6th September 1888

*Where is peace? It eludes me so. Death would be such a
release from this torment of perpetual agony. I have such
a headache, throbbing in my skull. There's laudanum in
the house. Took some. Better, much better. Saw no-one
today, watched the world passing through the window,
pretty girl selling flowers on the corner, clean girl,
young, innocent as the blooms in her basket. Coaches
and carts and barrows and life. All life, but not for me. A
cacophony in my head, a kaleidoscope in my mind, why
so tired, why? I turned my head from the bitter glass and
poured the laudanum into my throat.*

So the laudanum was taking hold of him! I couldn't know
how much he'd taken since his first purchase of the drug, but it
was clear to me that he'd been far exceeding the safe dose of the
stuff. It was clouding his thoughts, numbing his senses, and,
though undoubtedly helping to alleviate the pain of his
headaches, it was also helping to fuel his depression and his
sense of isolation by its mind altering and hallucinogenic
effects. I couldn't help but note his reference to the 'clean and
innocent' flower seller in the street. What a complete contrast
to his previous references towards the other women in his life,
'the whores'. This was a minor eye-opener to me; here was the
man who may have been one of the most notorious killers in the
history of British crime revealing not a wicked bloodlust, but a
desire for peace, almost inviting death. This wasn't the picture
of Jack the Ripper as envisaged by history, or by the so-called
informed public, or the venerated historians who had given so
many varied opinions on the murders over the years.

How soon could one become addicted to laudanum? I
wasn't sure. As a drug it had barely been used for years, but I

was well aware that the more one took in a short time, the faster would be the addictive process, and I'd no doubt in my mind that he had become addicted. It must also be borne in mind that at the time of the Ripper murders, there was no National Health Service in the UK, no Community Psychiatric Programme as exists today. Many people in Victorian London would have lived their entire lives without having access to qualified medical care, such as it was at the time. People moved around from address to address with far greater frequency than would be expected today. I had found the answer to one of my questions. If the writer had so chosen, he could indeed have lived his life in splendid isolation, with little or no contact with his fellow citizens. If he worked alone, or with little regular contact with colleagues and family, it would have been quite possible for his symptoms to remain unnoticed by those around him, particularly if he was able, (as I expected he could), to display a veneer of respectability and normality during his working days. The man would have developed the ability to become a consummate actor when faced with everyday life, displaying a public face far removed from the persona that took over when darkness fell, and when his 'voices' would awaken in his mind, leading him down the blood-soaked paths of murder and mutilation.

Then again, another question surfaced in my mind. It could still be that the writer of the journal was an impostor, a poor disturbed soul anxious to achieve some sort of infamy and notoriety by constructing an elaborate and convincing account of events that had already occurred. It still remained within the bounds of possibility that the journal was written after the fact, but then, I realized that my great-grandfather still had a part to play in this story, that I would read his own version of events in good time, when I reached the end of the journey into the mind of the tormented soul which was being poured out in graphic detail in the words before my eyes. I felt that the answers, however painful, would be forthcoming if I remained patient, and saw the journal through to its conclusion. Perhaps at some point a clue would be exhibited which would place the journal firmly into the realm of actuality, the writer would reveal some information, no matter how small, which would prove his involvement both before, during, and after the fact. There'd been so many hoaxes in the past.

I turned to the next page, and the rage was back! The handwriting was once more that of the original character in this terrifying melodrama. I was once again pitched into the darkest side of the character of the man I was beginning to believe truly was Jack the Ripper, though not quite the Ripper of legend. This was a human, seriously flawed, perhaps, but still a human character, filled with angst and anger, riddled with uncontrollable psychoses, and seriously in need of the help which he so obviously would never receive in the world in which he lived. There was another significant difference. Whereas the previous pages had been written in what must have been a fairly standard black ink, the page before me was written in red, the colour of the blood which so clouded his life and his thinking!

7th September 1888

They think they're safe, they all think they're safe, but oh no, I'll show them. They laugh and posture in their effete and lurid decadence. Yes, they're decadent; decadent and immoral, damned whores! They offer their putrid selves for a shilling a time, bending over and lifting their skirts in dark alleys, pigs in a trough. They spread themselves and their diseases for the price of a doss for the night, filthy, rancid, damnable whores! The chancre of the streets, a festering sore, the defilement of all things woman. The voices are calling, louder and louder, they're with me every minute, and we know what we must do. They make my head hurt, but the laudanum is my friend, and takes the pain away. Need more, shall have more, must hone my blades, sharpen my thoughts, let the voices speak clearly, together we'll make them listen, all of them. Blood, blood, and more blood, only blood will rid the streets of the pestilence.

I'll slash you and rip you,
and you'll die where you lie.
I've sharpened my blades,
so you'll die 'fore you cry.

Look out little whores, I know where you are, and I'm coming, oh yes, I'm coming.

This entry, dated the 7th September was particularly chilling, no less for the use of the perverse and terrifying little verse. It was like a clarion call, a battle cry, announcing, to himself and his journal at least, that the Ripper was about to stalk the streets once again.

A glance at my reference notes confirmed the fact that on the night of the 7th/8th September 1888, the Ripper struck again. I couldn't escape the feeling that I was actually there, I was so wrapped up in the words of the journal. I was aware of the strangest feeling, as though I myself was being touched by the terror that stalked the streets of Whitechapel. I wished I could cry out, warn someone, put a stop to all this, but of course, such thoughts were stupid and illogical, I was removed from the scene by an insurmountable chasm, over a century of time, and yet, I could almost taste the chill of that night, feel the dampness of the early morning dew forming on the cobbles of Hanbury Street. As I placed the pages of the journal down on the desk in front of me, I shook with an involuntary shiver, for I knew, with the grim and unchangeable certainty of history, that time was rapidly running out for Annie Chapman!

TEN
LEATHER APRON

THE EVIL that was Jack the Ripper brought fresh terror to the streets of London with the murder of Annie Chapman, the brutality and savagery of her murder far exceeding that which had gone before. Her body was discovered by an elderly man, John Davis, shortly before 6 a.m. on the 8th of September in the backyard of number 29 Hanbury Street. Her dress had been pulled up over her knees, and her intestines were clearly visible, draped across her left shoulder. He summoned James Green and James Kent, two acquaintances from nearby, and sent them for the police.

The police surgeon, Dr. George Bagster Phillips, arrived at 6.30 a.m. and on inspection he found evidence of the most serious mutilations so far in the series of killings which were now beginning to appear as the work of one crazed individual.

Chapman's throat had been cut, again the wound so deep as to almost sever the head from the body, the abdomen had been sliced cleanly open, and, most horrifically, certain internal organs normally present within the abdomen were missing. The killer had removed them and taken them with him! Her face was swollen and her tongue slightly protruding. Could the killer have suffocated her prior to inflicting the fatal wound to the poor victim's neck?

A witness had placed Chapman at the entrance to 29 Hanbury Street at approximately 5.30 a.m. If she was to be believed, it meant that the Ripper had met, murdered and butchered Annie Chapman in less than thirty minutes, indicating either an attack of great frenzy, or an act of consummate skill. Close to the standpipe which served the backyard of the building, the police discovered their first clue in the case, a neatly folded, but waterlogged leather apron. At last, they had something to go on! No-one had seen the killer; he'd disappeared like a wraith into the night.

Those were the bare facts of the case as far as I could ascertain from my printed notes. Would the journal confirm any of the facts? There was only one way to find out. I turned to the next page.

8th September 1888

Another whore in Hell. Blood's still under my nails. Wash, wash, wash, it'll clean away soon. Vile, filthy, whore blood! My, but she bled a lot, fat, dumpy little whore. This one tried to scream, not a sleepy whore like last one. Had to silence the bitch first, took her breath away, haha. She sliced up well, bit too much fat though, or her head would have come right off.
Now that would have been a sight! Oh yes, the blood would have really run then. Took some of the bitch's entrails and fed them to the street dogs near home, a feast, haha. Left something behind, the apron, not to worry, plenty more, and they'll never know it's mine, it's new though, such a shame, a waste, but had to go, there

were people nearby, just made the sewer, my invisible shield. Didn't realize the blood would stick to the leather like that. They can scour the streets for ever more, they'll never find me, never take me. Wish I hadn't had to go without it, they cost good money. Good money better than whores. Won't be long until the next one, the voices are pleased, they want more. More headaches, more laudanum.

So, he was celebrating the death of another poor woman while at the same time bemoaning the loss of an apron that had cost him 'good money'. The callous reference to 'good money better than whores' reduced poor Annie Chapman's life to less than the value of a cheap leather apron. As to the apron itself, this was the beginning of the police and public's fixation with 'Leather Apron', the name now given by the popular press and the people at large to the killer. The name Jack the Ripper wouldn't be given to the murderer until some weeks from now. How sad that the police of the day had no forensic scientists available to them The apron, left behind in Hanbury Street would surely have yielded fingerprints, DNA evidence, and perhaps more clues to enable an identification to be made, if not immediately, then at some point in the future. The lack of scientific technology at the time of the ripper murders was in itself one of the killer's greatest assets. As for the journal, well, I felt as I read the entry that the writer was becoming more and more disassociated with reality. He saw the act of killing as little more than a ritual required by his 'voices' in order to satisfy their need for blood. He was enjoying the 'slicing' and took some amusement from the fact that the poor woman's head was almost severed from her body by his blade. True to his plans, he'd used the sewers as his escape route, taking some of the victim's internal organs with him, before feeding them to the ravenous dogs that roamed the streets of London by night. What an awful and terrible confession! It seemed so logical to me that he'd used those dank underground passageways to evade the police, and any potential witnesses; I couldn't think why the police themselves hadn't immediately thought of the sewers as the killer's possible escape route.

There was the reference to his headaches again as well. Then even more laudanum. He was without a doubt hooked on the drug. It would probably have helped to anaesthetise him even further against the horrors of the deeds he was perpetrating.

I placed the journal on the desk once more and rose from my chair. I was getting stiff again and needed to stretch and relax my limbs. For the first time in what seemed an age, I looked at the clock. It was only eight o'clock. It certainly felt much later. It was pitch black outside the window, the wind had managed to blow itself up into a wicked storm, and rain had begun to lash the panes. If ever a night was fit for the revelations of one of the most evil killers ever to evade British justice, I felt that this was it. The moon had been obliterated by cloud, and there was little or no natural light visible through the window. I felt cut off from reality, from the world of 'normal' society, much as the writer of the journal must have felt during that awful, terrifying autumn so long ago. I was on my own, with no-one to talk to, just my own thoughts and fears for company. To tell the truth, reading the journal was having a profound effect upon me, far greater than I would ever have thought possible. I'd never been a fanciful person, not given to thoughts of the supernatural, and certainly not easily spooked by things I didn't understand, but I was more than a little unsettled as I paced around my study, trying to increase the circulation in my stiff and aching joints. Every sound in the room, from the ticking of the clock to the rain against the window panes was being amplified inside my head, the tension of the written words, and the loneliness of my situation only serving to add to the overall feeling of detachment I was beginning to feel. There was a similarity in our situations that wouldn't easily leave me, which I simply couldn't dismiss.

How many nights, I wondered, had he sat in his room alone, as I was at that moment, surrounded by the sounds of the night, with just his twisted thoughts for company? He may have welcomed the voices in his head, they were his solace, his companions, and he felt less alone when they were there with him. Thank God, I had Sarah, our parting was only temporary, I had never been alone in my life, and I dreaded to think of how lonely a life could be if one were so isolated from society, from friends and family, that one could possibly begin to retreat into a fantasy world, where imagined voices in the head could take on the reality of an individual's only confidantes, a person's only 'friends'. As an only child may invent an 'imaginary friend' in order to alleviate loneliness and isolation, so the writer of the journal, though certainly not inventing the voices, had come to see them as real entities, as his closest and most trusted allies in a world which certainly could not at the time, and probably never would understand his mental torment in the future.

He'd stated towards the end of this latest entry that it wouldn't be long until he struck again. A glance at my notes told me that it would in fact be a day over three weeks before the next Ripper murder, so assuming him to be telling the truth as he saw it at the time, that he was about to strike again, and quickly, something must have happened to delay his next foray into the dark streets of Whitechapel. Only the journal could tell me, and yet, I was becoming so tired, my eyes were heavy. There were too many pages in the journal still to go. I'd never stay awake long enough to absorb them all, not accurately. I needed sleep, perhaps after a few hours in bed, I'd be able to start refreshed, be less affected by the things I was reading, and approach the horrors of the Ripper murders with more logic and detachment than I was feeling at the moment.

I promised myself that I'd read just one more page, just one, then I'd retire to the bedroom and grab a few hours of much-needed sleep. As I turned the page and looked at the date, I noticed he'd missed a day.

10th September 1888

Almost slept the clock round. Been working much too hard. My, but the streets are alive with people. Walked amongst the throng in Whitechapel, poor lame fools. They think they can catch 'Leather Apron' just by walking the streets and shouting for justice! Never mind, haha, I cried for justice too. Berated some poor fool constable for not catching the awful fiend, "Why officer, can you not catch this evil malodorous person in our midst? Have you police no clue?"

"Move along sir, move along, now. You just let us do our work, and you see to your own, we'll catch the killer, never you fear."

I could have laughed aloud, there in his face. But he has told me to go on with my work, so I'll never fear as he says, and I'll get about my work, for it's crying out to be done. So many whores, so much pestilence upon the streets. I wonder what they're thinking now, trembling in their dirty shoes, waiting for the knife, waiting for me, waiting, waiting. Next time, I'll not just let the whore blood flow, I'll taste it's warmth upon my lips, just a taste, a morsel no more, I promise I shall.

The bare effrontery of the man! To walk amidst the crowds of concerned citizens, joining in with their calls for justice and police action, he was as brazen as they come. Not only that, but I could just imagine the poor constable being harried by this man, seeking some way to move him on whilst trying to do his job without upsetting an 'anxious and worried citizen'. The fact that the writer had gone so far as to quote the short conversation with the hapless constable showed his complete disdain for the officer of the law, his total contempt for the forces of law and order, and his absolute belief that he was untouchable by them. He so obviously felt himself immune from capture. I suspected that he would even have believed absolutely that the officer's words to 'get about his work' had given him free licence to carry on his killing spree with official sanction from the officer himself, if not indeed from the whole police force of London. He had obtained the approval he sought.

I was concerned most of all by his threat to taste the blood of his next victim. Shades of Count Dracula, I thought at the time. Though I was sure he wouldn't go as far as to drink the blood, I felt that he was beginning to personalize the murders a little more by this threatened action. Once the blood of his victim came into contact with his mouth, once he felt and tasted the warmth of his victim, he would feel in total possession of the body, she would be his to do with as he liked, and, as history has revealed to us, the worst was yet to come.

Finally, I was now sure of one thing. The writer of the journal was an intelligent man, well-schooled, as his words, phrases, and use of the English language were demonstrating to me. Assuming that he was indeed The Ripper, in my mind I was able to dismiss as suspects the Polish Jew Kosminsky, the boot maker Pizer, and the Pole Severin Klosowski, another suspect I had read of but not previously mentioned. To my mind, the words of the journal were those of an educated man writing in his own language, as he displayed so much familiarity with the phraseology of his English. A foreigner, no matter how well educated would surely not have played so adeptly with his sentence construction as the writer of this incredible journal. No, this was a home-grown killer, of that I was now sure.

That was it, it was now almost ten thirty, I didn't know quite where the time had gone. I'd been so engrossed, so carried along by this strange and macabre day that time had almost lost it's meaning for me. As I placed the journal on the desk, relieved to be taking my leave of the dark and murderous world of Jack the Ripper for a few hours at least, I remembered that I'd unplugged the phones a little earlier. Sarah may have been ringing, trying to call me back as she'd promised. I plugged them back in, checked for messages, and there she was, just a quick "Hi darling, presume you're busy, I'll call tomorrow, goodnight I love you," before I climbed the stairs, quickly undressed and found my way under the warmth of the duvet, and quickly fell into a deep, though disturbed and dream laden sleep, haunted by dreams of the dark, blood-soaked world of terror that was the realm of The Ripper.

ELEVEN
FROM HELL?

THROUGHOUT MY LIFE, I've always been fascinated by the human brain, by its sheer capacity for achievement. Though relatively small in stature it is without doubt one of the wonders of creation. Like a great computer, the brain has many functions. It generates the subconscious signals required by the body to maintain temperature, breathing and blood flow, it tells us when we're hungry or thirsty, thus acting as a fuel reserve indicator. It has the in-built facility to absorb and store myriad items of information, cataloguing them in order of priority, some being required as instant recall items, others to be stored away for future use, somewhere within its vast and largely unknown memory banks. It never sleeps, never rests, a constant stream of data impulses being produced to maintain and regulate the life of its host, the human body. The brain is a vast storehouse of information, ready to be accessed as and when we require it, and, housed somewhere deep within that storehouse is the complex and almost unfathomable entity we call the mind.

Unseen, without physical form, made up entirely of little

understood electrical impulses, chemical markers and countless thought processes, the mind is the great unknown; compare it to an iceberg, with less than ten percent of its form above the surface, the majority hidden, mysterious. So it is with the mind, so complex in its entirety that we understand so little about it. Unable to be seen, touched, or at times rationalised, it is the one thing that individualises us, makes us different from one another. The mind in it's similarity to an iceberg is composed of three sections, the conscious, which is the part floating just above the surface, which we can see, sometimes smooth, sometimes shards of daggers bearing witness to the shearing forces that so shaped it, and then there is the preconscious – alike to torpor, the rippling water of the surface where items are on the tip of conscious recollection, and then, lastly, there is the vast and unimaginable unconscious which stretches into the abyssal depths, unfathomable and dark, where we store all the data that we cannot consciously recall, or repress the memories that pain us so. It is the breaking off of fragments of repressed memories which bubble to the surface and become neuroses – manifesting themselves in some outré manner, seen or unseen, to the detriment of the individual, and on rare occasions – those sufficiently unfortunate to find themselves in the company of such an individual.

Psychiatrists and psychologists who use fundamentally different approaches to reaching into the mind to identify and treat the causes and effects of mental illness will often work hand in hand for many years in order to alleviate the symptoms of just one patient's neuroses. None of the information and resources available today was available in the 1880s, when a faulty or malfunctioning brain had little or no chance of repair by the medical profession.

Unfortunately, when these neuroses rise to the surface it is possible that, as in a computer, there are times when the mind itself acts as though infected with a virus. Its programming exhibits signs of being scrambled or interrupted, normal functions are disturbed and disrupted, and the result can manifest itself in what we term mental illness, disease of the mind. Psychiatrists and psychologists have spent decades attempting to understand the workings of this most complex component of human nature, the psyche, the thing that makes us who we are, yet even today, we've barely scratched the surface. An imbalance of chemicals in the brain, a 'short circuit' in the brain's electrical impulses, can all lead to various aberrations and breakdowns in the thought processes that keep us on life's even keel. In extreme cases, meltdown can occur, and the sufferer can descend into ever deeper troughs of illness and psychosis, what was once termed unsympathetically, 'madness'. Such is the frailty of 'the mind'.

As I slept, my own subconscious mind swept me away into the vast untapped world of dreams. Less understood than the mind, the power to dream is, in some specialists' opinions, a safety valve, a means of releasing the conscious tensions and anxieties of the mind while the body lies in its recuperative, self-refreshing state, sleep. That night, however, was anything but a release. Disturbed in my waking hours by the horrific and graphic tableau being played out in the pages of the journal, my dreams were a series of ghastly vivid nightmares. The faces of the victims and the suspects, all recognisable from the printed internet facts I'd obtained earlier, floated in a never ending grotesque merry-go-round in front of my eyes, victims screaming, bleeding from the throat, from their mouths, the suspects all laughing a crazed, high pitched laugh as they brandished gleaming, flashing knives, slashing wildly at my face as they were carried past my line of sight by an unseen demonic wind. At times, victims and suspects almost melded into each other, until the faces became indistinct, a blur, fading in and out of focus, dissolving into fog, into nothingness.

As the last of this grotesque gallery finally receded from view, I found myself standing alone in a typical nineteenth century East End street. I looked upwards, the street sign at the corner proclaimed it to be Dorset Street. I was rooted to the spot, just outside the door of a public house, its name clearly displayed as The Britannia, one of the haunts of at least one of the Rippers victims. From within came the sounds of music, an out-of-tune piano by the sound of it, accompanied by raucous laughter and singing. Try as I might I couldn't move, and then, the doors of the pub opened towards me, and, instead of the light from within flooding out to meet me, instead there poured a river of blood, a deluge that swept me off my feet and carried me along the street, screaming in terror, my arms flailing about in an attempt to find some hand hold, anything to grab in order to pull myself from the mad torrent of sickly sweet copper scented blood. I was being swept along at such a speed that the buildings of the street were indistinct, indeed my eyes, my mouth, my nose were rapidly becoming filled with the terrible red liquid that carried me inexorably towards ...towards where? I knew that I was drowning, drowning in the blood of the Ripper's victims, and I screamed, and screamed, and screamed, but no-one seemed to hear.

Just as it seemed my lungs were on the point of bursting, as I felt that I could take no more, I felt a hand grasping mine. Slowly, with a great strength behind it, the hand pulled me from that thick, viscous ocean of blood. As is the nature of dreams I suddenly found myself standing, completely dry and unsullied by the blood which moments ago had saturated my clothes and my body, in the grounds of the hospital where I had worked for five years, and there, beside me was my old friend and mentor, Doctor T J O'Malley. O'Malley had taught me almost everything I knew about modern-day psychiatry and had been my teacher and my friend until his untimely death from cancer three years before. Now here he was, rescuing me from the blood, from the terror, from the fear. I reached out to touch him, to thank him, and he just wasn't there anymore, he was gone!

There were other, less distinct dreams, but all of a similar nature, the theme never varying from the all-encompassing terror of the murders, and then, suddenly, I was awake.

I hadn't heard the window opening, hadn't felt the wind blowing the curtains into the room, or sensed the shadowy figure that now stood towering above me, oozing menace. In the darkness I could just make out the outline of the figure of a man, leaning over me, his eyes as red as the blood of my dreams. The eyes seemed to glow in the dark, they penetrated into my very soul, and the fear and terror I felt in that moment were indescribable. He was clad in black from head to foot, the bottom half of his face masked by a black silken scarf. On his head he wore a black top hat, and in his hand he carried a long, gleaming, wicked looking knife.

I was paralysed with fear. I couldn't move. He leaned ever closer to me, and he spoke with a voice direct from the grave.

"So Robert, you know me, do you not? You know who I am. You know too much Robert, far too much. As you have seen inside my soul, so have I looked into yours. I cannot let you go any further, you are mine now, Robert, mine forever."

Before I could reply, he swiftly raised his left hand and swept the scarf from his face. As it fell away, I was gripped by greatest sense of shock and revulsion I have ever experienced. I peered into Hell itself. The man opened his mouth, and there appeared a huge gape, and the smell of rancid decay and putrefaction poured from within that chasm, and I knew that he was death itself. His right arm rose, and even in the darkness of my bedroom I could see the flash of the blade as it came down swiftly towards my throat. As the knife pressed into my trembling flesh I tried to scream, and then....

Sweating, shaking, and trembling uncontrollably I really woke up. It had been that most terrifying of experiences, a dream within a dream. I reached out and turned the bedside light on. The reality of that last encounter had been so utterly terrifying that it took me more than ten minutes to regain some semblance of composure. At last, I felt confident enough to remove myself from the bed and make my way tentatively down the stairs to the kitchen, where I turned the lights full on, and switched on the kettle. I needed an extraordinarily strong cup of coffee.

Sitting at the kitchen table in my shorts a few minutes later, I concluded that the journal had taken some sort of hold over both my conscious and subconscious mind. I had become totally absorbed into the strange and murky world of Jack the Ripper, as perceived through the eyes of the writer of this incredible document. Nothing had ever affected me so profoundly before. There was something other-worldly about these sheets of old paper, the faded ink, the wild rantings of the words placed on each page. I felt as though he was there with me, in the house, in my head, in my mind. Although I knew it to be wholly irrational, and without sense or logic, somehow I was tuned into, and in the presence of a great evil. Though I knew no-one would ever understand what I meant, I knew I was not alone in the house that night. I looked at the clock. It was only 2.30 a.m. I'd barely slept three hours, yet I knew I must return to the journal, I had to continue the journey, had to see it through to the end. I would start to read again, there and then in the dead of night, quietly and carefully, watched over, so I thought by the soul of the man I was now sure was...Jack the Ripper!

I made my way to the study; coffee in hand, turned every light in the room on, and once more settled myself down at the desk. With my hands trembling far more than I would have thought possible just a few hours ago, I reached out and took up the journal once more.

TWELVE
RELATIVE CALM

12th September 1888

*What a night! No sleep, just dreams, red dreams, warm,
cloying redness everywhere. The headaches are worse
than before. Even the laudanum didn't stop them. See
what these foul whores have done to me. Now they've
robbed me of my sleep, my rest. They'll pay, oh yes, I'll
make them pay. I walked miles today, no cabs, and the
streets were filled with little insignificant people, worms
and insects. The smell of the streets was an assault on
my senses, but I had to go. If the laudanum won't work
any more, I need something else, must stop the pain.
Thought of visiting 'T', but he knows me too well.
Instead found myself on the street where Cavendish
lives. What a grand façade, he does live well. Presented
myself and was shown to the drawing room. He seemed
pleased though surprised to see me. We're not close of
course, I often wonder how he sees me, and we hardly*

*know each other after all, though we've spoken often.
Told him the laudanum wasn't enough, the headaches
are worse. He pried into other 'symptoms' which I
denied and said I should make an appointment for a
proper consultation. Did he think me foolish when I
refused, said I just wanted something to help the pain?
Do I care? No, I do not. He suggested I take the air
somewhere, the country perhaps. Shall I see the coast,
the sea perhaps? I think I may. No good ripping whores
if I can't take pleasure from the work. Get rid of the
pain, and then gut the foul bitches again. The voices
agree, let's rest awhile. They'll return when the time is
ripe, when the whores' blood is ready to spill again.*

THIS HAD BEEN one of the Ripper's longest individual entries.
It struck me as strange that he was describing a night of dreams
almost on a par with those I had just experienced. The link was
almost too close for comfort. What bizarre quirk of fate had
brought me to this page immediately after undergoing the
series of nightmares from which I'd just escaped? There was
one significant difference, however. He had written, 'no sleep,
just dreams' and I thought that he was perhaps referring to
hallucinations. Certainly, in his drug fuelled state of mind, true
sleep would have been difficult, and he had probably lain in a
waking dream state for hour upon hour, his head filled with one
vivid image after another, until the pain in his head would have
made him feel as though it were about to explode. He thought
that the laudanum had failed to stop the headaches; in fact, we
now know that, due to the amounts he was consuming, it was
actually helping to perpetuate them by inducing the terrible
hallucinations from which he was suffering. He was on a never-
ending downward spiral of drug abuse, such as is often

experienced by modern-day addicts. He must have been existing in a half-world, somewhere between sleep and consciousness, beset by terrible blood-soaked dreams, a constant reminder of the orgy of destruction into which his life had been plunged by his rapid descent into multiple wildly obsessive murder. That spiral would almost inevitably lead him into a helter-skelter style whirlpool of self-destruction. For the Ripper, there could be no going back, never again for him a normal life, an ordinary day. He'd already passed the point of no return.

I was still shaking, unnerved by my own terrible nightmares, and my imagined, though psychologically very real, encounter with the masked killer. My own mental equilibrium had certainly been profoundly disturbed by the last few hours, the letter from my father, great-grandfather's note, the journal itself, and the dreams. Though I wouldn't have cared to admit it, I was being drawn deeper and deeper into a world far removed from the reality of normal life, into a darkness not of my choosing. In short, I was identifying with, and being given a taste of the madness of the Ripper.

I was intrigued by the mysterious 'T'. He'd mentioned the man(?) before, without a clue as to his identity. Once more he had referred to him simply by initial, whilst clearly identifying my great-grandfather by name. Why? He obviously felt a need to protect 'T' from exposure, even in his private journal. Was he a close relative, or perhaps a friend of some social standing? Maybe I'd find out as the journal progressed.

I had to admit that this entry was perhaps the most lucid so far. It certainly seemed to make more logical sense than some of his earlier entries; there was less rambling incoherence in his words. My great-grandfather had obviously offered to accept him as a patient, which he'd declined, indicating that he must have had the financial means to pay for any such treatment. The Ripper had however seen some sense in great-grandfather's suggestion that he 'take the air'. His words indicated to me that he perhaps had family or friends both in the country and on the coast. I doubted he would have explored either option without knowing of some accommodating and friendly potential host. Was he, I wondered, becoming bored with the whole business of killing? He suggested by his writing that he was deriving no pleasure from the murders and needed to refresh his blood lust. Even his voices were silent, his head probably so clouded by a laudanum-induced stupor that he was numb even to that part of his psychosis. I pitied the poor family member or acquaintances on whom he may foist himself in the near future. They would be totally unaware of the fact that the most notorious killer ever to walk the streets of London was their houseguest.

As for my great-grandfather, well, Doctor Burton Cleveland Cavendish did indeed live in a quite sumptuous residence. As a youngster I had been suitably impressed by old family photographs showing his house on a long-disappeared tree-lined avenue in the Charing Cross area of London. The house did indeed have an imposing façade, with five or six steps, flanked by polished iron railings, leading up to the heavy oak double entrance doors, complete with gleaming brass letterbox and door handles. Though black and white, the photographs left no reason for doubting the luxuriousness of the house, or the wealth of its owner. Burton Cavendish had begun his career as a humble general practitioner, rising to become a skilled surgeon, and eventually deciding to specialize in diseases of the brain, at which time he entered the branch of medicine which we now know as psychiatry. As his wealth increased, so did his sense of philanthropy, and he would regularly devote a portion of his time to providing free consultations at the Colney Hatch Asylum. I doubt whether his reasons were entirely unselfish of course, as his visits to the asylum would have brought him into contact with many patients who would be suffering from far more diverse afflictions than he would be likely to encounter in his comfortable private practice. In short, the asylum was filled to the brim with an abundance of research material, human guinea pigs! If that sounds callous, I should point out that in the nineteenth century there were few psychiatric text books, even fewer specialist hospitals for the treatment of psychological disorders, and the only way for a doctor to study and therefore learn to treat such illnesses, was by contact with the sufferers of such ailments, and the more severe the affliction, the greater the opportunity to study it's effects and causes, the better to discover a cure.

Bearing in mind that in terms of distance the Charing Cross area was not far from Whitechapel, though in terms of its affluence it was a world away, I had no reason to doubt that the writer of the journal had indeed visited the home of my great-grandfather, and that thought in itself caused me to shiver once more. Though I had only seen photographs of the house, and never actually visited it, it having been demolished years before my birth, it still managed to make me feel a strange sense of disturbance that the Ripper may have sat enjoying afternoon tea or some such social nicety with my ancestor while the entire population of London, and indeed the country, thanks to press reports in all the major newspapers of the day, were seeking his apprehension and conviction.

Then again, little was made, in his own words, of his relationship with my great-grandfather. They 'weren't close', he wondered how my great-grandfather perceived him, and yet he'd written that they saw each other often, though they 'hardly knew each other'. Was there a professional link, (some thought the Ripper to be a doctor or medical man of sorts), a social connection, or worst of all, could Jack the Ripper have some distant, tenuous link as a little known and (partially at least) ignored, distant family member? My senses positively baulked at that last possibility. I couldn't even countenance such a thing, though I couldn't totally disregard it. It is possible after all to 'hardly know' a relative as the writer put it, if one has little or no contact with that person for a length of time, or indeed throughout the course of their life. Perhaps my great-grandfather would explain all in his own notes, to which I'd come in due course of my study of this incredible, horrifying, yet riveting document.

A quick reference to my research notes showed that there was in fact a lull of twenty two days between the killing of Annie Chapman and the next, (and violently bloody) murder, or should I say murders, as, on the night of 30th September Jack the Ripper would commit not one, but two abominable atrocities. I was intrigued by what I may be about to discover. Could it be that between the murder of Chapman and the grisly double killing the Ripper actually went on holiday? Did he become so ill as to be incapable of continuing his murderous quest, was he indeed hospitalised, and, horror of horrors, released back into the community in time to kill again? What twisted path would the journal lead me down, what revelations might be lying in wait for me on the next, and subsequent pages of the astonishing story unfolding in words before my eyes? Was I about to discover the secret of this missing three weeks in the murderous career of Jack the Ripper?

Though tired, and to some extent numb from my broken sleep, my nightmares, and the horrific thought that I may be connected by the ties of birth to the bloody slayer of defenceless women, I stretched my arms, reaching towards the ceiling, forced my eyes to open, despite the unconscious desire to drift off again into slumber, and, almost afraid to know what would come next, yet at the same time caught up in the intrigue of the journal, as the clock continued its inexorable ticking on the wall I prepared to turn to the next page.

THIRTEEN
A PAUSE FOR THOUGHT

Don't ask me why, but, just as I was about to turn to the next page in the journal, something stopped me. I couldn't to this day say what it was, perhaps it was the tiredness, the after-affects of the nightmares, or just a basic need to escape the intensity of the situation for a few minutes, but I decided to lay down the journal and instead look further into the environment, the world inhabited by the Ripper and his victims. Perhaps as well I was becoming more unsettled than I imagined by the journal and it's recurrent theme of bloodthirsty murder, the potentially insane ramblings of a man reviled by history, and the fact that here, in my study, on my desk, was a document that may have been handled by, and written in the hand of the notorious Jack the Ripper. Was I handling the same papers he had held, placing my own imprint, my fingerprints over those of the Ripper himself?

Of course, it was obvious that my own father and those before him had handled the documents, and that there would be various prints upon the pages, but it seemed ironic that somewhere on these pages, was the potential means of identifying the Whitechapel murderer conclusively, if only there had been a fingerprint record, a database of sorts from the time of the murders. No such records existed of course, and any fingerprints on the pages were irrelevant as a source of identification, and, at best, if made public, would merely have curiosity value. 'The fingerprints of Jack the Ripper', I could see the headline, and yet, what would it do to reveal them? At best they would only serve to add further mystery to the case and could only be of interest to those seeking to sensationalise the whole affair. To a serious student of the murders they could be of little value except perhaps to establish that the prints were male or female, if that were possible, and I wasn't expert enough in the field of forensics to know whether that were entirely possible.

Enough of this speculation! I wanted to know and understand more of the world as seen through Victorian eyes, including those of my great-grandfather. I turned once more to the computer. Much of what I'd already gleaned about the Ripper and his victims had been found at www.casebook.org, an internet website devoted to the study of the Jack the Ripper case. With hundreds of members worldwide, The Casebook furnished those with an interest in the case with not only details of the crimes themselves, but also with a wealth of detail and information relating to Victorian London, accompanied by a collection of informative and evocative photographs. I clicked onto the site once more and delved deeper into the world of the Victorians.

Certainly, the London inhabited by my great-grandfather would have seemed like another world to the average inhabitant of the East End. My grandfather's wealth and social standing in the community enabled him to live a privileged existence. He was able to afford the best of food and clothes, was attended by a retinue of domestic servants in his quite palatial London home, and his social life would probably have revolved around visits to friends, the theatre, the races, and of course his private gentlemen's club. My great-grandmother would have filled her time 'receiving' guests, taking tea with her visitors, and perhaps engaging in a little charity work. Even the slightly affluent middle classes would have thought nothing of employing at least one, and perhaps more servants in their comfortable homes, far removed from the slums of Whitechapel and its like. As for the real gentry, the royal family, the lords, ladies and gentlemen of the royal court, their lives would have been even further removed from the reality of the everyday drudgery that was the lot of their most humble fellow Londoners.

The vast majority of those poor unfortunates unlucky enough to inhabit the East End of London in the late nineteenth century lived in an almost continual state of abject poverty, if not complete penury. Housing, where it existed was of poor quality, and whole families would often be forced to live in one, cold, cramped, unheated room. Windows would often be glassless, and to keep out the draughts, many would stuff the gaps with old newspapers, or rags, anything indeed to keep out the biting cold of winter. Work was often transient, and always hard, with wages often barely enough to live on. Disease and general ill-health were rife, hardly surprising when one considers that the streets themselves were little more than the most squalid open sewers, and that personal hygiene was virtually non-existent.

Many of those with no home of their own would move from place to place, often sleeping in 'Doss' houses where a bed could be purchased for a few pennies a night. There would quite often be sixty or seventy people sharing a communal bedroom in these houses, which were more like hostels than homes. Many itinerant workers and the women who prostituted themselves on the streets of the East End would utilize the Doss houses on a regular basis.

A number of dignitaries and celebrities of the day visited the East End, only to be appalled by the degradation and deprivation that existed there. The authors Jack London and Beatrix Potter, and Charles Dickens no less, had all attempted to draw attention to the poverty and poor standards of living of their fellow human beings in Whitechapel and it's surrounds, but little was done to help alleviate their daily struggle for existence.

Women of course, fared even worse than the men in this vast melting pot of disease and poverty. In the nineteenth century, a working-class girl was considered as suitable for nothing more than the most menial of work, and then for eventual marriage. What little education was available was directed towards boys, there being no considered necessity for girls to receive any such knowledge. With a prolific death rate, and the possibility of widowhood at a young age an everyday occurrence in this cess-pool of humanity, it was little wonder that so many women, either by choice or circumstance, were drawn into the murky and dangerous world of prostitution.

I felt it important to remember as I read these facts however, that the Ripper's victims, like all those poor unfortunates who plied their trade on the streets by night were not born into prostitution. In fact many were born to respectable families, grew up to be married, bore children, and prostitution tended to be the last resort for many as their lives disintegrated around them through death, divorce, abandonment, alcoholism, or for many other reasons. I was struck particularly during my reading of The Casebook's files on the victims, to see a beautifully posed formal portrait photograph of Annie Chapman and her husband John, a coachman, taken in 1869, and further photos of her children.

The picture of normality, of domesticity evoked by these images served to remind me, and should remind others, that, like all the victims of both The Ripper and the system that produced them, these were normal everyday women, not some kind of misfits or rejects. History has, the thought struck me, dehumanised the victims of The Ripper to some extent. We've forgotten that they were living breathing, warm and vital souls, wanting nothing more than to live, to eat, sleep, and exist alongside their fellow human beings, no mater how sad and squalid their lives may have become.

Annie Chapman had had her own fair share of unhappiness. One of her daughters had died of meningitis aged just twelve years, her son was a cripple, and her marriage disintegrated, (both she and her husband were reputed to be heavy drinkers). John Chapman apparently paid his wife maintenance of ten shillings (fifty pence) a week, which continued until his death from cirrhosis of the liver and dropsy on Christmas day 1886. Annie was said to be distraught upon hearing the news, and it was only after his death that Annie is known to have taken to prostitution, as the only means left to her to maintain herself. At the time of her death she had been living in a lodging house on the infamous Dorset Street in Spitalfields, a street comprising a labyrinth of poor quality lodging houses, the location of three taverns of less than good repute, and a notorious site for the operations of local prostitutes. Here, in these smoke-filled microcosmic dens of iniquity, the jangling sounds of old, out-of-tune upright pianos would merge with the raucous voices of gin-soaked prostitutes and their equally drunken clients, where fights amongst the customers were a regular nightly occurrence. Whatever domestic normality Annie Chapman may once have enjoyed; it was sad to realise how far this once respectable woman had fallen in the two years prior to her eventual murder at the hands of The Ripper.

These facts were inescapable. I could at last identify with one of the victims. Annie had become quite real to me. The photographs in particular seemed to call out to me. They evoked happy days in the life of a young family. In those grainy, sepia-toned images there was no hint of the tragedy that would soon overtake those pictured. So far, in the course of my journey through the journal, I had only seen the events through the eyes of the writer, and through my own thoughts. Now I was able to think of the victims themselves, not just as the Ripper's victims, but as very real, quite ordinary people. Having read and digested the details of poor Annie Chapman's life and death, her marriage, her children, eventual grief and degradation, I knew for sure that I would be able to find similar circumstances if I were to look into the backgrounds of the other victims, and, indeed, I promised myself that I would do just that.

The room was becoming stuffy, and I opened the window, just a crack to let some much-needed fresh air into what had become quite an oppressive atmosphere. I read the final details about the funeral of Annie Chapman, and the fact that her grave was long buried over, which I found quite sad, and as I gently laid the information sheets on the desk in front of me, my heart felt heavy with sadness for that sad, lonely victim of Jack the Ripper.

I decided that I'd been putting it off long enough. My hands reached out to take up the journal once more, but, as I did, a minor draught from the window must have caught the Chapman pages, and they rustled slightly where they lay on the desk, and almost hovered above the surface. Using one hand, I reached out and gently patted them down onto the desk, putting a paperweight on them to keep them in place.

Were there other-worldly presences in the air that night? I was definitely in a receptive enough mood to feel their presence. Trying not to let my nerves get the better of me, I returned to The Ripper's words. Where, I wondered, would those words, his mind, take me next on this dark, windy, sleepless night?

FOURTEEN
WHERE IS HELL?

13th September 1888

The road to Hell is a one-way street, once entered upon the path, there's no way back. I walk the same path each day, following the whores as they too stagger blindly towards the oblivion I provide. Their deaths are pre-ordained, each one foretold by the voices that guide me on the way. Their blood must flow; their lives must end on the streets where they ply their filthy bodies, their rancid flesh. I shall continue my work, until the whores are gone, and the filth is gone, washed clean.

***

14th September 1888

I dare not leave the house. The temptations are too great, but I cannot work whilst I suffer such pain. The latest supply of laudanum seems not so strong as the last. I

*need more and more just to hold the pain at bay. I want
so for the pain to stop. I could but slay just one whore
tonight, but I cannot. I must wait until the sleeping
voices rise within and give me strength and purpose.
The whores must wait. Let them think they're safe.*

***

15th September 1888

*I wish that I could avoid the pain that I know must
come, yet every day I must live with that knowledge. It's
easy for the damned whores. Their pain is brief, as I
dispatch them to eternal Hell, while I must live in my
own version of that foul wretched place. There is so
much more to come, yet every day I wake with the fear,
the knowledge of certainty of the end which one day
must be mine. No one knows, nor can they, I must suffer
alone, for my sins, my earthly indiscretions which now
must take me deeper into the foulest depths of despair.*

So, something at least was different. For the first time The
Ripper, (I shall dispense with 'The Writer' now), had placed
three entries on one page of the journal. All the previous
entries, no matter how short, had each had a whole page
devoted to them. For whatever reason, he had chosen to place
these three short entries together. Was he short of paper? He'd
written that he'd been unable to go out or was it that he was
simply placing them together because they so closely followed
on from each to the other. Perhaps there wasn't any deep
reason for it; he'd just changed his writing format. Whatever
the reason, the entries were revealing.

He was on a rapidly descending path towards destruction,

and he knew it. His vision of a living hell was evident in virtually every word he'd committed to the paper. Strangely, he appeared to see himself as sharing a common road towards his ultimate oblivion with his victims, guided along the way by his voices. Would the voices therefore tell him when it was time to stop, or when it was time he ended his own personal descent into Hell? The first entry concluded with yet another threat to the 'whores', intimating that their deaths must take place in the very places where they sold their bodies for a pittance. The streets were where they worked, and the streets would be where they died, their blood spilling into the gutters of London, their lives meaning nothing more to The Ripper than that of an insect. As far as he was concerned, they were already in Hell, with him! That he wanted to kill again, and badly, I was in no doubt, and he was almost desperate to return to his deadly task. Yet, he was held in check by his pain, the headaches were growing worse. He thought the laudanum was weaker; in fact, it was probably no different to that he'd taken before, his body was by now simply accustomed to the drug and it's effects. He could now absorb larger and larger quantities of the opium-based drug before feeling any effects at all. He was probably so intoxicated by the drug that he couldn't 'hear' his voices. They were 'sleeping', perhaps his hallucinations were also lying dormant, he was certainly in a state of some confusion, and felt his life to have become nothing more than a living Hell. I felt that he was reaching a point of deep desperation.

Apart from all else, The Ripper was deeply depressed, his unhappiness and his fear screaming out from the page. Fear? Yes, he was afraid of pain, afraid of dying. He wasn't referring just to the pain from the headaches either, of that I was certain. I'd suspected earlier, and now I was sure that he was suffering from the later, (tertiary) stages of syphilis, probably contracted as I'd previously suspected from some long-ago liaison with one of those ladies of the street he now so despised. If that were the case, he was in all probability suffering from painful lesions on various parts of his body, his very tissues beginning to break down as sores developed on his face (though perhaps not yet), hands, and other extremities. (That was why I'd seen the vision of a facial mask over the bottom of his face in my dream). In my subconscious dream-state I'd anticipated the syphilis! He was possibly quite severely brain damaged by this point, and without doubt the man was gradually going insane. I'd begun to believe that he was an intelligent man, and would thus have known the prognosis of the disease, and that would have added to the terror he felt, knowing exactly what was happening to him, yet being unable to do a thing to prevent it. There were no drugs for the treatment of the disease. If he did seek help, he would in all probability be confined to an asylum, and I could understand his reluctance to seek medical help. He'd long ago passed that point anyway. How strange to think that today the disease can be effectively treated with modern antibiotics. Then, it was akin to a death sentence.

Perhaps, also, he refused to leave the house, particularly in daylight, because of those physical deformities by which syphilis would make him easily recognizable as a sufferer. He had however recently paid a social call on my great-grandfather, so I thought that unlikely. His pain though was undoubtedly real. How he must be suffering, being unable to find relief from the constant headaches, and the other equally painful symptoms he was undoubtedly experiencing.

These three entries convinced me that The Ripper was not a married man. Surely no wife would have missed the symptoms he must be exhibiting. His words screamed of loneliness and a life of solitude. Perhaps he had been married at some time in the past, but I was sure he had no partner in life at the time he wrote this sorry journal of his. After all, by his own words, he must suffer alone for his sins and indiscretions (an affair whilst previously married perhaps), or worse still, by Victorian standards, a homosexual dalliance)?

Whatever the answers that would surely reveal themselves as I delved ever deeper into the journal, I knew that the case of The Jack the Ripper murders was probably far more complex than many scholars and Ripperologists had previously thought. Was I the first to think that perhaps The Ripper was as much a victim of his own crimes as those he so brutally murdered and mutilated? The purists would probably think me as insane as he undoubtedly was to even suggest such a thing! Yet, that feeling wouldn't leave me; it grew with every passing minute, with almost every word I read. I couldn't, wouldn't, ever try to excuse his crimes, oh no, but, in light of what I was learning about his state of mind, the terrible diseases of the brain with which I was becoming more and more sure he was afflicted, the more I could perhaps begin to understand what lay behind the crimes of Jack the Ripper.

16th September 1888

Vigilantes in the streets! Jews, butchers, cobblers, all accused, ha! What next? Shall I join the throng, like before? Scream at the police, at the poor unlucky butcher's boy as he passes in the street wearing his blood-stained leather apron?

I grow tired of this game, my head hurts again, I feel dizzy, expectation crowds my thoughts, and I think the public too have expectations of me. They wait to see when I shall strike again. They want to see and hear of my work. They pretend to fear my flashing blade, yet deep beneath they want to hear and read of bloody murder. They won't admit it, oh no, they won't, but I know it's what they want. They want me to rip the next whore, but I'll keep them waiting, bide my time, the next whore won't bleed until I'm ready, then the river of red will flow once more, and I'll stain the streets with the blood of the foul-tainted whores. The crowds are too much; one cannot go about one's business without being accosted by the great unwashed, seeking retribution, ha, as if dead whore's need revenging. Let them die, let them bleed, let them cower from my cold, hard steel as it slices through their warm, sticky flesh. I want to see the horror on a whore's face as she gurgles and gags and chokes on the blood in her throat. The last one was too quick, too easy, let the next one die a little slower, yes, and let me taste her fear, foul despicable whore! I shall go on a journey, where? Tomorrow, I'll decide. Let London sweat, let the whores wait, just a little longer, but wait, shall I take my flashing blades upon this journey? Shall I let the streets of some new town run red, there are whores everywhere are there not, and do they not deserve to die also? My head hurts so much, I must try to sleep, tomorrow will be soon enough to decide such weighty questions. I feel sick, I need to sleep, to close my eyes, to rest.

His words seemed to reverberate inside my head. His chilling, matter-of fact references to the gory blood-letting of his killings, his apparent amusement at the public reaction to his deeds, and his obvious distaste for the crowds thronging the streets of London seeking the killer, as though they, not he, were the cause of public nuisance. He was becoming exasperated with the mob, with their need to find him, to exact revenge for the murders. After all, to his mind the victims;

those poor unfortunate women who had fallen into the lowest of professions were barely human, and so undeserving of public sympathy. They were after all 'only whores', and, as he'd previously written in an earlier entry, he was surprised to know that whores actually had names. They were nothing, little more than the 'raw material' for his 'work'. As an artist utilizes his canvas, and applies his paints diligently with his brushes, so those poor women were his canvases, his knives his brushes, and the resulting carnage he wrought with those blades became in his mind his masterpieces of creation, his 'work'.

Even more unnerving, as I sat reading this diabolical text in the dead of night was his stated desire to watch the face and hear the horrendous 'gurgling and gagging' of his next victim as her life ebbed away. Killing another human being in cold blood was one thing, but to take pleasure from his victims last agonizing painful moments was truly callous in the extreme. Despite his obvious psychological disorders I felt a positive sense of revulsion for the man who had written these terrible words, who had already killed three times, at least, and was destined to kill again, even more horrifically.

I shuddered and realised the lateness of the hour. My eyes were heavy, and I realised that I was reaching that point of half-sleep-half-waking, when the eyes start to lose their ability to focus, the words on the page begin to dance in a macabre ballet, and the brain begins to play mind tricks upon the unwary. Perhaps that was why I now felt as though the words on that awful page were changing shape, lengthening and swelling, swaying in front of me until they seemed to be oozing and dripping with small rivulets of blood, slowly trickling down the page, towards my fingers where they held tightly to the journal. I quickly shook myself into wakefulness, and simultaneously dropped the journal onto the desk as though it were red hot in my hand. I realised I was far, far too tired to be doing this at this time of night. The disturbance in my mind caused by my earlier attempt to sleep, and the ensuing nightmares that had accompanied the effort were as nothing compared to the painful fears and visions that now crowded into my mind, as though someone had opened a floodgate of irrationality in some deep corner of my psyche. This was worse than the dreams that come with sleep, for now I was in that awful place where reality and fantasy are too closely entwined to separate. Pictures of dark, shadowy figures flitted across my vision, though my eyes seemed unable to focus, it was like trying to see through a fog, a red, impenetrable fog, cloying, sticky, and the blood that formed the fog was itself filled with a life of its own, and it screamed at me in despair and agony!

I was awake, the room was normal, there was nothing to fear, and then, the strange dancing letters of the journal filled my head again, the fog grew ever thicker, and now, instead of the screams from within the dense cloud that gathered round me, the screams I heard were real, they were mine!

My head hit the desk with a dull thud. I had collapsed in a fit of nervous tension, and the impact of my forehead on the hard wooden surface brought me back to reality. I was shaking and, I was ashamed to admit, almost in tears. The whole process of my journey through the journal was becoming a trial for which I appeared to be singularly unprepared.

I needed Sarah. I wasn't one to feel lonely at the absence of my wife for a few days. It was quite usual for her to drive off to the Cotswolds from time to time to spend weekends or even a week with her sister. I had never felt the need to spend every minute of my life with her, nor she with me. We were in love, and that was enough. The time we were together was as precious and as special as any couple could hope for, and the occasional absence by Sarah had never bothered me until now. I'd never felt more afraid or lonelier than this in my entire life. What was happening to me? I wanted to pick up the telephone, call her right now in the middle of the night and tell her to come home, tell her how much I missed and needed her, but I couldn't. How would I have been able to make her understand that I was afraid of some papers my father had left to me, that I was so very frightened by the fact that I was sitting here alone in the dead of night reading the words of Jack the Ripper, and that I was afraid of every word in that awful journal? How could I explain to my wife that it was as if he were there with me, watching me, making sure I didn't miss a page, a single word?

I closed my eyes, leaned back in the chair, (I was afraid to go back up to bed), and I allowed a sudden, deep, dark sleep to overtake me. This time I slept without dreaming, or, if I did dream, they were those dreams that come in the deepest sleep, the ones you can never remember dreaming.

FIFTEEN
THE MORNING OF THE SECOND DAY

I awoke, stiff, aching, and feeling drawn and extremely tired. My body felt as if I hadn't slept at all, though a quick glance at the clock showed me that it was just before seven, a fact confirmed by the rays of weak early morning sunlight invading the study through the window. I'd probably slept for about two and a half to three hours; I hadn't checked the clock before being overtaken by the black sleep from which I'd now awakened. The wind and rain of the night before had gone, the house was still and quiet, and for a moment or two, I felt relatively calm, almost my normal self.

Then, the realisation hit me. I remembered exactly why I was here, sitting in my study chair, stiff and aching from head to foot. How could I have forgotten, even for a moment? There it was, the journal, on the desk in front of me, exactly as I'd left it. In the light of day it looked fairly innocent and innocuous, and yet, as I sat staring at it, it almost felt to me as if there was a malevolence about the thing, it almost seemed to me to be throbbing slightly, as though it held a life of its own. Was there a malicious spirit at work somewhere within the hidden depths of its words? Was I being irrational? In time I hope that you, the reader may be the judge of that. Berating myself for my foolishness I forced myself to return to a sense of reality, and it was then that I realised just how awful I felt.

My head ached, my tongue was dry and furred, virtually every muscle in my shoulders, arms and legs was sore and throbbing. If I hadn't known better I'd have sworn I had a hangover. No way, I'd only consumed a couple of whiskies the night before, certainly not enough to induce such feelings. In fact, the headache was quite severe, bordering on the intensity of a migraine, something from which I'd suffered very rarely in the past. I rose from the chair, stretching myself to try to induce an increase in blood flow to my tired and weary extremities. I staggered rather than walked from the study to the kitchen, reached for the first aid box and extracted a couple of paracetamol tablets, which I quickly downed with a glass of cold water. Maybe they'd help with the headache. I sat in one of the kitchen chairs, resting my chin on my clenched right hand, and I sighed a heavy sigh. My chin was rough against my hand, I was desperately in need of a shave, and I daresay that if I'd looked in a mirror at that moment, my unkempt uncombed hair would have added to an overall visual impression of a rough-looking homeless vagrant. I rubbed my eyes, they stung, I thought they were probably quite bloodshot. I was quite glad at that moment that Sarah wasn't there to see me looking as I did. My worst fears were confirmed when I mounted the stairs a few minutes later, made my way into the bathroom, and barely recognised the face that stared back at me from the mirror.

I showered, shaved, dressed in fresh clothes, and tidied myself up, until I resembled the me I was used to seeing in the mirror every morning, then, once more made my way to the kitchen. My stomach was empty; perhaps I'd feel appreciably better with some breakfast inside me. Somehow, though, when

I surveyed the contents of the fridge, nothing took my fancy. Food held little interest for me despite the pangs of hunger that were gnawing at my insides. I decided to settle for toast and coffee on the basis that something would be better than nothing, and I managed to consume three slices of hot buttered toast and two cups of steaming hot coffee before letting my mind return to the document that awaited me in the study.

It was strange to think that it had been less than twenty-four hours since I'd first laid eyes on the journal. Less than a day, and yet here I was, feeling more disturbed and aggravated than I could ever remember feeling in my entire life, such was the profound effect of its contents upon me. I thought about it for a moment. I'd read until I was exhausted, tried to sleep, been beset by outlandish dreams, given up on sleep, carried on reading, only to be haunted by what I could only describe as a series of waking nightmares, until I'd eventually collapsed into that dark slumber, more a state of exhaustion really, then I'd finally awakened this morning in this appalling state of both mind and body. All this in less than a day! What was happening to me? I was, after all, not a man prone to delusions or neuroses, I was a man of science for God's sake! I was a psychiatrist, not a patient, not one of those poor unfortunate souls who visited me for my own considered professional opinion. How would I diagnose myself at this time I asked myself? I didn't answer my own question. I couldn't. Whatever had happened to me in the hours since I'd come into contact with the journal defied any rational conclusion. I failed to understand how reading a few pages of aged and crumpled paper could have had such a deeply profound effect on my mind. It was illogical and unthinkable that the journal itself could manifest such feelings within my mind, wasn't it? They were just words written on paper, they couldn't house any external power, couldn't possibly be the depository for any lingering malevolence imbued upon the pages by the writer. The evil that was Jack the Ripper was *not* infused into the pages of his journal. Anyway, that's what I told myself at the time.

I remember thinking to myself that if there was nothing to worry about, why didn't I just go marching back into the study, pick up the journal, and read it to the end in one swift session, read great-grandfathers accompanying notes, then just return the whole thing to its wrappings and consign it to the safe or whatever, and just forget about it? Even as the thought crossed my mind, I knew that option was an impossible one. The journal wouldn't allow me to do that. I know that sounds stupid, but it's how I felt, I knew I couldn't do that. I had to continue my passage through its pages exactly in the fashion in which I'd done so far. Even the occasional break from the journal to study the facts I'd downloaded from the Casebook and other sources seemed to me to be part of the journal's plan, a need to be understood at every point along the way, for me to be aware of the facts of the case in a precise chronological fashion, as though to give the journal a solid foundation in my mind, in order that I might understand the mind that had controlled the hand that had written the diabolical words upon each terror-laden page.

Now, you may think me fanciful to use such a term as 'terror-laden', yet to me that's exactly what the journal had quickly come to represent. I was involved, almost against my will, (after all, I hadn't asked for the damned thing, had I?), in a journey into the mind, the thoughts and the twisted terrifying conclusions that had been wrought as a result of those thoughts, the thoughts of a deeply disturbed and very, very sick man. I supposed that most people, expert or laymen, had probably lost sight of the fact that Jack the Ripper, whoever he may have been, whatever evil he may have perpetrated was still, after all, just a man, someone's son, perhaps someone's husband, brother, friend. Though his crimes themselves may have been monstrous in both their substance and their execution, he was capable, at one time at least, of feeling love, affection and deep emotions. After all, it had to be remembered that his crimes themselves were committed whilst he was under the influence of an extremely deep emotional state, however warped and twisted it may appear to the rational mind. I was, I thought, bound tightly by the words of his journal to what I now realised to be the final few weeks in the murderous career of Jack the Ripper, I was tied to the history of his crimes, and believe me when I say to you that I had never known such terror, whether it be real or imagined, I was very, very, afraid of the revelations that may yet expose themselves to me as the Ripper's blood-soaked testimony continued.

I wished I could talk to Sarah, but I thought it too early in the day. Though I'd no doubt that she and Jennifer were up and about, the early morning demands of the baby would probably keep them occupied for quite some time. Perhaps in an hour or so I'd try calling, I knew that talking to Sarah would be the best therapy I could prescribe for myself.

Before returning to the study, I remembered something from my last night-time encounter with the journal, something that had been niggling away at the back of my mind. Half-forgotten since my awkward slumber in the chair, it came back to me as I cleared away my plate and refreshed my coffee cup.

He had said that he was leaving London! Why! Where was he going? Obviously, if the Ripper had left London early in September it would explain why the slaughter on the streets of the East End had been interrupted, why there were no further attacks until the night of the dreadful double murder. If that had been the case however, the question remained. Where had he gone? Had he perpetrated further atrocities elsewhere during his absence from the capital? From a comment made in his last entry, it appeared to me that he was incensed by the public's reaction to his crimes. The apparent sympathy of the press and the public for his victims seemed to infuriate him; the posses of Londoners thronging the streets in search of the murderer genuinely amazed him. After all, was he not performing a public service in ridding the streets of those he had consigned to the role of vermin? I thought that he probably found some amusement in the antics of the mob in the beginning, hence his originally joining in with the crowds; now the public outcry was becoming an irritation to him, and the sheer numbers of potential vigilantes on the streets were perhaps instrumental in his coming to the decision to leave the city, if only for a while. I may have been wrong, but the thought bore some weight of reason in my mind.

I decided that my first task should be to continue my factual investigations. I would try, by using the information provided by The Casebook and other websites, to ascertain if there were any Ripper style murders anywhere else in Britain during September 1888. Then the thought struck me that he may have left the country altogether. It was not implausible that he could have travelled to France, Holland, Germany perhaps, and laid low for a time, or used the time to perfect his 'art' by killing in a foreign land. Though this would perhaps be harder to establish, I promised myself that I would try to learn what I could about any related murders on the continent, if of course the journal confirmed that The Ripper had indeed left these shores.

What on Earth would I do however, if he failed to indicate his whereabouts during the days following his last entry? Would the journal inform me, or misdirect me? Would there be one of those gaps, days missed out, left blank, simply because he had nothing to say perhaps, or because he had left the journal at home, and had had no way of keeping it up to date? Would he suddenly return to it after an absence of days or weeks, ready to assault the pages with yet more bloody revelations? My head still throbbed, but I felt I could put it off no longer. I made myself a promise to phone Sarah in exactly one hour, no matter what the journal may be revealing to me at that time. The questions in my mind were beginning to absorb my thoughts, I wanted answers, I needed to know what happened next, to fit the next piece of the jigsaw into place, so, finally making my way to my chair once again, temporarily fortified by food and drink, and at least partially refreshed, I took up the journal once more knowing that there was only one way I was going to find out.

SIXTEEN
JACK'S SUDDEN ILLNESS

17th September 1888

A pleasant journey by all accounts. Left London early, a compartment to myself, clickety-clack, clickety-clack, the sound of the train as it clattered along the track. Such sights to see along the way, fields, trees, and factories. Houses in fields, and towns galore, I saw the world through the window, and still there was more. There were animals, cows, sheep, geese, and the smell of the smoke from the engine as it carried me away from the dismal city, ever onwards, further north. I saw the spires of the Minster, the great church of York, the splendid cathedral of Durham as it overlooked the city, and the great city of Newcastle, where it lies on the Tyne. I saw castles, great edifices of history, and white wave caps upon the sea as the locomotive pulled me ever nearer to my destination. At last, the city, with its grand castle towering above, what a sight, and the station, itself a wonder of the modern architecture, so grand and spacious. To walk in such a place! Such air. I breathe so easily. The people, though of a strange voice, are remarkably friendly to a stranger. The room is satisfactory, the bed clean, the staff attentive. I shall explore further tomorrow, I shall visit the great bridge over the firth, that iron wonder of the modern age, though it is not ready for the trains to cross I understand, I shall feast my eyes upon its massive girders, its grandeur as it stretches out across the murky waters below, but, for now, it is good to relax, to eat a hearty meal perhaps, and thence to sleep, refresh my bones. Tomorrow, yes, I'll visit the streets, tour the city, take in the sights, find a good pharmacist and walk the great mile. But for now, I'll rest, my work is waiting, but will not go away though I be absent from the city. It can wait. I am tired after all; I am so very tired. The headache is returning.

I FOUND this to be a revelation of monumental proportions. He had indeed left London, and there was no doubt from the description of his journey that The Ripper had headed north to Edinburgh. This discourse could have been written by a different person. There was evidence here of lucid thought, of what could only be described as normality. He had ceased to rant, save for the one small reference to his 'work' at the end. He had described his journey as full of wonders, York Minster, Durham cathedral, which, as he rightly described, sits upon a hilly outcrop overlooking the city, and the great city of Newcastle-on-Tyne, which, during the late nineteenth century must have been a throbbing scene of vast industry. He would indeed have seen Waverley station in Edinburgh as a marvel, even in Victoria's day it was one of the finest examples of station building in Britain. With its graceful arches and sweeping staircases leading from platform to platform, its open-plan vista as it opened up onto the street outside, it was a station of which the people of Edinburgh were rightly proud. And what of his promise to himself to visit the great Forth Bridge? He was acting more like a tourist than a seriously deranged killer attempting to lie low from the vast manhunt that was taking place back home in London. But then, he'd done no wrong had he? At least not in his own mind. He'd simply left town to recharge his batteries, so to speak, to escape the throngs of people crowding the streets, to rest and prepare himself for the next round of his task.

I don't know why, but something in his words seemed to reinforce my belief that he was a man of some substance; certainly no ordinary working-class East-Ender would have had the money to travel to Scotland by train, or to pay for a room in what sounded to me like a reasonably good quality hotel. He hadn't said much about it, I just felt it was a good establishment, as would be the case in a hotel where 'the staff are attentive'. Whoever the Ripper was, he was not a poor man, or one without a sense of culture. There was education in his background; this was a man with knowledge of the world.

He obviously enjoyed the change of air, for Edinburgh would have been so different to London. Smaller, with less industry and pollution, it was, by all accounts, a far cleaner and healthier environment than the great metropolis towards the end of the nineteenth century. He quite logically found the people 'of strange voice', as, to one who'd probably never visited the city before, the Scottish accent might have seemed like a foreign tongue.

Could it have been that he'd simply gone to Edinburgh for the good of his health, for a rest, for a holiday? At least, for the time being, his demons appeared to have left him in peace for a while. There was a definite sanity in his words, a sanity which had been conspicuously absent from every other entry in his journal. My immediate thoughts were that, for a short time at least, he was at peace, and as long as his 'voices' remained silent, he was probably no danger to those around him. Time would tell, and whatever transpired from his sojourn to Scotland's capital city I knew that in just under two week's time he would once again stalk the dark streets of London, where he would strike new fear into the hearts of the people of that great city with not just one, but two brutal slayings.

18th September 1888

*What a place of beauty. I found myself so at home today.
The fine parks and gardens of this fair city are wondrous
to behold. I took a ride upon an omnibus to view the
bridge; it is indeed a splendid testament to the engineer's
skill, though I should perhaps be a little unnerved to
actually allow myself to venture across such a mass
expanse of water even over such a sturdy structure. They
say it will soon be open to rail traffic. I looked through a
telescope I borrowed from a fellow viewer and saw many
small ships upon the firth and could see people so far
away that even through the glass they were as ants,
scurrying little ants, away on the far banks. The city has
a fine museum; I was enthralled by it, so many
wondrous sights to see. I must go further though, there
are things I must do, even whilst here, in this place, for I
was unnerved to hear some fellows on the omnibus
speak of the darker side of this fair city, and I must see
this for myself. I shall wait until the morrow, and when
the evening comes, then I shall go there.*

A sudden thought struck me. There were of course many

suspects, so many men who at one time or another over the years that had fallen under suspicion of being the Ripper. Had any of them I wondered, been documented as having visited Scotland during the time of the killings? I turned once again to my notes, such as they were. Though certainly not exhaustive, they were of course the results of many years of investigations by many scholars and lay persons into the case. I could find nothing to support any hint of a visit to Edinburgh by any of the popular suspects. Then again, there was extraordinarily little documentary evidence about the movements of *any* of the main suspects. Apart from the fact that the Royal Prince had been shown to be out of town at the times of the murders by virtue of a study of the Court Circulars of the time, there was no information on the movements or whereabouts of any of the others who had come under suspicion.

I was also disturbed by the latest entry in the journal. After his short description of his visit to the Forth Bridge, which, as he so rightly pointed out wasn't yet opened for rail traffic, (I quickly looked it up on the internet, it didn't open for business until 1890 though it would have appeared almost complete when he visited it), and general 'sightseeing', there was his sudden reference to an overheard conversation relating to the 'darker side' of the city. I had little doubt as to what this referred. Edinburgh would have been little different to any large city of its time. With its large population, and its associations with the sea due to the nearby port facilities, the great city would have its seedier side, red-light district, call it what you will, in other words, it would have a relatively large number of prostitutes working the streets at night. I had little doubt, but that Jack the Ripper was about to take a tour of the less attractive side of Edinburgh by night, and once again, I felt a prickle of fear beginning to travel up my spine.

I knew what I needed to do. Without doubt, the journal

was engendering a sense of fear and tension in my mind, the like of which I'd never experienced before. It was also teaching me to be a rather good amateur 'ripperologist', as those who follow the case are known. Before turning the next page of the journal, I would take a break, phone Sarah as I'd promised myself I would, and then delve into the research notes I'd assembled, and turn to others if need be. I needed to know if there were any unsolved murders of prostitutes in Edinburgh in September 1888.

Take a break! That was a first. Since I'd begun my strange journey through the journal, this was the first genuine, conscious break I'd allowed myself. I placed the journal back on the desk, rose from my chair, and strode purposefully out of the study, into the kitchen, where I made myself a quick cup of instant coffee, (I know, more coffee), then moved to the back door, opened it, and stepped outside.

The fresh air hit me like a slap in the face! It was the first blast of natural air I'd received since arriving home the day before with the journal tucked underneath my arm. There was a slight breeze, just enough to ruffle the leaves on the trees, and I sat down on one of the patio chairs and just allowed the fresh air to wash over me. It tasted good, that heady mix of coffee and cool autumn breeze, and after sitting on the patio for about ten minutes I felt sufficiently refreshed to venture back indoors to make my call to Sarah.

Fifteen minutes later I put the phone down on my lovely wife, feeling just a little sad, and slightly depressed. It appeared that my new nephew, little Jack had been taken ill in the night, and Jennifer had telephoned for the doctor, who was expected to call to see Jack any time in the next couple of hours. Sarah, after asking how I was after my trying day yesterday, (I of course said I was fine), had asked me if I'd mind her staying on for a few more days to help Jennifer with the baby, as he would be doubly hard to care for if he were ill, poor little mite. Without letting on quite how much I was missing her, I told Sarah that of course I wouldn't mind, I'd be fine, and there was always Mrs Armitage to call and make sure I was still in the land of the living. (I'd have to do something about Mrs Armitage I thought, to keep her from interrupting me without arousing her suspicions).

"I love you, Robert," Sarah said as she ended the call.

"You too, my darling," I'd replied, replacing the phone on the table and suddenly feeling very alone in the quiet stillness of my home, and, despite the warmth of the room I shivered involuntarily, and felt a sort of panic beginning in my mind, as though I were in some sort of danger from being here on my own. It took me a couple of minutes to fight that feeling of panic until it subsided, and I chided myself for being irrational and stupid. What on earth could happen to me here in my own home, after all I was just reading some old papers wasn't I? As horrific as their content might be they were just bits of paper, nothing more. I had to work quite hard to convince myself of that fact, but, having achieved it, I made my way back to the study, to continue my research, this time into unsolved murders in Edinburgh.

There weren't any! You can imagine my sense of puzzlement and frustration at making this unexpected discovery. Negative though it was, and obviously good news for the people of Edinburgh, I couldn't help but feel a little disappointed. Yet, there it was, in black and white, from a reliable source of information on the net. Not one of the newspapers of the day had reported a single unexplained murder of a prostitute or any women at all for that matter during September of 1888. I found it hard to accept that having read The Ripper's threat to visit the darker side of Edinburgh, he wouldn't have done something to release his own tensions and savagely sadistic bloodlust whilst he was there. I visited three more websites, all providing historical information and news from the relevant dates, and they all confirmed it, there was nothing! Could it be that he really was just taking a break himself, as I'd just done, maybe for a bit longer of course, or was there something more sinister waiting for me on the next few pages?

I leaned back in my chair, took a deep breath, picked up the journal, and, as the words of the Ripper reached out to me from the page once again, so my strange journey into history continued.

SEVENTEEN
WHERE MEN GO DOWN TO THE SEA
IN SHIPS

20th September 1888

Oh, what a night. Such fun! I took the road to the docks,
a long and tortuous path I confess, not a cab in sight.
Still the air was fine and filled me with vigour for the
task ahead. The docks were large, though not so as to
rival London. How unimaginative of these Scots, to call
the road to Leith, Leith Street. Oh well. What a fuddle of
a place. So many ships tied up, creaking hulls and smells
of the sea. And outside the gates, they were waiting,
whores aplenty for the seamen to pollute themselves
with. Brazen doxies all of them, with no sign of
propriety, so obvious in their intent to lure the
unsuspecting to a disease ravaged doom. I watched from
afar, in the lee of a warehouse, until the dock was silent.
The greatest insult to our sovereign, this was called
Victoria dock, and here did the whores ply their evil
trade. The last slut to leave the dock was not so old I
think, though the trade was poor last night, and she'd

found no sailor boy to tempt. Dark hair, quite slim, with swinging hips. She tottered on her way to find solace in drink I shouldn't wonder, but never made it to her drinking den. She walked right up to me as I stood waiting and had the nerve to ask me if I should like her company. I made no reply, save to drag the slattern into the shadows. I smelled her cheap perfume, so sweet. I moved so swift, her throat was cut in seconds, almost through and through, nearly removed the bitch's head this time, ha. She tried but couldn't scream, stupid little whore. I let her bleed into a drain; there are many drains along the dock. I gutted her as swift as I would a salmon, slit her wide and sent her entrails flowing along the stones. The legs moved awhile, none of the others did that. I sliced her well, and quick too, all warm and sticky, and her parts all exposed as befits a whore. I thought to leave her there where she lay, wide open to the world, but no, they might have thought it strange to find a ripp'd whore this far north, and clever police may have traced me here. Better to get rid, so I let the slattern bleed a while, then dragged her to a sort of pier, and threw her in. The tide will take her, and who shall miss a little stinking whore? Replaced my coat, though not much blood, good drains here, and returned to sleep, refreshed, and my voices came and bade me well. I have stayed here overlong I think, I shall leave soon. There are whores aplenty wherever I go. Will they give me no peace? Must I gut and rip the hearts and parts and spill the blood of every whore in the nation before they cease their filthy tempting of the innocent? My head is beginning to hurt fair badly, must take more laudanum and rest before I leave.

My hands trembling, I laid the journal down upon my desk. This had been the longest, and in truth, the most horrific entry yet recorded by The Ripper. He'd left a blank date for the 19th, but that was easily explained. He must have spent all of that day preparing himself for his visit to Leith that night, and the entry for the 20th I'd just read obviously related to his murderous excursion of the night before.

So he had killed in Edinburgh after all. I thought that perhaps he hadn't intended to, but that overhearing that casual reference by two locals had led to his obsession rising from deep within his black soul to compel him to carry out this latest act of savagery. His description of the killing of that poor girl, quite young by the sounds of it, was appalling, and chilled me to the bone.

My mind was full with the savage imagery that his words inspired within me. I could almost see his silent and vicious attack, the blade slicing viciously through the poor girls' throat, nearly decapitating her. What fearful terrible last thoughts must have passed through her mind as she coughed and spluttered her last breath on that cold and dark dockside all those years ago? I doubted she'd have known much about those last few seconds, at least, I hoped not, and then of course he'd described in the most intimate detail so far his demonic mutilation of the young girls' body. I thought it probably true that docks would have any number of small drains spaced along them and this had obviously helped him to dispose of his victim's blood, easily and quickly. That would also help to explain why he wasn't saturated in blood himself, particularly as he'd so obviously removed his coat before beginning his 'work'.

My pulse was racing, my heart seemed to be thumping

loudly in my chest, and I could virtually hear the throbbing of blood pumping in my veins, so horrified was I by this latest, terrifying entry. It seemed to me that he'd killed, then casually strolled back to his hotel to sleep and refresh himself, unseen and unheard as usual; he couldn't have been blood stained to any extent, as, surely even in 1888 there'd have been someone on duty in the hotel whatever time he'd returned, and he'd have been noticed if there'd been blood on his clothes, wouldn't he?

A red blur seemed to float before my eyes, as though the blood of this latest, poor hapless victim were floating into my very soul, clouding my brain, my thoughts. Why were there no records of this heinous crime? Was there even a police force in Edinburgh or more specifically, in Leith in 1888? My earlier research had told me that the Metropolitan Police force had only been formed in London in 1829, so I thought it possible that there hadn't been a police force in Edinburgh at the time of the girls murder, maybe there was no-one to investigate the bloodstained dock, for there must have been some sign left of his vicious assault on the girl. I would have to explore that avenue.

I quickly logged on to the internet once more and tried, unsuccessfully to obtain some historical information relating to the Edinburgh police force. My best hope was a modern-day reference to the website of Police Scotland, specifically the Lothian and Borders Division, the force which polices Edinburgh today. I quickly sent an e-mail requesting information on the history of the city's police force, and asking for details of any unsolved disappearances of young women around the time in question, all under the flimsy guise of researching unsolved crimes of the past for a historical record, then realised I could find out little more until they replied, if indeed they could be bothered to respond to such a request.

Meanwhile, I thought to myself that surely the girl would

have been missed by someone, parents, family, friends? Maybe she was an out-of-town girl, not known locally in Leith. I supposed that in Scotland all those years ago Edinburgh would have had the same attraction for the poor as London had in England. Perhaps the poor child was a country girl, recently arrived in Edinburgh and unknown by anyone in the city, or conceivably an orphan. Yet, why had her body not been discovered? There again the answer to my question was obvious. If he'd dropped her body into the water as he'd said, the tide would in all probability have carried her poor lifeless body quite quickly towards the sea. The Firth of Forth is itself a wide expanse of water and the open sea is only a few miles away. Yes, I could quite understand why the girl's body may have floated away, never to be discovered. The blood leaking from her eviscerated corpse would also have acted like a magnet to all manner of underwater creatures in search of food and would have been readily consumed. Were there sharks in the sea off the coast of Scotland? More questions, but few answers.

I couldn't help but feel an immense sorrow for the poor girl, probably one of many who'd made her way to the city from the outlying towns and villages in search of a better life, much like many of today's youngsters who head for London, Edinburgh, and our other metropolitan cities. Perhaps unable to find work, finding herself close to starvation, she'd turned to prostitution, selling her young body on the streets, probably for little more than the price of a bed for the night, or a cheap meal, giving herself to any man who offered the promise of a few pennies, the chance to live another day, to survive another night. Instead, she had ended her days on a dark, dank dockside wharf, her life- blood bleeding into a filthy drain, and her body viciously mutilated and literally thrown to the fishes. Whoever she was, she would probably remain as unknown in death as she had been in life. I knew with certainty that there was little if anything I could do to attempt to identify this new mystery victim of The Ripper; she would remain as anonymous throughout eternity as she had been in life. I glanced at my computer, willing some form of reply to arrive from the police.

I said a silent prayer for the poor girl's soul as I sat in my comfortable office chair, her soul after all was known unto God, if to no-one else. My own feelings at that time were a mixture of horror, revulsion, and a deep sadness, sadness for another poor lost soul, taken from life by the well-sharpened blade of a madman. Despite my own professional training, and though it wasn't a word much used by my modern colleagues, I knew that The Ripper was quite mad; sick, yes, with many symptoms of the most terrible psychological disorders, but madness was the only term I could use to describe these acts of wanton violence and mutilation. Yet, his own soul must have been troubled also; for he was also known unto God was he not, if God truly existed? Would his deeds have placed him outside God's good grace, or would he have been welcomed into Heaven, alongside the souls of his victims, despite his sins, when the time came? I thought it best to avoid the theological question. That was for others to debate.

I glanced again at my computer screen and saw the flickering icon telling me that I had incoming mail. I was amazed to find that the information section of the police force in Edinburgh had replied to my e-mail in double-quick time. It appears that my original request had been passed to a civilian clerk in the department who himself was something of an expert on the force's history, and an avid crime buff as well. He was incredibly pleased, so his e-mail said, to provide me with the information I'd requested, and also anything else I may require from him in the future.

The City of Edinburgh Police, as they were then known were established in 1805, meaning that Scotland's capital city was well in advance of London in the formation of their police force, the Metropolitan Police Force not having been established until 1829 you may recall. The Leith Burgh Police were formed a year later in 1806, as Leith was at that time a separate Burgh, (Borough). It was a fact that Edinburgh was much smaller in those days than it is today, and many of the suburbs lay within various county areas outside the city boundaries and were therefore covered by either the Edinburghshire or Midlothian Constabulary, formed in 1840.

I immediately saw that this could have led to certain logistical difficulties. If the various forces were anything like those in England, communication between them may not have always been of the highest degree, and if the girl had been killed in Leith, though she may have lived within the city bounds, or elsewhere, her disappearance may not have been recorded with any accuracy if at all. A curious fact was included with the information from my Scottish contact. Although the headquarters of the force was at Number 1 Parliament Street, most of the city's citizens and the police themselves would refer to the building as 'the High Street' and it was common parlance to predict the fate of potential arrests as, "ending up in the High Street". Obviously, the Ripper had been careful to avoid this fate.

The next fragment of information made my hair stand on end! In response to my query about unexplained or unsolved disappearances, my informant, with the fine Scottish name of Angus MacDonald, had come up with a tantalizing possibility.

As far as he knew, he said, according to all the records still in existence from those days, there was only one unsolved disappearance in the area which may be of interest to me.

On the 30th of September 1888, a young woman named Flora Niddrie had walked into the tiny police station in the village of Corstorphine, just west of Edinburgh to report that her friend, Morag Blennie, aged 22 years, had left for the city two months previously, and had never been heard from since, despite her promises to keep in touch. An orphan, Morag had been well-spoken, and with a little education, and had left the village in the hope of finding work in the city. Being a one-man station, the officer at the police station had taken the girl's statement about her friend, without placing too high a priority on it. After all, so many young girls followed a similar path, and just simply failed to go home, keep in touch, or make any form of contact with their former acquaintances. The constable was also aware of the possibility that Morag may have drifted into prostitution, and probably wouldn't want to be found by her friend or anyone else who knew her. Her disappearance would have been a low-priority item for the hard-pressed constabulary of the time.

The bloodstains on the dock had been found by early morning dockworkers, and investigated the day after the killing, and, in the absence of any evidence to the contrary, the Leith Burgh police had concluded that a fight had probably taken place on the spot, (a common occurrence around the docks apparently), and that after much blood-letting, but with no serious harm done, the protagonists would probably have crawled away home to lick their wounds.

On the night of the killing, a man on his way home from the pub had seen a man who he described as being in an agitated state, and with blood on his hands walking along George Street in the city of Edinburgh. He reported this to the police the next day, as he thought there may be a reward at stake if he'd witnessed anything of significance. With nothing else to go on, and no other reports of the man, or of any violent crime in the city, the Edinburgh City police had had no option other than to simply file the report and take no further action.

When taken individually, all of these seemingly unconnected events meant very little, and yet, what if...? What if the young girl described in the journal had indeed been Morag Blennie? What if the bloodstains on the dock had been reported by the Leith Burgh police to the headquarters of the City police at Parliament Square, and what if the City police had then made a connection with the man witnessed in George Street with blood on his hands? Although she wasn't reported missing until the 30th of the month, some ten days after her murder, there may just have been a chance that the police might have been able to do something. Maybe they would have checked the shores of the Firth of Forth, found some small piece of clothing, a shoe, just something that may have at least identified the poor victim of this senseless killing. Who knows what may have happened if they'd linked everything together, and traced the mystery man with blood on his hands to a hotel in the city, yes, I thought, what if...?

Not until 1920 did the Leith force become amalgamated into the City police force when the boundaries of the city were extended to include the little port town. Suddenly, every crime committed within the bounds of the city would fall under the auspices of one centralised police force. Not so in 1888. I knew in my heart that the police officers of the time, in every force involved, had done their jobs to the best of their ability, but that nagging little question kept repeating in my head, what if?

From 1920 every report of suspicious behaviour, unexplained bloodstains, or missing persons would fall under the investigative arm of that one single police force, and just maybe communication would have been faster and more effective. Had The Ripper visited the city of Edinburgh after 1920, he may not have been so lucky, as it seemed to me that he'd been a little sloppy in his actions this time, compared to his comparative invisibility in committing his heinous acts in London.

Though it hadn't answered any of my questions with certainty, I was grateful for the information supplied by Mr MacDonald, and, at least in my own mind, I was inclined to think of that poor girl, her body floating down to the ocean in the dead of night, as Morag Blennie. I thought it better to give her that name than none at all, after all these years I didn't think anyone would mind.

My mouth felt very dry, and my head throbbed. I looked at the journal lying on the desk in front of me, and I shivered, again. There was something very frightening about that collection of papers, almost as if it were carrying its message from the depths of Hell itself. The words themselves, the more I looked at them, seemed to be imbued with the life and the soul of the hideous hand that had written them down upon those worn, slightly faded pages, which, strangely, felt almost warm to the touch. Of course they were warm; I'd held them in my hands for so long that my own body heat must have transferred itself to the pages, giving that impression. I berated myself for such foolishness, whilst at the same time half-believing in my own irrational and very unprofessional fears.

That he was able to think logically was evident to me from his knowledge that to leave his victim on display, as he had with the women in London would have drawn an instant response from the police. Even though this latest murder had taken place far from the streets of Whitechapel, surely word of a mutilated prostitute in Edinburgh would soon have reached the ears of the Metropolitan police and brought investigators northwards. Even though he would have been long gone by then, it was evident that he wanted no trace of his visit to Edinburgh to be known to the police, or anyone else for that matter. Yes, I could see logical thought processes at work in his decision to throw the poor girl's body in the water, to float, bleeding and torn into oblivion.

He still saw the prostitutes as a pollutant in society, a scourge to be destroyed, and he doubtless saw himself as some sort of avenging angel, that was clear. He wouldn't stop until he'd rid the world of his targets, those poor unfortunates with one of whom he had probably poisoned his own diseased body.

I prepared to take up the journal once more, breathing deeply, my pulse quickening at the thought of just touching the thing, my sense of fear and loathing for what was yet to come growing by the minute. As I leaned forward towards the desk, I saw that my hands were shaking more than ever; I seemed to be gripped by man's ancient 'fight or flight' response. Should I pick it up or run from the room and seek sanctuary in the safety of the lounge. Sanctuary? Sanctuary from what? I asked myself. Forcing myself to think rationally, I slowly reached across the desk, still shaking noticeably and just as I was about to pick up the journal once more...

The door bell rang! Damn, I'd forgotten all about Mrs Armitage. It had to be her, come to check on my well-being. She'd be reporting back to Sarah without a doubt. If I didn't answer the door, she'd be thinking all sorts of horrible thoughts, and worrying Sarah with all manner of invented problems. Taking a deep breath, and, I must admit, almost with a sense of relief at having the excuse to leave the study for a few minutes, I left the journal in the middle of the desk, rose from my chair, and padded quietly from the study, almost too quietly I thought, down the hallway, and with trembling fingers turned the key to unlock the front door.

EIGHTEEN
A VOICE FROM THE GRAVE?

"Robert? Robert, what on earth is the matter, you look absolutely terrible, are you ill? Does Sarah know what a state you're in? Tell me what's wrong, why haven't you come round, or rung me, if you'd told me you were ill I'd have come to see you straight away."

Mrs Armitage stood there, barely drawing breath as she launched into her concerned neighbour mode. In truth I didn't realise I looked too bad at all, considering the mental trial I was putting myself through with each page of the journal I was reading.

"I'm fine Mrs Armitage, honestly, what makes you think I'm ill?"

"Oh, come now Robert, how long have I known you? You look as if you've been up all night (*which of course I virtually had*) and my dear boy, you look so pale! If I didn't know better I'd think you were one of those men who goes into a decline just because his wife is away for a few days. When did you last eat?"

"Actually, I ate breakfast a while ago and a good meal last night, so I'm fine as I said. There's nothing wrong, I've just been working on something and it's true I didn't sleep much but apart from that I'm ok, honestly."

"Well, you don't look it, that's for sure, you look so drawn and, well, you look as if you've seen a ghost. Nothing's happened to frighten you has it?"

"Oh, now come on, Mrs A, I'm a grown man for God's sake, what on earth would I be frightened of here in my own home? It's just work, that's all."

"Really Robert, you were supposed to be taking time off to sort out your poor father's affairs, not to get bogged down with work. You should be taking a bit of a rest you know; you've had a stressful few weeks recently."

"Yes, I know. Listen Mrs Armitage, I appreciate your concern, I really do, but I must get on. I'm ok, really I am, and I'll probably get a good night's sleep tonight, and feel much better tomorrow."

I didn't like to be quite so dismissive of our caring neighbour, who was a busybody alright, but at least she did have a heart of gold. She meant well, and I knew it. She had taken the hint though.

"Very well Robert, if you say so," she replied, "but I'll call tomorrow and see that you're alright, Sarah would never forgive me if I didn't make sure you were looking after yourself while she's away, now would she?"

"Ok, ok, now, please Mrs Armitage?"

"Alright Robert, but remember, you look after yourself, if you need me just call me, and I'll see you tomorrow."

At last, I was alone again. I watched Mrs Armitage as she disappeared down the drive, out the gate, and turned towards her own house, then made my way to the kitchen. More coffee was definitely in order before I returned to the study, and the journal. Another five minutes passed as I pottered around in the kitchen, making coffee, and selecting a handful of chocolate biscuits to accompany me to the study. I was a little shocked that Mrs Armitage had seen such a change in me as to be so noticeable. I would have to work hard to keep up my strength and not let the journal take me over too much, (or had it done that already?) I set myself a target of two hours at most to continue my exploration of the journal, after which, I promised myself, I'd stop for lunch and get myself a dose of fresh air, maybe take a walk into the village to buy a newspaper or something. At least, that was the plan.

As I walked back into the study, the atmosphere within the room suddenly seemed to me to be quite heavy and oppressive, as if a presence I couldn't explain was hanging in the air. I hadn't noticed it before, it was quite strange, I hadn't experienced anything like it previously. It was almost as though, in the time I'd taken to speak to Mrs Armitage and make my coffee, the room had been invaded by some all-pervading aura, a sense rather than a being. It was stupid, I told myself that, I was simply becoming spooked and anxious by the content of the journal, that was all. Stupid or not, the feeling was quite real and unnerving, and despite the sunlight pouring into the room through the study windows I switched on the desk lamp, it's warm radiance casting a comforting glow across the desktop. The room felt uncomfortably warm as well, which was unusual as there was no heating on in the study, and the weather was still not cold enough for the central heating to be running. I opened the upper lights of the windows to allow some fresh air into the room and took my place at the desk once more.

If the sound of the doorbell had been my first surprise of

the day, the second wasn't far behind it. As I turned the page of the journal, expecting to find The Ripper's next entry before my eyes, imagine my astonishment when instead I found, tucked between the previous page I'd read and the next entry, a page of old, good quality vellum inscribed in my great-grandfather's hand! It was smaller than the pages of the journal, thus ensuring it had stayed neatly in between the pages, undisturbed, probably since my father had first read the journal.

It was undated and addressed simply to 'My Son'. That would of course have been my grandfather. The handwriting was neat, very neat, as I thought befitted a Fellow of the Royal College of Surgeons. My great-grandfather had written as follows:

My Son

I write this after the event. As such, it is easy to say I should have acted sooner, but at the time I thought my diagnosis was correct, and that I was acting in the interests of the patient, the man who wrote the journal you are now reading. I have placed this note at this point in the journal for it is at this time by the journal's own chronography that I became involved in these tragic matters. That I am a wretch of the greatest magnitude is beyond argument, and I wish that I had had a little more foresight at the time, but, the past is history, and cannot be changed.

It was on or about the 23rd day of September in the year of our Lord 1888. Yes, the 23rd, I'm sure of it. I was at my practice in Charles Street, between patients, when

*there was a loud knocking at my door. I was visited by
two representatives from the Charing Cross hospital,
who had called to request that I visit there as soon as I
possibly could. It appeared that they had a patient,
recently admitted, who was in a state of much confusion,
almost delirium. He had been taken to the hospital by a
police officer after being found wandering around in
daylight hours displaying signs of being highly
disorientated, perplexed and disturbed. He seemed not
to know who he was, or indeed where he was, or had
indeed come from. He could recall nothing of his recent
movements nor where he lived, so had been removed to
the infirmary where he was seen by the doctors there.
Though he could speak little, he had managed to give
them my name as being of his acquaintance, and, with
no other means of identifying him and being unsure of
what exactly ailed the man, the doctor in charge of his
case, a Doctor Silas Malcolm, had sent them post-haste
to my door with this urgent request to attend upon him.*

*Now, Silas Malcolm was known to me from my days at
Lincoln's Inn Fields. We had studied together for a time
and qualified as surgeons at about the same time so I
recall, so it was natural that I should grant his request
for assistance in this case.*

*Imagine my surprise, my son, when I arrived at the
hospital and was shown to the patient. I had last seen
him some weeks earlier, certainly not long ago, and was
appalled at his state of collapse. Silas Malcolm greeted
me cordially, and, after I confirmed that I did know his
patient, he ventured his opinion that the man was
suffering from a brain fever induced by over indulging*

in the use of laudanum. I agreed, explaining that the patient, (I shall not name him here), had spoken to me privately some time ago and had indicated that he was suffering from severe headaches and tiredness, and that I had suggested a regular small dose of laudanum may prove efficacious. It seems however, that the patient had taken my words far too much to heart and had become addicted to the drug, which as you know can cause extremes of behavioural disorders if taken in too great a quantity.

It was the following day before the patient was sufficiently coherent to speak lucidly to anyone, and he was somewhat surprised, though obviously pleased to see me at his bedside when I visited the ward after my own surgery was over. He was still in a state of some confusion, he seemed to think he had been on a journey by train, though he could not remember where to, and he was obsessed with the thought that he had killed a girl. He said his mind was 'full of blood' and that he could not close his eyes without seeing the blood of his victim 'seeping down the drain'.

All these things I put down to the hallucinogenic effect of his laudanum overdose, blind fool that I was! I reassured him that he was suffering from a minor and temporary form of dementia brought on by the use of too much laudanum, and that he would be well again in a day or so. Doctor Malcolm had prescribed a series of purgatives which were rapidly driving the laudanum from his system and I said that I felt he would be allowed to leave the hospital within two days.

Why did I not believe him? Why, my son, why? Perhaps

if I had, so much pain could have been avoided, and so much less blood spilt upon the streets of London. But I did not believe him, I did not believe him, and I will always have to live with that knowledge. You may ask why I took such pains to visit this man who I have not named, to take an interest in his well-being. I tell you now my son, that if I had my time again I would have turned him away when I first set eyes upon him some few months ago, at my club. He approached me there and asked if I knew him. I did of course, not from his own countenance, but from his eyes. He had the eyes of his mother you see, and I have never forgotten that grand lady who gave birth to him all those years ago. In deference to her memory I was civil enough to him, and treated him as kindly as I could, and thought him a fine young man for the most part.

I know you must wonder at my words, who he was, who his mother was, and perhaps I shall reveal that to you in time, but not yet. For now, be aware that there are reasons why I keep this to myself. Continue with your reading of his journal my son, and I shall tell you more later, this I promise.

The note ended there, a tantalizing end to a puzzling statement. In truth I felt as though my great-grandfather's words had raised more questions than they had provided answers, though at least now I was sure of a genuine and solid link between great-grandfather and The Ripper. As for this woman, his mother, could she have been a paramour, a lover of great-grandfather before or maybe even during his marriage to my great-grandmother? Is that why he refused to name her? Could The Ripper have been his son, an illegitimate ancestor of mine? The thought made me shudder, for, if that were true, then the blood of The Ripper could be flowing in my veins at this very moment, for we would both share the genes of great-grandfather at the least if that were the case. I thought I knew everything about the history of my family, but perhaps there were skeletons in the cupboard of which I had never been made aware. I was quite afraid at the thought that I may be about to find them out.

Whatever sense of foreboding I had felt up to this point now doubled in intensity. Whatever the truth of the matter, whatever revelations remained hidden within the as yet unread pages of the journal, I sensed that my peace of mind, such as it was, would never quite return to the state of equilibrium it had enjoyed before I ever set eyes on this document of evil and sick depravity. I wondered where this strange journey was taking me, for though in truth I had not set foot out of my house since returning home with the journal, psychologically I had been transported into the dark and gloomy world of Victorian Whitechapel, been witness to mind-numbing acts of macabre and vicious murder and mutilation, had travelled to the Edinburgh of the nineteenth century to observe yet more scenes of untimely and ferocious killing, and now, my mind was besieged by thoughts that Jack the Ripper may in some way have been a relative of mine, that the seed of my great-grandfather may have been planted in that most cruel and inhuman unknown assassin, and may be flowing still within my veins.

My palms were sweating, my brow deeply furrowed, and my heart was thumping in my chest. I felt as if an explosion of previously untapped deep emotions had suddenly been released deep within my soul, and, despite my attempts to convince my mind that all was normal, that nothing had changed, I felt the beginnings of what was to turn into the longest and most fearful living nightmare I could have envisaged for myself. Believe me when I tell you that Hell exists in many different forms. In the words of his journal The Ripper felt he was already there, and my own descent to that fearful place was only just beginning!

NINETEEN
OF JOURNALS AND JOURNALISM

As THE WORDS of my great-grandfather's note began to sink deeper into my consciousness so the feeling grew within my own mind that I was being faced with innumerable questions, to which I had precisely not one answer. Firstly, there was not one piece of information in the note that explained exactly where the Ripper had been found wandering incoherently around the streets of London. Nor was there anything that provided me with an explanation as to when or how this sudden seizure of disorientation and partial memory loss had begun. Had he started to hallucinate whilst travelling back to London on the train? Had he reached his home first, only to succumb to this strange and sudden reaction on leaving the house at some time afterwards?

The last entry in the journal had been dated the 20th September, and my great-grandfather's note was dated the 23rd. I presumed from his words that the patient had been admitted either one or two days before that date, so perhaps the Ripper's collapse had occurred on the 21st, which was almost certainly the day he had returned by train to London. At the latest he would have been admitted to the hospital on the 22nd so there wasn't quite the gulf of blank dates that there could have been. It did explain why there were no journal entries for those dates. It wouldn't have been possible for him to access his journal if he were lodged in a bed in a hospital ward.

I must admit that I was wholly intrigued by the references to the Ripper's mother. Who could she have been? If she weren't a secret lover or a relative of my great-grandfather, then what would have induced this feeling of responsibility toward the man in my ancestor? Was it logical to assume that the man was the bastard child of an illicit relationship between great-grandfather and this mystery woman? Of course not, I told myself. There could have been many reasons for his feelings of benevolence towards this young man, though I admit that for the life of me, at that moment in time I couldn't think of any! I suddenly realised that I'd thought of the man as being young. Why? Great-grandfather hadn't mentioned his age, only that he reminded him of his mother, yet, somehow, I had the feeling that I was right. Jack the Ripper was a young man, probably younger than I was at that time, I just knew it, without any concrete evidence to hand, I just knew.

My research notes were lying on the desk in front of me, where I'd left them in readiness for my current excursion through the pages of the journal. Suddenly something on the uppermost page seemed to leap up from the paper and strike me straight between the eyes. It was a date, the 30th September 1888. It was of course the date of the so-called 'double murder', when both Elizabeth Stride and Catherine Eddowes would meet with their horrific ends. Yet, there was something else, I couldn't think of it at first, but there was a significance about that date that was eluding me for the time being. I wracked my brain, but it wouldn't come, no blinding revelation or realisation sprang to mind. I would have to hope that my memory would click into action before long, and that the significance of the date would reveal itself to me.

I suppose it was the lack of a good night's sleep, for, even though it was still quite early in the day, I suddenly felt my eyes becoming heavy, my thoughts seemed slurred, as if I were caught in a whirlpool of sudden drunkenness. I shook myself in an attempt to clear my head. As I did so, I thought I heard a sound behind me, a sort of quiet rustling, as though someone was treading on dry leaves. I turned quickly, knowing logically that there was no-one there, yet at the same time, my illogical fears and tensions were such that I just had to check that I was truly alone. I was, of course.

The uppermost thought in my mind at that time was simply; was it possible to be alone and yet not alone? Anyone who's been in love will probably recognize that concept, the feeling that, no matter how far apart they may be, two lovers can yet feel as though together across the miles. Unfortunately for me, the feeling in my mind wasn't one of togetherness with Sarah, that most beautiful lady with whom I shared my life, and who was many miles away at her sister's house; no, my feeling was one of togetherness with the malevolent force that I felt was somehow contained within the words and pages of the journal. Like a cancerous mass of gargantuan proportions, the sensation weighed me down, my mind was clouded by thoughts of death, of a crazed madness running out of control, toward an inevitable climax of destruction; but whose, his or mine? His destruction of course had been a fact of history. It was over a hundred years since the series of murders he'd perpetrated had taken place, and Jack the Ripper, whoever he may have been was by now long dead. So, why was I asking the question? Was it possible that my own mind was becoming scarred and twisted in some way by the words that were floating towards my eyes from those aged pages, from the paper itself, strangely warm to the touch, and horrific in content?

I shook myself once more in an effort to dispel the daydream, the feeling of other-worldliness that seemed to be hanging over me, hanging over the entire study, hovering just below the ceiling, a cloud of depression and fear, of evil intent and malevolent purpose. Why didn't I just give up, throw the damned journal in the waste bin, or better still, take it into the garden and burn it? I couldn't. No matter how much I may have wanted to dispose of it, to read not one more single page of the depravities committed by the Ripper, I was somehow being driven by a compulsion I couldn't deny, as though a will stronger than my own was invading my body and mind.

Though my head ached, and my heart throbbed noisily in my chest, and though every logical part of the man that was me screamed at me to leave it alone, I knew that I would never desert my strange voyage through the journal until I'd read every last blood-soaked, horror-filled page, until I'd discovered the secret contained somewhere within its pages or in the words of my own ancestor who had begun this curse upon our family by bequeathing the journal to my grandfather, who had, tragically continued the custom, or should I say, the compulsion? The thought entered my mind that perhaps my grandfather and my father had both experienced the same feelings as I was now being subjected to. If they had been, I wondered how they'd coped with whatever knowledge would eventually be revealed to me. I knew that my grandfather had spent the last few years of his life as a virtual recluse, seldom leaving his home, and turning visitors away from his door, except for the closest members of his family. I'd merely thought him a little strange, perhaps a little senile, now perhaps was the time to revise that opinion, though what to replace it with? Even my father had undergone something of a personality change in the later years of his life. His once permanently cheerful countenance had been replaced by one that seemed to me to be wracked and marked by worry lines, a furrowed brow, and a loss of his once almost legendary sense of humour. Maybe it hadn't just been the result of his long battle against cancer, as I'd thought. Maybe something far more malevolent had eaten at his very heart and soul, as it may have done to those who'd gone before him.

This was bad, unbelievably bad; I just couldn't shake myself out of this awful feeling of doom and gloom, of gathering depression and oppression. That was the word for it, oppression. The room was filled with a tangible sense of cruelty and tyranny, I felt as if I were no longer in control of events, a pall hung over me, and it wasn't going to go away until I had completed my task, and that meant reaching the last page, the last word in the journal, the last vestige of information from great-grandfather. Was I cracking up? I was beginning to think I was. Even my professionally trained and analytical mind was capable of being influenced by outside forces. I knew that, and I wondered just how much I would be affected by the remaining pages of the journal.

I must have fallen into one of those 'waking sleeps' again; you know, when you think you're awake, but you've actually nodded off for a short while, and wake up feeling as though you've been asleep for hours, when it's really only been a few seconds, or perhaps a minute. Anyway, I suddenly came to with a violent jolt, and for a moment I wasn't even sure where I was. I quickly gathered myself however and looked at the clock. I realised it had passed the time when I'd promised myself that I'd stop what I was doing and take a break, maybe get some fresh air in my lungs. As much as I wanted and needed to continue my expedition through the journal I knew that I needed to leave the study and collect my thoughts and give my mind and body the opportunity to refresh themselves, even for a short time. So, with a supreme effort, (and it was exceedingly difficult), I rose from my chair, leaving the journal and my notes behind, and walked out of the study without looking back at them. I think that if I had cast a glance back in their direction I'd have probably returned to the chair.

The walk into the centre of the little village where Sarah and I had made our home five years before wasn't a long one, but it was decidedly pleasant. I gulped in several lungfulls of fresh, sweet tasting air as I walked along the street. The birds were singing, a beautiful resonant chant that filled the air around me. Thrushes, sparrows and various finches were all joined in a harmonious concert of unbridled joyous birdsong, all seemingly choreographed and led by the tumultuously melodic voice of a sole blackbird, who I saw perched majestically on the top of a telegraph pole on the opposite side of the street, his neck stretched upwards, his yellow beak a conductor's baton as he co-ordinated the symphony of song. The sun was warm on my neck as I walked, and the hint of a breeze served to gently rustle the leaves on the trees as I walked, elms, rowans, and the single large oak tree that stood guard at the only crossroads in the village. For a few minutes, as I walked, the horrors of Victorian Whitechapel, the terrible crimes of the Ripper, all thoughts of insanity, dementia and the strange and unholy effects of the journal were left far behind me. My mind, which, for the last twenty-four hours had been filled with little else was suddenly set free, free to enjoy the simple pleasures of my walk, the symphony of the birds, and the soft and gentle accompanying serenade of the leaves as they danced and rustled in the breeze, and the wonderful warming rays of the sun.

I crossed the main street and approached the solitary newsagent the village possessed. As I got closer to the little shop the words emblazoned on the news hoarding by the door jumped out at me. *WOMAN BUTCHERED IN VICIOUS KILLING!* My escape from the horrors of the Ripper's crimes hadn't lasted long. All thoughts of birdsong, rustling leaves, and warm sunny days were immediately dispelled by those stark words, written in bold black felt pen, on that virgin white paper background. I was surrounded by death, by the awful truth of reality, that here, in the midst of our so called enlightened modern society, brutality and murder were still just around the corner, waiting like the Ripper in the night, to strike and destroy the lives of the innocent.

I walked into the shop to be greeted by the friendly smiling face of Rashid, the proprietor, who, despite his foreign name and background had apparently lived in the village longer then the vast majority of its current batch of residents. I tried to respond to his jovial "Good morning, doctor" with a cheerfulness I certainly didn't feel, and quickly purchased a copy of the Daily Mail, and the local paper, whose front page was devoted to the brutal slaying heralded on the hoarding outside the door.

Five minutes later, I was sitting on the small wooden bench which overlooked the small village pond, populated by it's usual compliment of resident ducks, all innocently paddling contentedly across its gleaming surface, their shadows reflected as rippling upside-down ducks in the clear water. Leaving the Daily Mail on one side, I quickly scanned the lead story of the local paper. A thirty-year-old woman had been found in an alley in the town of Guildford, not far from my peaceful village. The poor woman had had her throat cut and had been horribly mutilated. The report concluded, *"In a crime reminiscent of the Jack the Ripper murders in nineteenth century London, the police are urgently seeking the perpetrator of this heinous and barbaric act, which at the moment appears motiveless. With little evidence to go on at present, the officer in charge of the case asks that the public remain vigilant and that women in the area take extra care if going out alone after dark."*

My head was spinning, the shaking in my hands had returned, and the newspaper visibly quivered as I attempted to hold onto it, as if it were the last solid object in a rapidly crumbling universe.

"Why now?" I asked aloud, though to no-one in particular, (I was alone after all). Why did this have to happen at this exact moment in time? My heart went out to the poor victim of this horrible and sadistic crime, and to her family of course, but it was almost too much for my mind to cope with, that this should have taken place just as the journal had fallen into my hands, on the very night in fact, that I had begun to explore it's sinister, ancient pages. Add to that the newspaper's reference to the Ripper himself, and the coincidence was uncanny, as though the present was reflecting the past in some way.

No, I couldn't accept that. Jack the Ripper died long ago, and no-one knew of the journal's existence, therefore the murder of this poor unfortunate woman had been nothing more than a grisly coincidence, that's all. I kept repeating that fact to myself as I walked slowly home, my feet and legs leaden, my heart heavy, and my mind in a whirl. The birds were probably still singing, the leaves quietly rustling, and the sun was likely as warm as before, but I never heard or felt a thing, I swear it. I must have been like a zombie as I made my way back into the house, threw the newspapers onto the kitchen table, and sat in Sarah's fireside chair with my head in my hands, as that pall of gloom and depression oozed its way from the study into the kitchen and quickly wrapped itself around me. In truth, I had never felt quite so wretched, so disturbed of mind, and so lacking in confidence. I felt as if my wonderfully crafted and carefully constructed world were being wrenched away from me by some power, some force that as yet I couldn't even recognize. I knew that before long I would return to the study, pick up the journal once more, and delve ever deeper into the mind and the world of Jack the Ripper. What I would find there was anyone's guess. I certainly didn't want to try to foresee what may hit me when I next peered at those pages; I was still so disturbed by the strange coincidence of the murder of the poor woman just a few miles from my home on the previous night. As I'd sat reading the words of the Ripper, someone had dragged her into a dark and terrifying alley, slit her throat and committed acts of great cruelty and horror on her body. I remember thinking that though the Ripper may be long dead, something of his cruelty must exist in each and every one of us, buried deep within the subconscious of seemingly rational men and women, but there all the same, waiting to be released by the right catalyst if and when the time comes.

Sensing that I was being drawn by a strange inevitability and feeling more tense and nervous than I would have believed possible in myself just twenty-four hours ago, I rose from my chair. The journal was waiting...

TWENTY
'DEAR BOSS'

25th September 1888

Confusion reigns within my head. I am troubled by events. They had me there, in that place, that bed, and I was in such pain of forgetfulness. Thank God for Cavendish! He is my rock, my anchor, he at least understands, and did not decry me for my folly. They have kept me though from the one thing that helps this pain within my head, my laudanum.

Hours have passed and I am better than before, much better. My head is clear, and once more I may focus my thoughts on what must be done. I was not so clear in the hospital; I cannot in truth remember how I got there, I felt so ill upon the train and then, my senses failed me, though I do remember blabbing to Cavendish. He blamed it on the laudanum, ha. What did I say? Of that I can't be sure. Did I say too much of things that should not be spoken of? I know I told him of the Scottish whore, but little else. His sense of logic, his professional judgement and his loyalty will keep his silence.

Now I have much to do. The streets are fair ripe with whores in need of execution, to be consigned to their rightful end. I shall have some sport this time, for I remain invisible and the plodders of the official force are impotent to catch me.

I fancy I shall write to them, immediately, no, not to them direct, for that would be no sport. The press shall have my words, and let them print the promise I shall make, and the public read those words and tremble, and the police read those words, and squirm in their inability to take me. I shall disguise my hand, more to confuse them, and I'll need a name that befits my task, and the ink shall be as red as the blood of the whores I rip. There it is; the name with which I shall tease and taunt the poor fools. For am I not the original Jack so nimble, Jack so quick, do I not rip the whores so swift and slick? Bit long? Perhaps. Then I shall give them 'Jack, the Ripper', the ripper of whores, let them chase shadows, as I spread my paths through the most wondrous grottos of Mr. Bazalgette, who has so kindly provided me with the cloak of invisibility with which I evade the uniforms and the whistles, the plodders and the takers. I must return to the streets, they have slept too long, the voices, they must speak to me once again, and together we shall reap the harvest of blood that is rightfully mine.

I shall begin my letter at once; I shall send it to the boss, not of just one publication but to the biggest agency in town! Let them know me and fear me. I shall give it to them in the colour of the whores' blood; I wish I had the real thing with which to write it, but maybe in the future I shall. My words shall reach deep into the hearts of the filthy whores, and they will tremble, for they will know that I am coming for them, one at a time, one after the other. Yes, tremble little ladies of the night; hold on to your innards while you can, Jack is coming for you all.

So THERE IT WAS, before my eyes. I felt as though, in those few words I had witnessed the birth of Jack the Ripper! Yet how mundane, how casual had been his decision to use that name, now synonymous with the deaths of those poor women so long ago. Of course, the name Jack had been almost a Victorian institution. Almost every fiction of the era had a 'Jack' somewhere within it. There was also Jack Tar, for a sailor, and the rhyme the Ripper had alluded to in his writings was of course the old 'Jack be nimble, Jack be quick, Jack jumped over the candle-stick'. He'd taken that most innocuous of children's rhymes and added it to the terrible action of his crimes in order to invent a name that would go down in infamy and take its place in the history of crime.

I felt sick, my head throbbed even more violently than before, and I knew without looking at them that my hands were trembling. He had passed off his stay in the hospital so lightly, being almost unconcerned that he'd confessed his guilt to my great-grandfather. He simply seemed amused and disdainful of my ancestor's failure to believe him. Was it a ploy, I wondered, this stay in the hospital? Had he engineered it deliberately in order to gain some sort of attention. Could he have been brazen enough to know that great-grandfather would come to his bedside, and that he would put his confession down to a hallucination caused by the laudanum he was taking? I didn't know, I doubted that I'd ever know, but I had my suspicions that the Ripper might have been arrogant enough to do just such a thing in the fullest of confidence that he could confess to my great-grandfather and not be believed. He may have been seriously ill, indeed seriously mentally deranged, but he was clever, very clever indeed.

It was also obvious from the tone and content of this latest entry that the Ripper was preparing to strike again. I knew from my notes that he was drawing ever closer to the night of the 30th September, when he would commit the gruesome double murder. That's when it came to me, the thing I'd been trying to remember! The 30th had a significance to me in the light of what I'd already read. I now knew that on the very night he was out upon the streets of Whitechapel slaughtering his latest victims, two hundred miles north of London, a poor Scottish lassie was walking into a police station to report that her friend, Morag Blennie was missing. Flora Niddrie never saw Morag again, nor did anyone else, and I felt such a bleak sadness, an emptiness in my soul such as I can't begin to describe to you in these pages.

I felt sick at his fulsome praise for the work of Joseph Bazalgette. I didn't need to look that name up to know the significance of the name. The 'wondrous grottos' to which the Ripper referred were in fact the new (at that time) sewers of London, which had been designed and engineered by Bazalgette, and had done much to alleviate what was known as 'The Great Stink', the awful stomach-churning stench that had pervaded every home and building in London until their introduction. London had turned from being little more than an open sewer into a sanitized and modern city as a result of his work, and Joseph Bazalgette is well deserving of a place in any list of England's great engineers and innovators. For Jack the Ripper however, his system of interlinking tunnels and channels was obviously once again to be put to quite another use, and I couldn't help but think that the carriage of thousands of tons of raw sewage and effluent would have been a far more noble and virtuous purpose than to be used as the escape vehicle, the means of avoiding detection used by the notorious Whitechapel murderer.

As to the letter, well, so many 'experts' have for so long derided the 'Dear Boss' letter as being a fabrication, the work of a journalist, or someone seeking to sensationalise the murders at the time, here was my proof that it was genuine. You will note that I now had no doubt about the journal's authenticity. Though it was true I had no scientific proof that it was the work of the Ripper, I knew in my heart that this journal was no attempt to capitalize on the crimes after the event, nor was it a modern fake, my great-grandfather's notes confirmed that for me. For those who have never seen or heard of the letter, I have taken the time to copy it out here, in the colour used by the Ripper, and using his original spellings, the 'mistakes' in grammar an obvious attempt to misdirect the authorities as to his origins and intelligence. It read as follows:

25 Sept 1888

Dear Boss

I keep on hearing the police have caught me but they wont fix me just yet. I have laughed when they look so clever and talk about being on the right track. That joke about Leather Apron gave me real fits. I am down on whores and I shant quit ripping them till I do get buckled. Grand work the last job was. I gave the lady no time to squeal. How can they catch me now. I love my work and want to start again. You will soon here of me

*with my funny little games. I saved some of the proper
red stuff in a ginger beer bottle over the last job to write
with but it went thick like glue and I cant use it. Red ink
is fit enough I hope haha. The next job I do I shall clip
the ladys ears off and send to the police officers just for
jolly wouldn't you. Keep this letter back till I do a bit
more work, then give it out straight. My knife's nice and
sharp I want to get to work right away if I get the
chance. Good luck.*

Yours truly
Jack the Ripper

At the request of the police the Central News Agency did in
fact keep the letter from the public until the 1st October, after
the double murder, after which of course the name on
everyone's lips in London was that of Jack the Ripper. He had
achieved his fame, exactly as I suspected he had intended to! It
was also true that he would, in the course of one of his two
murders on the 30th, cut the ear from one of his victims. As the
letter was received by the news agency on the 27th, how could a
journalist have written it with such foreknowledge of the
Ripper's plans? Unless of course, the Ripper were the
journalist? Now there was a new possibility to ponder! My
thoughts were becoming crowded, closed in, and I could feel
the pulse in my head throbbing in my temples. There was a
sudden imperceptible flash of light outside, which I sensed
rather than saw through the window of the study, followed by
an immense and quite frightening clap of thunder, the loudest I
could ever recall. It seemed to shake the house, the study itself
seemed to reverberate to the immense crash of that thunder,
and then, as if a horde of ear-piercing demons had been
unleashed from the gates of Hell itself, came the screams and

shrieks of numerous house and car alarms all along the street. It was a disharmony the like of which I'd never heard before, the lightning flashed again, there was another immense thunderclap, the room shook, and then the heavens seemed to open, and the rain began to lash against the windows with the intensity of a thousand devils trying to batter their way into the house. I sat, almost paralyzed in my chair as the storm raged outside, the alarms shrieking, daylight became darkness, and I was adrift in sea of disorientation. With subsequent flashes of lightning and terrible crashes of thunder, my desk lamp flickered on and off, as though imbued with a life of its own, and that life was fighting for its existence. For over twenty minutes it continued, that raging storm, and I couldn't escape the thought that this awesome display of nature's wrath had been launched from the depths of some outlandish nightmare. As suddenly as it had started, the storm abated, and the sun crept back out from behind the dark clouds, bringing its light and warmth back to the world. Somehow though, it failed to reach into my room. One by one the automatic cut-off systems switched off the alarms, and a strange stillness and quiet swept along the street, only the sound of the rainwater dripping from the gutters and the leaves and branches of the trees reached my ears through the glass panes of the windows.

The room felt cold, as though I were no longer in my warm, comfortable study, but instead entombed in the darkest crypt, shut off from any source of heat and light. I also thought that I could detect an odd aroma in the room, a fetid, dank, stale smell, like the stench of death, or just the scent of evil. That was nonsense of course, it was my own mind playing tricks on me, it had to be. There was nothing in the room that could be the cause of such a smell, I was sitting in my study, alone, surrounded by my own personal possessions, as I had done a thousand times before, nothing had changed, there could be no strange smell, unless of course, it was the smell of my own fear, permeating my thought processes, and invading my conscious mind.

And I was afraid, that much was certain, though as yet I had no idea why. Every ounce of logic within me told me that there was nothing to be afraid of; I was simply sitting reading some old papers, what could be more harmless? A few sheets of old parchment couldn't harm me, could they? So why the fear? What could be causing such a reaction to these words that now almost seemed to be gaining some sort of life of their own in my increasingly fevered mental state? I was beginning to believe, however irrational it may have seemed and still does today, that there was far more to those old and crumpled sheets of paper than I had originally perceived. What that something was I had no idea at that point, but I was determined that I would not give up, I would see the journal through to its ending, whatever it may be, and wherever it may lead me.

I promised myself to utilise my own logical thought processes, my professional and analytical mind, to try to avoid being caught up in the almost ethereal aura that seemed to emanate from the journal. I felt stupid at the time, for even thinking such thoughts, for believing that there could be something dark and sinister about the journal, and yet, at the same time, my heart was attempting to override my mind, it was sending out a warning, a warning that I should ignore at my peril, but of course, as a doctor, a scientist no less, the warnings of the heart were not tangible enough for me to heed, I placed my trust in logic and science, in the realities of the twentieth century, and to this very day, I wish that I had listened to my heart.

TWENTY-ONE
THOUGHTS OF PAST AND PRESENT

My lunch was a sombre affair that day. Though the fridge was well stocked, (Sarah had made sure of that before she left), I grabbed the first thing I saw, a packet of ready sliced chicken, made a quick sandwich, poured myself a large glass of fresh orange juice, and dawdled as long as I could in the kitchen, slowly devouring that meagre repast. In truth I had no interest in eating, the sparse meal was simply a means of ensuring some form of nutritional intake reached my stomach, I was eating out of necessity, not for pleasure.

My head was awash with thoughts, none of them particularly pleasant ones. Only yesterday, my life had seemed ordered, tranquil even. Despite the recent loss of my father and the pain that came with it, I was happy, at least as happy as any man had a right to be. Now, through my exposure to the journal, and the strange, compelling power of its words, I felt as though I were trapped in a downward spiralling whirlpool of illogical thoughts, horrific mental imagery and a sense of confusion that had left me teetering on the edge of the thin dividing line between reality and fantasy. With every page that

I read, with each new horror described in the Ripper's own hand, I was being drawn almost imperceptibly into a darkness, a world apart from my own, where the sights, sounds and smells of the foul, rank smelling streets of Victorian London were becoming horrifically real, where I could see, rather than imagine, the blood of the Ripper's victims as it gushed uncontrollably from the gaping wounds imposed upon their bodies, almost tasting the copper-sweet smell that accompanied the flow of that precious life-blood. Without knowing why, I had even imagined that I could feel the final moments of terror and panic that must have flashed through the minds of both Polly Nichols and Annie Chapman, and the poor Scottish girl, (Morag Blennie?), as the fatal realization had dawned upon them that they were living the final seconds of their lives. That was the most frightening part of all this, that I really could feel all those things, I really could see them happening, as real as if it were being enacted right there, in my study, like some bizarre and unworldly panorama of death, a masque of horror and revulsion staged just for me, a private vision of Hell!

Was it any wonder that my mind was confused? There was of course no logical reason for me to be feeling these things, it was nothing more than a trip into the depths of my own imagination, a daydream of sorts, fuelled by the intensity of the contents of that infernal journal. At least, that's what I kept trying to tell myself. As time wore on however, I realised that I was subconsciously trying to delay the moment when I would return to my study and take up the journal once again. Why didn't I just ignore it? I could have sealed it up, thrown it away, done any one of a dozen things that would have wrenched me away from the unnatural nightmare world I had entered, but I didn't. With my limbs feeling heavier by the second, and with my heart rate increasing due to the strange thrill that seemed to be coursing through my veins, I made my way back to the study. Yes, there was a thrill attached to all the horror I was exposing myself to, not, admittedly a pleasant thrill, but a thrill, nonetheless. This private insight into the mind of the Ripper was becoming obsessional, an addiction as strong as the pull of the opium laced laudanum had been for the killer himself.

As I took my place in my leather office chair once more I reflected on the fact that even my walk to the village had done nothing to relieve the stress and tension that was gradually increasing within me. Admittedly, the walk there had been agreeable, but all thoughts of peace and tranquillity had been immediately dispelled by the news of the horrific murder virtually on my own doorstep. The similarities between it, and the contents of the journal were just too disturbingly similar. Though the victim hadn't been a prostitute, (the report described her as a barmaid), she had been waylaid on her way home from work late at night and horribly mutilated by all accounts; 'butchered' being the word used by the journalist to illustrate the point. In addition to the disquieting affects of the journal, it was also quite clear to me that somewhere in the local vicinity there was a new and equally sadistic killer on the loose. I hoped that the police would make an early arrest, that this latter-day ripper-like murderer at least would be apprehended, and the streets made safe for women to walk freely once again.

All these thoughts and more were rushing through my mind as I settled myself as comfortably as possible into my leather office chair and prepared to continue my journey through the world of The Ripper. As I reached out to pick up the journal however, I paused in mid-action, and consciously stopped myself from doing so. Instead, I picked up the telephone and dialled my sister-in law's number. Perhaps if I spoke to my lovely Sarah, just for a couple of minutes, it would give me added heart and help to dispel some of the aura of gloom that had rapidly begun to descend upon me as soon as I'd walked back into the study. The phone rang and rang until Jennifer's answering machine clicked on. Dammit! No-one at home. I left a brief message for Sarah, nothing too detailed, just told her that I loved her and missed her and would try her mobile number, and if that failed, I'd call again later. Her mobile phone was switched off! I presumed they were out and probably in a place where mobiles had to be turned off. I hoped that little Jack hadn't had a turn for the worse, that he wasn't languishing in a hospital bed, or should that have been cot? I thought all manner of bleak and unhealthy thoughts about the baby, but then decided that Sarah would have called me if things had got too bad. I would just have to wait and speak to her later.

Deciding that I'd put it off for as long as I could, I redirected my shaking hand toward the ominous-looking journal on the desk, picked it up once more, and turned to the next, grisly page. There was a gap of one day, as was a frequent occurrence to which I was growing accustomed, and then the journal continued:

27th September 1888.

Does theatre echo life, or is it the other way around? Last night I paid a visit to the Lyceum Theatre and witnessed a performance of the new stage play, 'a phenomenon of the stage' they call it, Mr Robert Louis Stevenson's 'The Strange Tale of Dr Jekyll and Mister Hyde'. A wonderful performance by Mr Richard Mansfield, the great American actor, in the title role, and yet, how so like my work. Am I not the perfect gentleman, this 'Dr

Jekyll, and yet also the instrument of fear and terror that is 'Mr Hyde'? Oh, to see the looks of shock upon the faces of so many in the audience! I could have laughed aloud at their pitiful shrieks and gasps, but I did not. If only they had known, what would they have thought, how would they have reacted? I shall obtain perhaps a copy of the book, so that I may study in more detail the author's words on the subject, so obviously cut short by the needs of the stage.

I wonder, have the press received my letter yet? What shall they make of it I wonder? Will they dismiss my words as a hoax, or a fanciful lie perhaps? Ha, they will soon see that I do not lie. The time is fast approaching when I shall go to work once more, the streets are too dry of the blood of the whores, they must run once more with the river of life, I shall release the flow from the wells of their wretched bodies, they will bleed, and they will die. The voices are getting louder once more, my head is aching terribly. The laudanum helps but won't stop it altogether. The pain is sometimes more than I can bear. Only the blood of the whores will make it go away. I shall take a larger dose, feel the warmth coursing through my body, and the sleep will come, if I am so lucky, a lovely long black sleep, and then, my work may begin once more.

A visit to the theatre? I could scarcely believe what I was reading. Here he was, just three nights before he would commit the ferocious double murder of Liz Stride and Catherine Eddowes, happily enjoying an evening enjoying the most celebrated play in London. My own notes had shown that at the time the ripper murders began, Richard Mansfield, a renowned American actor was starring at the Lyceum in that very play, and that subsequent to the double murder, the play was cancelled as people had thought that its content might possibly inspire the murderer to strike again. Today we would find such a thing ridiculously naïve and childish in the extreme, but, to the sensitive factions of Victorian society, it seemed the right thing to do at the time. Whether Mr Mansfield was ever compensated for the cancellation of his starring engagement I cannot say, as I was unable to obtain that information. The Ripper was also richly mocking in his view of his fellow theatregoers. To say he felt like 'laughing aloud' when witness to their shock and horror at the more lurid scenes of the play was yet another example of his total disdain for his fellow citizens, who he so obviously held in ridicule and contempt. I was intrigued by his allusion to the similarities between the character of Jekyll and Hyde, and himself. He knew enough to realise that the similarity existed, so he obviously had not as yet passed the point of no return, the final descent into the madness towards which I knew he was spiralling with grim inevitability. Had that point been passed, I doubted he would have had the clarity of thought to make such a comparison. For now at least, I felt that he was just holding on to a vestige of reason and sanity, though by little more than a thread.

Deep within him the rage was building once again. The voices were back, presumably guiding and goading him. Whatever psychosis was acting upon his mind, I was sure that he would soon have little control over his own actions. The blood lust was getting stronger, he now saw the bodies of his victims as 'wells' which would provide him with the blood he needed to satisfy his, and 'his voices' crazed need for blood. I was still certain that he was in the tertiary or final stage of syphilis, and that the damage to his brain was now irrevocable. I couldn't yet understand how he hadn't been diagnosed with the disease. Surely, over the years he had consulted a physician, and would that doctor not have noticed the tell-tale signs? Then again, though the early sign of the disease are evident to the sufferer, they are not outwardly visible, and if he had chosen not to seek help, the initial stage would have passed with or without medication, and the second phase would have allowed the disease to lie dormant, possibly for years, before finally rising like a phoenix from the ashes to begin its awful, terminal stage.

He was obviously ignoring the symptoms as much as he could, and also ignoring the doctors, including my great-grandfather, who had treated him for his latest 'attack' of temporary amnesia and partial dementia. This was evident by his intention to increase the dosage of laudanum, which by now was probably already at dangerous proportions. He was totally addicted to the opium in the drug, and like any addict, any attempt to wean him from the drug would have been a fruitless exercise without some form of support and medical assistance. He knew that the laudanum would induce what he described as a 'dark sleep', a deep hallucinogenic sleep, during which he would 'see' and 'hear' all manner of aberrations, which would fuel his sadistic passions as soon as he returned to a waking state. I had had this type of so-called sleep described to me on many occasion in the past by patients far less disturbed than the writer of this awful text. Already driven half-crazy by the syphilis which was spreading through his body and his brain cells, he was now also a drug-crazed junkie, and possibly subject to other forms of psychological disorders too. I was amazed to some extent that he managed to function at all in the everyday world, though it was certain that he did, and that no-one saw through his external façade, his mask of normality. Yes, in many ways he was like the actor Richard Mansfield, who had created such a stunning and frightening stage persona that people often ran screaming from the auditorium, such was the fear he engendered in them, but Mansfield was just an actor, who, at the end of each performance could wipe away the greasepaint and make-up, wash his face and hands, go home to his lodgings and become his own self once again. The Ripper was different, vastly different.

To put it simply, unlike the character portrayed by Richard Mansfield, unlike Robert Louis Stevenson's Doctor Jekyll and Mr Hyde, Jack the Ripper was no figment of the imagination, no fictional creation of a literary brain. No, as the words of his journal screamed from the page his threats of further mayhem, as the streets of London waited unsuspectingly for the blood to flow once again, the character with two minds, two personalities, but one single, simple aim, that of horrific and brutal murder, was all too real, all too genuine, and about to go down in history under the name by which the newspaper and penny broadsheet sellers would soon be shouting on every street corner. Within days everyone would know him by his self chosen terrible and blood chilling name. The 'Whitechapel Murderer', and 'Leather Apron' were about to be consigned to the pages of history, 'Jack the Ripper' was about to announce himself to his public!

TWENTY-TWO
AN IMAGE OF HELL

My father, God rest his soul, always told me that psychiatrists are among the most ignorant of doctors. When I asked him why, he told me that, although the range of illnesses, psychoses, and other ailments we attempt to treat are huge, virtually limitless in fact, the clinical and factual knowledge at our disposal is minute by comparison. We cannot for example, peer into the human psyche, we cannot understand how the thought processes of the human brain really work, or how it can be that one set of circumstances can lead one individual into, say, the deepest pit of trauma or depression, when the self same circumstances have no effect whatsoever on millions of other individuals. Psychiatry is not, and probably never will be an exact science. In most cases we treat, rather than cure the patients in our care, managing to alleviate some of the worst and most disturbing symptoms of their illness without ever managing to totally cure them.

Compare that to a surgeon treating diseases of the heart for example, where so much knowledge is available on the workings of that particular organ, where the science of heart surgery is such that we can now transplant a healthy heart from one person to another, giving those otherwise fated to an early death a new lease on life, and you will perhaps see what he meant, and why I for one, understood his reasoning.

Not only that, but my own experience had taught me that it is wholly possible for two or even three or more psychiatrists to make different diagnoses, and to prescribe different courses of treatment for an individual patient, despite being presented with exactly the same symptoms. Such then, is the imprecise nature of my profession. Patients entering the world of psychiatric medicine are always treated with the best intentions and with the utmost professionalism by their psychiatrist, but what we can do is limited by our knowledge of those precise workings of the brain, the mind, and the psyche.

I make these observations for you so you may appreciate, (as I did not) what was happening within my own mind at that time. Under normal circumstances, reading the journal of a long-dead miscreant should not have had an adverse effect on my skilled professional mind, and yet, here I was, feeling more and more disturbed with every page I read of the journal of the Ripper. In hindsight I was perhaps beginning to show signs of cognitive dissonance. Humans cannot think two opposing or clashing things at the same time, e.g. we know that cigarettes are harmful yet continue to smoke. To be able to do so the mind rationalises the thought or perception which goes against the behaviour. So, as a psychiatrist, did I think I was 'above' being affected by such a written record. Was it because my own father, grandfather and great-grandfather had read those pages, and had each kept whatever secret they hid to themselves for years and years, never breathing a word about its very existence until after their deaths? Would I, on reaching the last page of the journal, feel compelled to keep that secret myself, as they had done? Or was there something far more sinister at work as I read the words of the Ripper? What strange thing was happening that was drawing me deeper into the past, a past that was becoming so real that I could almost see myself walking beside the man as he waited in shadow, only to reveal himself to his victims from the darkness before committing his wicked acts of murder and mutilation? As I sat, preparing to continue, I could feel an even stronger throbbing in my head, and I realised that it was the beating of my heart!

There were no entries on either the 28th or 29th of September. Could I assume that the Ripper had indeed entered that 'deep sleep' to which he had previously alluded? Was he at that time lying at home or in some opium den perhaps, in a state of total opium intoxication? The thought of the opium den had just struck me as a possibility. Though he hadn't mentioned it in the pages of the journal, I thought that if he wasn't receiving the palliative effect he desired from the bottled laudanum a direct infusion of pure opium would maybe have been his next logical (!) step. Then again, my hypothesis could have been entirely wrong, and again, there was only one way I was going to find out.

30th *September 1888*

How I slept! Never have I known such a feeling, I was asleep yet not asleep, and the dreams, oh such dreams. I walked in fields bedecked with hanging whore corpses, hanging from trees and dripping blood upon the green grass that grew at their feet. The sky was blue, yet tinged with red, the clouds suffused with the blood that rose in a mist from the grass and swallowed up the corpses and sent the whores' damned souls soaring upwards in their twisted agonies, reaching for Heaven, only to send them crashing downwards, spiralling as they fell, screaming as

*they descended into Hell. There are too many for I alone
to rid the world of, but I shall strike down as many as I
can, and I shall strike again tonight! The voices are here,
they whisper gently in my ear, they tell me that the time
is right, tonight shall be my night!*

This was the first time since I'd begun my odyssey through
the journal that the Ripper had made what I termed a 'daytime'
entry, announcing his intentions for the coming night, as
opposed to a simple after-the-fact rendering of his murderous
deeds. Not only that, but the graphic imagery conjured by his
words describing his dream were horrific in the extreme. There
was no mention of opium dens, just an allusion to a strange
sleep, 'asleep, yet not asleep', he called it. In other words, he
was hallucinating, probably not truly asleep, but in that state of
opium induced hallucination I had thought probable. He used
so few words, and yet they depicted a scene of such demonic
horror that my sense of revulsion was exceeded only by the
terror such a scene induced in my mind. His description of the
'rising souls' of those poor women, reaching out to the heavens
only to be cast down into the depths of Hell was akin to a scene
from Dante's Inferno, a picture of the descent into Hell, of
screaming, twisted souls in agony. Somehow, the Ripper's
version, though described solely in words as opposed to
pictures, served to horrify and terrify me far more than Dante.

What disturbed me most about this depiction was the fact
that I could see the whole scene in my mind as if I were there, a
spectator to the grisly panoply that had played out in his mind,
like a grotesque x-rated movie. The words on the page had
somehow brought the scene to life in vivid intensity, and I
couldn't shake the images from my mind. Nothing in my
experiences had ever had such a profound effect on me as this
terrible demonic collection of words, or the sights and sounds

that they were able to conjure in my mind. If it were possible, (which of course would be absurd), I would have said that the words themselves, the ink with which they were written, had assumed the character and the soul of the one who had written them, that they'd taken on a three-dimensional quality, and that by holding the pages, by reading the words, I was being sucked inexorably into a world between worlds, where my own sense of reality was gradually being eroded, where the words reached out from the page to touch me, to invade my thoughts, my mind, to infect my thoughts as a virus would infect my body.

Though I knew from my research notes, which lay innocently and quietly on the desk before me that this was the night of the double murder, though I knew that all this had happened over a century ago, I was somehow gripped by a fear I couldn't explain. I wanted to be there, to walk those dark London streets, feel the rain that had fallen that night as it splashed my face, hear the sounds of the late night hansoms and broughams as they carried their wealthy passengers home, and then to make my way into the meaner streets, to feel the demi-silence that descended upon the thoroughfares of Whitechapel, watch the Ripper's victims as they walked towards their inevitable doom, the heels of their boots clattering along the uneven cobbles, their feet splashing in the puddles, and somehow, I wanted to shout, scream, warn them of their impending fate, I wanted to save them, though I couldn't, could I?

Those women were dead, and had been for over a hundred years, they were a footnote in history, having achieved a fame in death that they could never have attained in life. Had they not been murdered that night in Berner Street and Mitre Square respectively, Liz Stride and Catherine Eddowes would have eventually passed into the afterlife as anonymously as they had lived. So, why was I so concerned, why was I reacting this way?

My mind was full of incomprehension as I battled with the illogical desires within me, and the impossible assault on my senses that was heightening by the minute.

Fear of the unknown is perhaps the greatest fear that can stalk the mind of man. Though I was, and still continue to think of myself as a rational and sound thinking human being, I had to conclude that something beyond my comprehension was taking place as I sat in my comfortable chair, surrounded by the trappings of my comfortable existence; I was no longer myself in the true sense of the word, I was a spectator, (quite how, I couldn't explain) and rapidly becoming a willing one, to the crimes of a 'madman', and, as I shivered with the realisation, I wondered whether perhaps that madness was not also invading my own mind. Was I losing control, was I going mad? I shall continue this narrative to its conclusion, and then perhaps you can be the judge of that question.

TWENTY-THREE
WITH THE COMING OF THE NIGHT

As I STRETCHED my aching limbs, I realised that the day was
drawing in. It was late afternoon and darkness was beginning to
descend on the world, as it had so long ago on the streets that
were the Ripper's stalking ground. My own intense immersion
in the matter in hand, and the light from my desk lamp, which
had burned faithfully on my desk all through the daylight
hours, had helped to disguise the gathering gloom outside my
window.

Feeling cold and weary, I rose from my chair and crossed
the study, and, for the first time in many months, I turned on
the antique design, log effect gas fire. Its instant warmth
suffused the room, bringing a degree of light and cheer to my
self-imposed cloistered environment. I reached for the dimmer
switch on the wall by the door, and turned it up to halfway, and
the overhead ceiling lights came to life. The room looked warm
and inviting, though I must admit that despite the warmth and
the glow of the fire, and the illumination provided by the lights,
I still felt as though I were gripped by a coldness that had now

spread throughout my body, my hands were visibly trembling, and my legs felt heavy and leaden.

I thought of retaking my place at the desk and continuing my strange passage through the corridors of the Ripper's mind, but decided instead, as I was on my feet, to make for the kitchen and fix myself something to eat. Fifteen minutes later, having partaken of a meagre repast of cheese and biscuits washed down with a glass of sparkling spring water, (just about all I could stomach at the time), I was back in my chair.

As I was about to take up the journal once more, the telephone sprang into life. It was Sarah.

"Robert, my darling, I got your message, I'm sorry we were out. How are you? Mrs Armitage phoned me a few minutes ago and said she'd called to see you and that you looked awful! What have you been doing to yourself? Honestly! I can't leave you for a few days without you going to rack and ruin can I? What is it Robert, what's wrong?"

Sarah paused for breath, and I seized my opportunity to reply.

"Sarah, calm down, please, there's nothing wrong, really. Yes, I looked a bit rough when Mrs A called round but that was because I hadn't slept very well. I've been going through some more of Dad's papers, and some case files that needed bringing up to date, and I burned the midnight oil a bit, that's all," I half-lied. "If I was ill my darling, you'd be the first to know about it, don't you worry about that! Now, how's young Jack?" I enquired, attempting to deflect the conversation into a more manageable direction.

"He's much better Robert, in fact, I should be able to get back home in two or three days, Jennifer says it's not fair to keep me here when you've just lost your father, and that I should be at home to look after you."

"That's wonderful," I replied, "I can't wait to see you, my darling. You know how much I love you don't you Sarah?"

"Of course I do Robert darling, listen, are you sure you're alright, you do sound a little strange you know?"

"Sarah, really, I'm fine. Now go, enjoy your time with Jennifer and little Jack, and don't worry about me."

"But Mrs Armitage said..."

"Sarah!" I almost shouted down the phone. "I know she's a kind hearted old soul, but she can also be an interfering old busybody, who obviously reads too much into things. Please believe me, I'm ok, really I am, and I'm looking forward to you coming home, now go and give my love to your sister and Tom, and give the baby a kiss from his uncle, and I'll call you later to say goodnight."

"Alright then Robert, if you say so darling," she replied, "but you'd better ring me, or I'll be calling Mrs Armitage and sending her round to make sure my gorgeous husband is as well as he says he is!"

"I'll ring you; I promise."

"OK my darling, I'll talk to you later then, I love you very much, Robert, "bye my love."

"Bye, Sarah, I love you too."

The silence in the room was tangible after I'd hung up on Sarah. For a brief moment, I was impaled upon the twin horns of loneliness and desolation, I wanted to ring Sarah back, tell her to come home immediately, tell her how disturbed I felt, how much I needed with her right then, but, just as the terrible emotions threatened to overwhelm me, I took a very deep breath, looked at the assorted paraphernalia of the Ripper's journal, great-grandfather's notes and father's letter upon the desk, and I knew that the only way to complete my trek through these pages of history was by being alone. I couldn't expose Sarah to the words or emotions contained within the pages of the Ripper's journal, and, in that moment, I began to understand why possession of this fiendish work had been kept such a close secret by my forebears.

Outside, the last vestiges of daylight were fast disappearing, and a light breeze had begun to disturb the branches of the trees in the garden. I noticed a few spots of rain beginning to appear on the window, and another involuntary shiver ran through my entire body as the day gave way to evening, and night approached with the same inevitability as the bloody crimes that I knew would soon be described in the journal. Almost imperceptibly, I felt as though the whole room were being gently suffused with a faint red hue, as though the 'red mist' of the Ripper's dream was somehow flooding into my study, giving the task in which I was engaged the rather droll and gory title in my mind of, 'a study in red'. Reality dawned upon me with the realisation that the redness in the room was simply caused by the reflection from the darkened window of the dancing flames of the gas fire, the colour highlighted by the low lighting I had settled for when turning on the lights. At least, that's the way I rationalised it at the time. There couldn't have been any other explanation, could there?

1ˢᵗ October 1888

Two in one night! A glorious if unintended double.
Tracked one whore and tempted the bitch with grapes.
What whore can afford grapes? She could not resist my
gift, and I should have had great sport with her carcass
but for interruption. I slit her easy enough, though in the
dark used the shorter knife, not so quick or sharp, and
saw the blood spurt in a copious river from her neck.
Then, damnation, couldn't begin to gut the whore.
Heard sounds outside the yard, and horses footsteps on

*the stones. Had to flee, and quick, kept close to the wall
as a horse and cart came close by and slipped away
before the man raised the alarm. Had no blood upon me,
so slipped into the nearest tunnel and kept invisible,
rising soon in Mitre Square. God Bless Mr Bazalgette!
Another whore soon made herself available to me, and
this time I made no mistake. This one bled as a stuck pig
would, and the blood gurgled as it left her gashed throat.
I ripped her face apart and gutted her as easy as you like.
The street was stained fair red, even in the dark I saw it.
I could swear she moved as I sliced her innards, poor
bloody little whore! Maybe not. Took no time at all, and
this time sliced the ear as promised. Used the whore's
own apron to wipe the knife, this one's blood was too
sticky. Left the whore on display and tripped off home.
The voices were so pleased with what we'd done, slept
well, and woke as a new man, though my head throbs
with the headache again, I shall dose myself once more,
and sleep again until the pain subsides.*

*Woke later, felt better, sent a card to the boss, wanted
him to know it was me who did the deed as promised. I
shall rest awhile, and sleep again, my exertions tire me.*

Two women, two murders, vile mutilation, and here was
the killer dismissing the deeds in a few words. I admit that I
was surprised by the lack of emotion shown by the Ripper to
the double murder. There was a mild elation, yes, but more a
sense of frustration in his words. I thought he was perhaps
angry at being interrupted in his 'work' on Liz Stride, and that
he felt grievously inconvenienced at having had to seek out a
second victim, Catherine Eddowes. Perhaps, if a man named
Louis Diemschütz had not walked into the yard on Berner

Street at the moment he did, thus allowing the Ripper to perform his grisly mutilations on Liz Stride, then poor Catherine Eddowes might never have become a Ripper victim. Such, I mused to myself, were the vagaries of fate.

He had indeed used the sewers again, Bazalgette's fine creations, to effect his escape from Berner Street, but, just how close was Diemschütz to him as he slipped out of that yard, perhaps only feet away? Many experts have pondered over the years as to how the Ripper managed to get from Berner Street to Mitre Square so quickly between the murders, unseen by a soul. The answer was always there, staring them in the face. The sewers! He'd been able to travel below ground, in a series of straight lines, without having to make recourse to the highways and byways of Whitechapel, thus probably shortening the distance and journey time considerably. It was also a fact that a piece of Catherine Eddowes apron had been found at 2.50 a.m. in the doorway of Wentworth Model Dwellings, underneath the so-called 'Goulston Street Graffito', the message scrawled in chalk on a wall which so baffled many criminologists of the time, and which was ordered to be removed without being photographed on the orders of Sir Charles Warren, the Metropolitan Police Commissioner. It has long been thought that the writing on the wall was not, in fact, the work of the Ripper, and this thought became reinforced in my mind by the absence of any reference to it in the journal. I felt that, if the Ripper had indeed written the message, he would have made some reference to it in his journal. He did not; therefore I was sure the graffito was not his work.

The journal did, however, confirm the horrific assault on Eddowes, in particular the horrific mutilations to her face, and the severing of the ear. He was so matter of fact about the mechanics of his crimes that one couldn't help but shudder at the sheer barbarity of his actions. Catherine Eddowes had in fact been subjected to the most vicious assault so far, and her injuries were many and various. Her intestines had been drawn out and placed over her right shoulder, the right ear had been almost severed, her face had been severely mutilated, her throat had been cut, as in all the victims, and the poor woman's abdomen had been opened from the breast bone to the pubes. The list of her injuries was in fact far longer and more detailed but I have avoided listing the full extent of the atrocities committed upon the poor woman. Let it suffice to say that no-one, police included, had ever been witness to such horrific mutilations.

There was also a reference in the journal to the postcard received by the Central News Agency, postmarked 1st October, written in red, which read,

I was not codding dear old Boss when I gave you the tip, youll hear about saucy Jackys work tomorrow double event this time number one squealed a bit couldn't finish straight off, had not time to get ears for police thanks for keeping last letter back till I got to work again

Jack the Ripper

Many senior police officers felt that the previous letter and the postcard, which appeared to be in different handwriting, were hoaxes, but I thought that if that were the case, how on earth did the hoaxer know what the Ripper was intending to do, particularly the severing of poor Cathy Eddowes' ear? No, their dismissal was too quick and too illogical. The handwriting was easily solved. Here was an intelligent and devious mind at work, and it would have been a simple matter for him to disguise his handwriting, or to vary it as he did with the letter and the postcard. Though there were a number of apparent errors in punctuation and grammar, both were obviously written by someone with a good knowledge of the English language, as evidenced by the correct spelling of words such as 'straight' and 'squealed'. A person from an uneducated background would have found the spelling of such words difficult and would have been expected to make more spelling mistakes than appeared in either the letter or the card. No, I was sure they were genuine, and that the Ripper had applied a good measure of guile and cunning in his clever deceptions of the different handwritings and his so-called grammatical imperfections. I deduced that the major problem for the police investigators of the time was their complete unfamiliarity with mental illness, or the effects it could have on an otherwise normal, and possibly highly intelligent personality. They were simply looking for 'a madman', a merciless killer who cut these poor women up for fun, 'just for jolly'. They unfortunately had no conception of who or what they were dealing with. Jack the Ripper was, I am sad to say, probably far cleverer and devious, as a result of his education and his illness, than those whose job it was to attempt to apprehend him.

Suddenly, a wave of sadness welled up inside me. I felt an immense sorrow, firstly for the poor unfortunate victims of the Ripper, murdered, mutilated, and left to bleed upon the filthy, decay riddled streets of Whitechapel, and secondly, surprisingly perhaps, for the Ripper himself, the poor individual, wracked with an illness he couldn't control, undiagnosed, with no help available to him, and who was rapidly descending into irrevocable insanity, an individual who, despite his crimes, was a sick and tortured human being. Despite myself, and contrary to my better judgement, I found myself quietly praying for the souls of the Ripper, and for his victims, each by name.

How much more could his brain take, I asked myself? The insanity was gathering pace every day. I knew that, and I guessed that there might come a time when his journal entries would become fewer, and less coherent. The journal itself was becoming thinner with each page I read, and I knew that I was drawing ever nearer to my great-grandfather's final revelation/confession, whichever it was. I needed to know more about his connection with the Ripper, how much closer he became involved before the end of the Ripper's killing spree. I still didn't know, but I would soon find out.

TWENTY-FOUR
'MURDER, 'ORRIBLE MURDER!'

I MUST ADMIT that my own brain felt close to overload at this point, so much so that despite my ever growing need to continue my strange journey through the journal, I felt in need of a break from the gruesome, grisly depictions which were being brought to life for me within its pages. Outside my window, the rain was beginning to increase in its intensity, the breeze had developed into a strong wind, and darkness had fallen like a pall upon the outside world. Despite the lights in the study, it was the darkness that gripped me and held my attention, as if, regardless of the illumination provided by the electric lighting, the power of the external darkness, of nature itself, was overpowering the man-made light, and the power of the night was invading my warm sanctuary.

Leaving the journal lying in the centre of the desk, I decided to do a little more research into the case and once again logged onto the Casebook website. I wanted to know more about the contemporary reactions to the murders, and the Ripper's letters, to get the feel of how London and Londoners received the latest news at the time of his latest crimes.

The Casebook website contained a welter of facts and general information about the case, and I soon found references to the information I sought. The Ripper's 'Dear Boss' letter had been printed in the *Daily News* on the morning of October 1st, and it wasn't long before the shouts and calls of the newspaper sellers on the street corners were announcing to the world the name of 'Jack the Ripper'.

"Murder, 'orrible murder, read all about it!" I could almost hear the shrill tones of the young boys as they stood screeching excitedly at the passers-by, entreating them to purchase the paper, to read the latest reports on the killings that were shocking the whole of London, rich or poor. *"Jack the Ripper butchers two more"*, and *"Jack the Ripper, Jack the Ripper, Ripper taunts police,"* went another. Later that day the 'Saucy Jacky' postcard was reproduced in *The Star* adding yet more fuel to the fire of hysteria that was beginning to grow ever more rapidly with each passing day. It could perhaps be said that the streets of London, and the Whitechapel/Spitalfields areas in particular were ablaze, not with the flames that had razed much of the city to the ground some two hundred years previously, but this time with fear and uncertainty, with citizens looking over their shoulders as night approached, and with a growing anger at the seeming inability of the police to lay their hands on the heinous and bloody murderer who now had a name that the public could identify with, a name that had now, with the publication of the letter and postcard announced to the world the grand entrance of the character whose name would forever be synonymous with murder and infamy. Jack the Ripper had made his grand entrance, and his public now knew his name!

With the newspaper sellers shouting his name on virtually every street corner, it could reasonably be supposed that there were very few Londoners who hadn't heard of Jack the Ripper by the end of that day. What the police thought of this new development is hard to say. Throughout the Ripper investigation there was much disagreement among the investigating officers as to whether these, or any of the other countless communications received, were actually penned by the Ripper himself. Of course, they were not blessed by the hindsight of history, nor were they privy to the words of the journal which now lay on my desk. Certainly, the leading detectives at the time were reported to believe that the publication of the letter and postcard would do little to help their investigations, merely seeing them as whipping up yet more public anxiety and animosity towards the police, who were being quite clearly taunted by the Ripper. There were now vigilantes on the streets of London, gangs of so-called 'citizen peacekeepers' roamed Whitechapel by night, often roughly abusing anyone they considered to be acting suspiciously. Most prominent amongst these groups was the *'Whitechapel Vigilance Committee'* whose president was a man by the name of George Akin Lusk, owner of a building and decorating business, specialising in the restoration of music halls. Lusk would be brought closely into connection with the case some time hence, so I shall leave that aside for now.

The double murder had of course resulted in uproar, and feelings of resentment toward the police were such that many noisy and rebellious gatherings took place on the streets of London that day, and in Whitechapel in particular. Extra officers were drafted in to keep the peace under fear of general public disorder, and this in itself merely served to hamper the efforts of the police in their primary need to bring the Ripper to justice. The streets of the city were a ferment of fear, agitation, frustration and anxiety, and strangely, I could feel those sentiments being echoed within my own mind as I realised that once again, I felt as though I could see the demonstrations in the streets, hear the calls for action by the police, and most of all, I could hear the shouts of the newspaper sellers calling out *"Murder, 'orrible murder"*

More than anything, I knew that the time had come to escape from the study for a while. For the first time in over twenty-four hours, I ventured into the lounge, my legs shaking as I walked, and, without thinking too much about it, absent-mindedly switched on the television and sagged wearily into the corner of the sofa. At least the TV would provide a welcome distraction for a while. I could return to the journal soon, but I desperately needed a brief respite from its intensity, its power, from the strange hold that it seemed to be asserting over my mind.

I had chosen that moment to tune into the news, and it wasn't long before I was plunged into yet more mental turmoil. Following reports of various international crises and a hurricane in the Caribbean, the newsreader switched to more local, national issues.

There'd been not one, but two murders in Guildford the previous night! The second victim had been found less than a mile from the first, and was another woman, also a barmaid, and she too had had her throat cut, and been subjected to what the newsreader referred to as 'a series of wanton and appalling mutilations'. Her body hadn't been found until close to noon, having been dumped in a rubbish skip behind a restaurant which was temporarily closed for refurbishment. Two workers had discovered the body when they'd arrived with their truck to remove the skip for emptying at a local refuse site. So frenzied had been the attack upon her, that her body when found was virtually bloodless, the contents of the skip stained deep red by the outpouring from her numerous and viciously inflicted wounds. Identified as Angela Turner, a 32-year-old mother of two young children, her family was reported as being 'distraught', an understatement if ever I'd heard one. The police had no suspects at this time!

I was incredulous! Two murders in one night, the news of the second killing coming just as I'd read the Ripper's account of his own double killing. My head throbbed; I could barely take it in. This was stretching coincidence too far, surely, and yet the reality was there, staring me in the face, being reported in the cold, matter-of-fact words of a newscaster who had probably reported on hundreds of similar killings in the course of his career. Somewhere in the vicinity of my home, a few miles away at most, someone was slaying innocent women with all the hallmarks of the Ripper himself clearly in evidence. Who, in this day and age, would be so callous as to commit such acts? Sadly, there are all too many disturbed individuals in the world capable of such wanton and terrible murder. Perhaps even more so than in the Ripper's day, today's killers may be motivated by greed, lust, drug or alcohol dependence, or simply by a thrill-seeking need to gain attention. Whatever the motivation for these latest killings, the result was shattered families, motherless children, and untold grief and loss. I turned the TV off; I could watch no more. My entire body felt as though it were shaking, not visibly perhaps, but certainly deep within. I could barely comprehend what was happening to me. Was the Ripper somehow reaching out across the years, his soul embedded in the psyche of some poor, sad individual of the modern age, driven by his impulses to commit these horrific crimes? Impossible, at least that's what I told myself. I tried to force myself to be rational about the latest killings. They could have no connection to what had occurred back in 1888. I decided that obviously, reading the Ripper's journal had set my perception towards such events. Such news must obviously have been a common occurrence, not in my village of course, but rather on the national news, and it was merely that I was perceiving these events more readily than I normally would have, just as a pregnant woman suddenly notices so many women with children, so many other pregnant women, there are no more than before, but she perceives it as so. It was all a ghastly, gruesome coincidence, and yet, at the back of my mind, a fear and a nagging terror that there was something other-worldly about the whole situation in which I found myself just wouldn't go away. I had to ask myself if I was attempting to rationalise where there was no rhyme or reason but only a cold hand reaching out from the murky mists of centuries past. I had no real answers.

You may think me crazy, but I just couldn't shake that feeling, and as a cold, grave-like stillness filled the room, and me with it, I felt a physical sensation of all-pervading helplessness and terror take hold of me. I felt as though I was sliding ever downwards, like an out of control aircraft as it dives headlong toward the earth before smashing itself into a thousand pieces from the destructive impact as it finally collides with solid ground. Though not yet close to that final impact I knew that I was falling, and could feel tiny pieces of my normal self, my sane and rational self, breaking away as I careened toward an unknown inevitability.

Nothing in my own training as a psychiatrist could have prepared me for this situation, primarily because no-one had ever experienced such a thing, except perhaps my own father, and his before him, and I had no idea how they would have dealt with it; or had they been immune to the effects of the journal, was it just me, was I so susceptible to the Ripper's words that I had allowed myself to fall under his long-dead spell? I doubt that there was even a satisfactory name that could be given to what I was undergoing at that time; my own experiences had never identified any such phenomenon. All I knew was that I was alone, afraid and becoming more and more disturbed by the hour, as the events of a century ago and those of the present day appeared to be merging into one long, waking nightmare!

I could take no more, not that night, and leaving all the downstairs lights on and the documents in the study lying exactly where they were, I surmounted the stairs, stopping long enough in the bathroom to take two rather strong sleeping tablets that had been prescribed for Sarah some time ago, and, with my mind in a state of almost complete mental exhaustion, I slipped into bed, and, perhaps because of the poor night I'd suffered the night before, I slept long and hard, without dreaming.

If I'd thought that sleep would cure what ailed me, that the morning would bring a bright and refreshing light to my newly disturbed world, I was to be severely disappointed, but for a few hours at least, my mind and body were at rest.

TWENTY-FIVE
THE MORNING AFTER THE NIGHT BEFORE

I DON'T KNOW how long I slept that night; I'd made no reference to the time before my head hit the pillow and the sleeping tablets took over, sending me into that long, dreamless sleep. I know that I looked at the clock when I woke, and it was seven a.m. give or take a minute. My first sensation on waking was that my tongue was stuck to the roof of my mouth, which itself felt as dry as the Sahara Desert. My head ached, and I felt a degree of disorientation akin to that accompanying a severe hangover, though I swear that not a drop of alcohol had touched my lips the previous night. It was the sleeping tablets of course. They'd been prescribed for Sarah some time ago after she'd suffered from severe back pain caused by an injury received playing squash with her best friend Chris, and our GP had prescribed them to try to help her get a good night's rest from the pain. She had taken a few, and then left the bottle on the shelf. I should have known better than to take them, but it was too late for that now.

It seemed to take an age to hoist myself out of bed, into the bathroom, and dress, finally managing to make my way to the kitchen, where I drank copious cups of coffee, and four slices of toast. I wasn't particularly hungry, but I thought that the food might help to counteract the after-effects of the sleeping tablets.

I switched the radio on as I ate and waited to hear the eight o'clock news. When it came, the report on the local murders stated that the police had made an arrest! 'Acting on information received', a twenty-five-year-old man had been arrested at his home late the previous night, probably while I'd slept. I was glad that at least the streets of Guildford and the surrounding villages, mine included, were safe for the time being, presuming of course that the police had got the right man. Perhaps my own disturbing emotions might now subside; no more murders in my town would surely mean no more grisly coincidences.

As the news came to an end I was disturbed by a loud knocking at the front door. Still feeling quite groggy from the after-effects of the sleeping pills, I walked slowly from the kitchen to the door, and peered through the security porthole. Standing outside were a uniformed police constable and another man dressed in a blue suit. Wondering what on earth the police were doing at my house, I unlocked and opened the door.

"Doctor Cavendish?

"Yes?" I replied, questioningly.

"I'm Inspector Bell; this is Constable Tenant, Surrey police. Could we come in for a few minutes please?"

"What's this about, Inspector?" I asked.

"I'd rather discuss that inside, if we may doctor."

"Right, well, you'd better come in then hadn't you?" I replied rather ungraciously. My head still throbbed, and my furred tongue had barely resumed its normal functions within my ultra-dry mouth. The last thing I needed was an unexpected visit from the local constabulary.

I led the two officers into the kitchen and bade them sit down.

"Now, inspector, what's this all about?"

"Well doctor, you may have heard about the two murders that took place in town two nights ago?"

The hairs on the back of my neck suddenly stood to attention.

"Yes, of course, but what has that to do with me?"

"Well sir, you may also have heard that we picked a suspect up late last night. It just so happens that he claims to be one of your patients."

At that, my heart almost missed a beat, and I could swear to this day that my pulse rate virtually doubled. Certainly, the thumping in my head increased, I thought that the policemen must surely be able to see the pulse in my temple visibly throbbing, though they obviously couldn't.

"Go on, inspector," I gulped.

"His name is John Terence Ross, his own mother called us when she saw blood on his shoes and on his trouser hems after he'd gone to bed last night. Seems he's had a history of psychiatric disorder for some time, and as I said he and his mother claim you're his psychiatrist."

"It's true I've seen him a few times, his mother paid for him to see me when the doctors at the Farnham Road hospital seemed unable to make much progress with him."

"What can you tell us about his illness, doctor?" asked the inspector.

"Come now inspector," I replied, "you know I can't breach doctor/patient confidentiality."

"I know that doctor, of course, but I thought that maybe you could come down to the station on Margaret Road, maybe talk to him, see if you can get him to talk to us. He's been virtually silent so far."

"Has he told you anything?" I asked.

"Only that he did it, and that they deserved to die. If he needs psychiatric help, we need to know exactly what we're dealing with."

"Alright inspector," I sighed. "Give me an hour and I'll drive into town to see him. Is that alright?"

"That will be fine sir; I'll be there at the station to meet you. Just ask for me at the desk."

This couldn't be happening! Yet it was. After the police officers left the house I sat in the fireside chair in the kitchen, my mind racing, my head throbbing, and my hands, my whole body in fact, shaking like a leaf. The mirror image with my great-grandfather's situation stared at me with grim reality. How could such a series of events have conspired to happen at just such a time? Like great-grandfather, here I was being summoned to examine a man I knew, who could well be the murderer of two innocent women. Unlike my ancestor however, this time the man was in custody, though that did little to alleviate the feeling of impossible coincidence that filled my mind. John Ross was indeed a disturbed individual, though I wouldn't have thought him capable of such a heinous double crime. His medication should have served to keep him psychologically stable, if he'd taken it as prescribed, which perhaps he hadn't!

Not only that, but a strange and unsettling thought suddenly leaped into my brain, striking home like a lightening bolt. His name, well, not so much his name as his initials. They'd never meant anything to me before, why should they? All of sudden however John Trevor Ross became JTR, easily translated into 'Jack the Ripper'.

· · ·

The drive to the police station took me about half an hour, but it felt like hours as I drove in a state of fugue, barely aware of who I was or what I was doing. I certainly had no idea what I would achieve by talking to John Ross, other than to further confuse and disturb my own increasingly fragile grip on reality. I couldn't tell the police that though, could I?

I parked in the visitors section of the police station car park, entered the station, and reported to the reception desk. I identified myself and asked for Inspector Bell, who arrived a minute later and led me through a door, down a corridor and into an interview room where I came face to face with John Trevor Ross.

TWENTY-SIX
"WELCOME HOME, ROBERT"

JOHN ROSS LOOKED QUITE a pitiful creature as he sat at the table in the interview room. His solicitor, Miles Burrows, hired that morning by his mother, sat beside him, with Inspector Bell beckoning me to sit next to himself on the opposite side of the table. A police sergeant was also present in the room to operate the tape recorder which was used to record the interview and was now a part of standard police procedure.

Ross's clothes had been taken away for forensic examination, and he was dressed in a simple one-piece boiler-suit type garment provided by the police. He was the smallest man in the room, though his size belied a sinewy strength gained from many hours spent working out at his local gymnasium. I had held four consultations with him in recent months, and had diagnosed him as suffering from a mild schizophrenia, with a latent tendency towards violent behaviour, though the medication I had prescribed for him, and which his mother had promised to ensure he took regularly should have regulated his behaviour and enabled him to live a reasonably normal life. Obviously, things hadn't gone according to plan, and Ross's illness was far more serious than I had perhaps perceived. Unfortunately, schizophrenics can be highly adept at hiding their symptoms from their doctor, and it seemed John Ross was no exception.

Though I wouldn't reveal any of my patient's medical details to the police at this stage, I did my best to encourage Ross to talk to the inspector, to try to explain to him why he'd done what he'd done. I was no more successful then the police themselves had been. Despite my assuring him that I, and the police wanted to help him, and help was what he required without a doubt, he refused to co-operate with his questioners. I knew that, when his case came to court he would probably face a life sentence, to be served in a secure institution, yet I could have felt a little sympathy for him if he'd only opened up to someone. Even an illogical, insane explanation for his actions would have been preferable to his sullen silence. Perhaps in time, as the interviews progressed, he'd feel less intimidated, and begin to talk to the police or the battery of psychiatrists who would now surely be brought in to interview and examine him.

I left the police station after almost two hours, two of the most depressing hours of my life. Ross's rigid stare, his silence, and the feeling that the police could somehow see straight through me to my own internal disturbances made me want to run from the place as though I were the criminal, as opposed to the man in the white boiler suit.

On arriving home, I unlocked the front door, entered the hallway, quickly locked it again, and sagged against the door, my back against its solid oak panels. The house felt cold, and I was shivering. Perhaps I was shaking rather than shivering, by then it had become difficult to tell one from the other.

I made my way to the study, I'd lost valuable time by visiting the police station, and I wanted to complete my exploration of the Ripper's world before Sarah returned in a day or two. It wouldn't do to have her exposed to the strange phenomenon that was the journal itself, or for her to see me in this state of heightened anxiety, bordering on panic.

I opened the study door, (I couldn't remember closing it when I left) and peered across the room towards my desk. The journal lay exactly where I'd left it, but, as I looked at it I could have sworn that I'd heard a hushed whisper from within the room, and that the pages themselves were moving, gently rising and falling, as though infused with life, breathing softly on the desk. That was nonsense, I told myself quickly, the movement was obviously caused by the draught I'd caused by opening the door, and the sound was just my imagination. Rooms didn't whisper nor journals breathe, did they?

Despite the early hour, I poured myself a small whisky, I felt I deserved it. I sat in my chair once more and reached out to take up the journal. It took quite an effort to stop my hands from shaking as I did so, but the warm pages of the Ripper's secret confession were soon in my hands again.

He had omitted to make any entries for three days since the 1st October, and the next entry, dated the 5th October was surprising in its literacy and in the revealingly chilling message it carried. Written like his letter to the press in red ink, with word-perfect spelling and punctuation, it read:

5th October 1888

Blood, beautiful, thick, rich, red, venous blood.
Its colour fills my eyes, its scent assaults my nostrils,
Its taste hangs sweetly on my lips.

Last night once more the voices called to me,
And I did venture forth, their bidding, their unholy
quest to undertake.
Through mean, gas lit, fog shrouded streets, I wandered
in the night, selected, struck, with flashing blade,
And oh, how the blood did run, pouring out upon the
street, soaking through the cobbled cracks, spurting, like
a fountain of pure red.
Viscera leaking from ripped red gut, my clothes assumed
the smell of freshly butchered meat. The squalid, dark,
street shadows beckoned, and under leaning darkened
eaves, like a wraith I disappeared once more into the
cheerless night,
The bloodlust of the voices again fulfilled, for a while...
They will call again, and I once more will prowl the
streets upon the night,
The blood will flow like a river once again.
Beware all those who would stand against the call,
I shall not be stopped or taken, no, not I.
Sleep fair city, while you can, while the voices within are
still,
I am resting, but my time shall come again. I shall rise
in a glorious bloodfest,
I shall taste again the fear as the blade slices sharply
through yielding flesh,
when the voices raise the clarion call, and my time shall
come again.
So I say again, good citizens, sleep, for there will be a
next time...

Any doubts I may have harboured about the Ripper having been an educated man were dispelled by this horrendously gloating entry. He had written almost poetically of his crimes, and this one entry, perhaps more than any other so far, gave me a vivid and terrible insight into the mind of the notorious Whitechapel murderer. I presumed he'd written it immediately after the night of the double murder, (though I supposed it could have been written after any of the murders) and transferred it to his journal later. His reference to making his escape *under leaning darkened eaves* did however bring to my mind a picture of the yard in Berner street from which he'd so narrowly escaped detection. His illness was now plain to see, his mind probably beginning to finally give way under the weight of his appalling crimes. Having killed two women in one night, and with the mutilations and atrocities against his victims' bodies growing in ferocity with each murder, I knew that he was approaching a point where, even allowing for his disturbed state of mind, the sheer immensity and horror of his own wrong-doing would eventually overflow and lead to a massive breakdown. Though it was over three weeks away, I knew in my heart and mind that the murder of Mary Kelly, probably the most vicious and visually horrifying of the Ripper murders, had probably 'sent him over the edge', and that whatever came afterwards, hopefully to be explained either by the Ripper himself or in my great-grandfathers notes, would prove that final deterioration beyond a doubt, and reveal the reason for the Ripper's disappearance after the date of Kelly's murder. After all, there had been no arrest, no rumours of a strong suspect, and the murderer had simply seemed to fade away, back into the darkness from which he'd come, never to be heard from again. Why? The journal was getting thinner, I knew that the final answers couldn't be far away, and as I sat reading and re-reading the latest terrible entry, I was once again gripped by an inexplicable tension and a fear that I may not be prepared for what I was about to learn.

This last poetic entry had said that he was 'resting'. Was it a conscious and deliberate ploy on his part to disappear from view, escape the public's attentions before perpetrating his last and most gruesome killing? He'd written that the voices themselves had left him for the moment; that they too were at rest. It was clear that the voices were his motivation for the killings, '*the bloodlust of the voices again fulfilled*' his own control over his actions by then were severely diminished, and his mind, close to its final descent into insanity was in need of time to recuperate, to regain a degree of normality, in order for him to plan and execute his next, and ultimately his last appearance on the streets of Whitechapel.

As I replaced the journal on the desk I found myself asking when my great-grandfather would make another 'appearance' in the journal. Would there be any further notes inserted into the pages of the Ripper's words, or would I have to wait until the end in order to decipher whatever secret had been held so closely in the family for so long? Surely, the identity of the Ripper was there, waiting to be revealed to me when I reached that last page, the last note. Not only that, but my family's involvement, however small, must be there. How I resisted the temptation to flip through to the end at that point I don't know, but something stopped me doing so. I had to continue as I was, page by page, reading about and 'seeing' the horrors of the murders as they happened, before I could be allowed to witness the final revelations of the journal.

My head had begun to throb once more, as I realised that the Ripper had made no reference to laudanum in the last entry. Had he weaned himself off it? Surely not. Perhaps he was by now so used to taking it, that he considered it irrelevant to include in his journal. More likely, his addiction was such that he barely knew he was taking the drug; it had become a part of his every day life, a part of him! Had the headaches stopped? Maybe I'd find out in the next entry. He certainly must have been fairly lucid and in control of himself to write that last macabre entry. I was so full of questions and devoid of any answers, that my own senses were reeling.

I felt as though a gust of wind had suddenly swept through the room, and I turned to see where it could have come from. There was nothing, no open windows, and no doors that could admit such a gust. With the irrational fear that I was alone, yet not alone, growing in intensity in my own overloaded mind, I raised myself from the chair, left the study, and began a search of the house. I know you'll think me crazy, and perhaps I was, but I thought that, illogical and impossible as the thought may seem, it wouldn't hurt to check, would it?

There was no-one there, of course there wasn't, the house was empty, apart from me, and I chided myself for my foolishness. I returned to the study, and as I walked in through the door, I swear that once again, those damned pages were rising and falling, and that the room whispered a welcome to me as I sat in the comfortable leather chair, and reached out to the journal.

TWENTY-SEVEN
RUSSIAN ROULETTE

THE LIGHT of day was already fading, the sky turning a dirty autumn grey as I turned the next page. Instead of the hand of the Ripper, the next thing I saw was another note from my great-grandfather, once again neatly tucked in between two of the journal's pages. Perhaps now, I thought, the whole thing might begin to make sense. This note was undated, though its content was plain enough. The Ripper had suffered another amnesiac seizure!

Great-grandfather had added a note across the top of the paper, scripted by a different pen, in darker ink, obviously written on a later date than his original writings. The note read:

> *Had I known later the true nature of what I now know to be fact, I guarantee to any who may read this that my actions would have been wholly different. I apologize for my short-sightedness, my stupidity, my rank failure to see what lay before my eyes.*

Note by Doctor Burton Cleveland Cavendish, November 1888.

Once again I have been called to attend upon this sad pathetic young man. He has allowed his life to be destroyed by not just one, but two unfortunate addictions! Despite having had a decent, God fearing upbringing, with many of the advantages denied to so many in our society, he has led a dissolute existence. It appears he has been too fond of visiting those poor unfortunates who inhabit the dark streets of our metropolis and suffers from that vile disease so often associated with men who avail themselves of such women. He is in the terminal phase of the illness, and insanity is not far away I fear, though for now, I consider that he may live as he does, alone in his home, without recourse to hospitalisation. In addition, I fear that he may have taken my previous advice too literally, and had developed an addiction for the laudanum, which I had suggested he take to alleviate the symptoms of his headaches, though at the time I gave such advice I was not privy to his deeper problems.

He is languishing once again in the day ward of the Charing Cross hospital, having been sent there once more after being found in a state of near collapse in the street. He appears to know nothing of how he came to be there and was pleased to see me. I thanked Malcolm for sending for me once more, as I would not have wished a stranger to have perhaps requested that he be confined to the asylum, as surely he would never have exited from such a place, once admitted. His mother surely would never have wanted to see him in his current position, it would have broken her heart, as it would do to see him in the pitiful state in which he now lies.

He has no recollection of his previous seizure, or his insane 'confession' to a murder no-one has any knowledge of. He does however, this time confess to a hatred for the woman who infected him with the syphilis, and all her kind, and has stated that he will not rest until all her kind are gone from the earth. He is fixated with the need for the trade of prostitution to be eradicated from the streets of London, though his language is quite coarse whenever he refers to this subject.

On my second visit, he once again 'confessed' to having rid the world of what he calls 'the whore pestilence', but this I take to be the ramblings of his dementia. He has no doubt been reading the horrific tales of the atrocious crimes currently being committed in Whitechapel, and I fancy that in his delusional sate, he may believe himself to be the murderer which all London is now calling Jack the Ripper! I fear that if he fails to show improvement in a short time, Doctor Malcolm may recommend him for committal to the asylum, and, in truth, as I am not in fact his physician, I will be unable to prevent such measures being carried out.

I have advised him on yet another visit to cease his rantings, to believe that he is hallucinating as a result of an excessive intake of laudanum, and to accept medication to help alleviate the worst symptoms of his other illness, on the premise that by so doing he may achieve his discharge from the hospital and be allowed to return to his normal life, though I fear for the length of time that is left to him before the syphilis begins to eat away at his body, as it is already doing to his mind.

He has, I believe, listened to my entreaties, and Doctor Malcolm professes himself much satisfied with his progress. I too found him much improved, though not particularly talkative; though this I took to be a part of his desire to recover from his illness by refraining from his previous nonsensical rantings. Malcolm suggests that if such progress remains evident, the patient may be allowed to return home in two days, to which suggestion I concurred, and offered to keep a watchful eye on him after discharge, which benevolent gesture was much appreciated by Malcolm, and, it seemed, by the patient.

He was subsequently discharged from the hospital after a stay of almost two weeks, quite a long time in my opinion. I will endeavour to pay occasional visits to his home and have asked that he will see me in my consulting rooms on a weekly basis, to which he has agreed.

There now followed another added note, again in the darker ink:

Oh, what a fool I was, to fail to recognize his words for the truth. I will be forever damned, and my name would surely be held in vile scorn by the whole profession of physicians were I to confess my transgression. Believe me, whosoever reads this, that this journal did not come into my hands until it was too late, had I known the truth, I would have acted sooner, though that is of no

*consequence nor help to anyone now. Whatever blood is
on his hands is without a doubt shared by mine, I am
complicit by my shame, and I am broken into many
pieces by the force of the knowledge I must take to my
grave. My wretched soul will surely burn in Hell, as
unquestionably as will his, if that is any consolation.*

I placed the journal down upon the desk with trembling
hands. My heart was heavy with sorrow and a sense of grief
directed toward my great-grandfather. Whatever else he may
have been, I was sure that he was no fool, and yet, it appeared
as though he had allowed the Ripper to walk free from hospital,
after hearing him confess not once, but twice to his crimes. I
was sure that his humanitarian instincts and his belief in the
fact that the man was simply delusional had clouded his
judgement. Added to that was the as yet unrevealed connection
between himself and the Ripper's mother. Whatever that
connection may have been would also, I was sure, have given
him an added incentive to attempt to treat the man in the
hospital, rather than see him admitted to an asylum, surely a
most dreadful fate for any person in those unenlightened days.

Yet I couldn't escape from the thought that my ancestor
could at least have discussed these strange 'confessions' with
Doctor Malcolm, or indeed with the police, bearing in mind
that the Ripper was not actually his patient. At least if he had
done so, and the authorities had believed as he had, that the
confessions were mere delusions, he would at least have been
absolved of the terrible burden of guilt to which he obviously
fell prey on discovering the truth. I could see that he had made
what today would be thought of as glaring omissions, both in
his role as a doctor, and as a citizen, but I couldn't help but
sympathise with him to a great extent.

After all, was I not myself becoming severely affected by

my exposure to the words of the Ripper, merely from my reading of his journal? Was I not finding it harder and harder to keep a grip on reality? Indeed, I was experiencing the terrifying sensation of being somehow drawn into the nightmare world of the mind of Jack the Ripper from simply handling his infernal writings. Was it therefore not possible that my poor great-grandfather, exposed as he was to a first hand personal relationship of sorts with the man, could have been completely taken in by his words, by his voice, which, though I hadn't heard, I somehow imagined to be quiet, soft and hypnotic, not at all threatening and monstrous as some may imagine the Ripper's voice to have been? No, I was certain that his voice would have been soft and inviting, capable of captivating and charming his poor victims into the awful, final embrace of death. If the mere feel of his journal in my hands could elicit such a response of fear and terror so long after his death, what beguiling, charismatic qualities must he have possessed in life?

My great-grandfather may not have been a fool, but I was sure, knowing what I had already learned from my exposure to the journal, that he may well have *been* fooled. The Ripper was knowledgeable and intelligent; I had no doubt on that score, so his confessions may have been a clever ruse. By confessing in such a way that he would be thought to be delusional or hallucinating, he would have the pleasure of openly admitting his crimes, boasting of them in fact, safe in the knowledge that the doctors wouldn't believe him, so granting him a twisted, warped sense of satisfaction, and above all superiority over those self–same doctors who thought they knew their profession, and who to some extent he was granting the power of life and death over him. I couldn't escape the feeling that Jack the Ripper was playing a kind of Russian roulette with his physicians, and he was winning!

Feeling a sense of great sorrow and sympathy for the

dilemma that had gripped him, and that perhaps my great-grandfather had assumed too much in the way of guilt, (though of course I was still unaware of the final outcome of his involvement with the Ripper), I stretched my aching limbs and looked up for a moment to see that all was dark outside my window. It was raining again, and, feeling once more that I wasn't quite alone in the study, and with a sense of mounting trepidation, an irrational fear of what was to come, I slowly turned to the next page...

TWENTY-EIGHT
CONFUSED THOUGHTS

26 th October 1888

*Jack's back! What fools, what stupid blundering fools, to
have me there and then to let me go? They know
nothing. Even that blind fool Cavendish, I told him of
my cause, my great mission, and he still thinks me mad!
So I'm hallucinating am I? I'll show them. I'll show
them all! My voices speak to me of blood, rivers of
flowing blood, and ripped flesh upon the floor. I will
outdo myself on the next occasion. The next job shall be
my greatest yet. They shall never take me, for I shall
wear once more my cloak of invisibility and disappear as
quickly as I appear from the filthy streets where the
whores walk. I am cursed forever by the thing inside me
which even now eats away at me. My head hurts, but
now my body festers as I breathe, and I must be wary of
being seen. The pestilence the whores have wrought has
made me a monster, so I will choose the youngest,
prettiest little piece of whore-flesh I can find, and I shall*

*rip, gut, and fillet the slut as she lays spread before me.
This one shall be hand-picked, for sure. The streets are
filled with me, my name spoken and shouted on every
corner. The newshounds smell a good one, and they shall
yet receive still more. The people fear me; they gather in
huddles in every public house and tremble in their
hovels as they whisper my name. Soon they will scream
my name in louder tones, and I shall grip their hearts in
an icy vice, and all the world will know all too soon,
Jack's back!*

THE THREAT and the menace contained in this latest entry
sent shivers through me. Though not perhaps as dark and
ranting as his previous entries, this was in some ways all the
more chilling because of that. There was a premeditation about
those words that made me believe that the Ripper knew
without a shadow of a doubt that his own days were numbered.
There was of course the usual mocking of the medical
profession, who, my great-grandfather included, in seeking to
help and understand his illness, had in fact released the
monster back into the world, the fox being given free run of the
hen-house. It was now clear to me why Mary Jane Kelly had
been his last victim. He was beginning to suffer from some of
the worst effects of his syphilis. Though he failed to describe
them in detail I knew that he would by now have visible lesions
on his face and body, which eventually would become open,
suppurating sores, making him appear as the monster he now
described himself as. People would turn from him in the street,
cross the road to avoid him, and only by wearing a scarf or some
other device over his face could he hope to disguise his grievous
appearance from the world. My thoughts went back to my own
horrific dream, when he appeared to me wearing just such a
scarf, and the shakes returned to my hands, a panic gripped my

heart, and I felt as though I had really been visited in that disturbed night, only two nights ago, though it seemed an age, by the disturbed and troubled soul of the Ripper himself. It was as though he were unable to find rest, even in death, and that he was somehow able to reach out from beyond the grave, across the years, and steal a way into my thoughts, my dreams, and my life.

Returning to my thoughts of Mary Kelly, I felt that she was chosen purely because she was young and attractive, not the usual description to be applied to a Whitechapel whore of that era. Most of the poor unfortunates who fell into the dark and sullied world of prostitution were old before their time, often riddled with disease, and with their best years, and their looks long gone. Kelly was different; she still had a youthful prettiness, and was described as being vibrant, attractive, and full of a zest for life. Her meeting with Jack the Ripper would put an end to that life and leave a lasting impression on all those who were unfortunate to witness the evidence of his last and most gruesome killing. The Ripper now appeared eager for fame, as though the insanity which accompanied his terminal phase was now beginning to take a firmer hold of him. His voices were louder, his head probably felt as though it were ready to burst apart, and his mind was filled with the image of 'rivers of blood, and ripped flesh upon the floor'. I thought that, even allowing for his state of mind, such images in themselves would have served to unnerve even his disturbed mind and lead him further down the path towards total breakdown. The rising corpses of the dead women from his earlier hallucinatory dream leaped into my mind, and I found myself wondering just how any human being could cope with such mental imagery *without* going totally insane. My own mind was in such a ferment as I attempted to assimilate the information it had been receiving over the last two days that I knew I was becoming unnerved and disturbed myself, so what of the Ripper himself? He had actually experienced and lived through these terrible seizures of the mind, had perpetrated some of the most vicious and gruesome crimes ever recorded in London's long and at times bloody history, he had to have been so deranged and confused that he would barely have recognized himself, had he been given the opportunity to return in some way to his original state of mind before all this began. Would he have condemned himself if he could have been a spectator to his own descent into the Hell that was by then his path toward oblivion?

My own thoughts were reeling, I was trying to make some sense of it all as, unbidden by my conscious mind, my great-grandfather and his involvement in the life of the Ripper came to the forefront of my consciousness. The Ripper only had one more murder (that I knew of) left to commit. How much more would be revealed by great-grandfather's further notes, assuming them to be tucked elsewhere into the ever-dwindling pile of pages that made up the journal? What was his connection to the killer? That question still hung perilously close to the front of my mind, so far without satisfactory explanation. I couldn't escape the thought that the wildly deranged and degenerate murderer of women whose name still haunts crime researchers today could be a relative of mine, however distant. Why else would my great-grandfather have gone to such pains not only to try to help the man through his illness, but to seemingly do all in his power to prevent him being admitted to an asylum, where, though his treatment may have been brutal by today's standards, he would at least have been prevented from committing further atrocities upon the women of Whitechapel? But of course, my great-grandfather believed the Ripper to be merely imagining the murders, seeing him as one who was hallucinating as a result of his addiction to the laudanum, intermingled with his syphilis and what today would be termed a pathological hatred of prostitutes. Oh, how I wish my ancestor had delved a little further into the mind of the man, or just simply believed that his story might have been the truth and brought it to the attention of the police. Of course, he didn't, and the result was the terrifyingly grisly murder of yet another woman. Though still refusing to blame him for his actions, I just wished he'd done things differently.

And what of me? Was I really in a position to pass judgement after all those years? I was after all blessed with the power of hindsight and backed by the knowledge and experience that modern-day psychiatric training gives to the medical profession. Despite that, I was beginning to believe the wildest theories imaginable; I was seeing things I knew to be impossible and sensing the presence of an entity I knew to be unreal and a fantasy of the mind. I had begun to manifest somatic, (physical) symptoms of these delusions, (and that was the only word for them), such as the tremors in my hands and body, the irrational fear that was growing in intensity with each passing hour, and the frightfully lucid and very real dreams that transported my to a nightmare dimension that must have been so close to the one encountered by the Ripper himself. In short I was falling under the spell of the journal, if a spell it was, and despite my better judgement, despite all my powers of logic and reason, I couldn't stop myself. I was as much on a downward descent as the Ripper had been, except that I wasn't going out at night murdering innocent women, was I?

I was losing track of time, and I realised that evening had given way to night. I was aching all over, I felt cold and stiff from sitting in the chair for so long, and hunger had begun to gnaw at my stomach. My headache had intensified to such an extent that my temples felt as though they were throbbing, and the muscles in the back of my neck were hard and contracted from the joint acts of sitting for so long, and holding myself in a stiff and unmoving position. I needed to rest, to eat, to regain some strength and composure. The journal would still be there after I'd refreshed myself, I knew that, and yet, as I looked at it yet again as it lay on the desk, I couldn't help but feel as though a malevolence of awesome proportions was slowly emanating from its pages, and like an invidious virus against which I had no control, was seeping slowly into my every thought and action. I was becoming addicted to its words, its grisly gruesome tale, and I had to physically force my eyes to look away from the infernal thing, force myself to rise and leave the room, as though it were continually pulling me back, refusing to let me go.

Before I knew it, I'd made it out of the study, and I stood trembling uncontrollably, propped up with my back against the kitchen door, as though its solidity could keep at bay the demonic thing that I felt was contained within the pages of the journal. I moved to Sarah's fireside chair, meaning to sit and relax for five minutes before getting something to eat, but, such was the state of nervous exhaustion into which my own mind had descended, I fell instead into a deep sleep. It was to be almost three hours before I awoke, to the shrill imploring sound of the telephone ringing.

TWENTY-NINE
A TIME TO WAKE, A TIME TO SLEEP

THE SOUND of the ringing telephone boring into my brain brought me out of my slumbers with a start. I had that feeling of disorientation one sometime gets on such occasions, not being quite sure where I was, or even what day of the week it was. I literally stumbled from the chair, and walked across to the wall, and lifted the phone from its cradle as though it were a thing on fire. Holding it with just my fingertips, I gingerly held it to my ear.

"Robert darling, are you there? Are you alright my darling, you took an age to answer? I thought you might be asleep."

"Hi, Sarah, my gorgeous darling, yes, actually, I was just having a lie down," I lied, not wanting Sarah to know the exact circumstances surrounding my latest sojourn into that cavern of deep dark dreamless sleep.

"You sound awful darling, I'm sorry I woke you. Why don't you get your head down again and try to get back to sleep? I only called you to say that I'm having an early night myself. Little Jack has worn Jennifer and I out, he's been quite fractious poor little mite. I suppose he's still feeling a bit unwell, but we've just got him off to sleep, so we thought we'd get some rest while we can."

"Good idea," I replied. "You do that, and yes, I'll do the same I think."

"That's good, darling."

"Sarah?"

"Yes Robert."

"I miss you, darling."

"Oh, Robert, I miss you too, of course I do. I'm sorry; you must be feeling a bit lonely there all on your own."

I tried to sound as upbeat and cheerful as I could.

"Don't worry darling, as I said before, I'm just tired, that's all, I'll be a lot better after a good night's sleep."

"Of course you will, now, off you go, and remember how much I love you. It won't be long until I'm home, and then we can make up for lost time together."

"I love you too, Sarah, more than you know. Sleep well my darling, I'll talk to you in the morning."

We said our goodbyes, and I sat in the chair for a good two minutes before I rose and replaced the wall phone on its cradle. The tiredness in my body was all encompassing, there didn't seem to be a muscle or a joint that didn't ache. I felt awful, though it wasn't just the effects of the tiredness. I felt guilty at the thought that I was misleading my wife into thinking I was perfectly alright when in fact I was anything but. I tried to console myself with the thought that in some way I was protecting her, though from exactly what I wasn't sure. I just didn't want her worrying about me, and at the same time I was glad she was at Jennifer's and nowhere near the influence of the journal, whatever that might be. The journal was definitely having an influence over me, I knew it, I had never known such feelings before as I was now being subjected to. If I'd been a patient of my own at this moment I would have thought I was heading for some sort of breakdown and would probably have prescribed a strong sedative and a course of anti-depressants.

I needed to keep Sarah away from what was happening to me, at least until I had some answers, and that meant completing my reading of the journal. She wouldn't understand quite what it was all about, and I didn't want her to have to try. Sarah and I had met in medical school, though she'd dropped out in her third year. By then of course, we were madly in love, and we were married a year after I'd qualified as a doctor. Sarah had gone on to forge a successful career as an interior designer, and I suppose it was due to the nature of her work that she tended to see things in a clearer, more linear fashion than I. The intricacies of the human mind were something she couldn't quite grasp, and often expressed astonishment even now at my choice of psychiatry as a career path. If she could see me now, far from her world of exact measurements and angles, immersed in an unholy quest to discover some hitherto unknown family secret tied into the Jack the Ripper murders of over a hundred years ago, she would probably have thought me quite mad, which, at the time, I perhaps was!

What exactly is madness? Is it a permanent state of mind, caused by a combination of internal and external forces? Can it be temporary, or is it inherent in the sufferer, always there, though perhaps not always manifesting itself outwardly? Does madness exist at all? Just because another human being fails to live according to what the majority of us perceive as 'normal' should they necessarily be classified as 'mad'? Perhaps in some way we are all slightly 'mad', able to be influenced by various events and pressures into behaving in ways deemed abnormal to our fellow beings. Whatever the answer, and it is of course an extremely complex question, open to many interpretations and theories, I had to carry on, complete my strange passage through the pages of the Ripper's words, and reveal the secret held for so long by my various ancestors before I could entertain any hope of finding once again the peace of mind that had been mine such a short time ago. Until then, I was trapped in this strange time-warp, one minute sitting cosily in my own study, sipping a fine malt whisky, researching the events of long ago, the next I seemed to be whisked away into a world inhabited by the ghosts of those times, where I could almost see and hear the sights and the sounds of a bygone age, smell the stench of the Victorian sewers, the cheap perfume of the ladies of the night, and feel the grip of the river fog as it drifted landward from the reaches of the Thames. Perhaps worst of all, I was totally convinced that, somehow, I was being led by the words of the Ripper, as a parent leads a child, to be a witness to his gruesome crimes, to be a part of them, and my eyes suddenly welled up with tears, as the faces of those long-dead victims rushed from nowhere to fill my mind with sadness and melancholia.

Those faces, (I had seen only the mortuary photographs, apart from Annie Chapman), whirled around in my head, as though part of some grotesque merry-go-round, and from somewhere in the deepest recesses of my mind, another figure suddenly appeared, at first dark and shadowy, growing clearer as it came closer, until the figure of a cloaked, half-masked man superimposed itself onto the grotesque montage in my head. As the figure got closer to the back of my eyes, (that's how it felt in my brain), despite the mask, I could see the eyes, and the recognition that went with the realisation of whose eyes they were chilled me to the bone, and shocked me to the core of my soul. I screamed into the room, I was alone, but not alone, I felt as though someone was watching me and laughing from somewhere far away as that recognition hit home like a spear through my heart. Those eyes burned bright, with an intensity of resolute determination, and a blazing hatred emanated from them, directed at everything and everyone in their sight, But the most frightening thing about the awful apparition that almost overwhelmed me in the midst of this appalling and dreadful waking dream was that those eyes, those terrible, hate filled, murderous eyes, weren't the eyes of a stranger, they were mine!

THIRTY
AND SO TO BED

EXACTLY HOW LONG I sat in stunned silence I'm not sure. Eventually, a sort of calmness asserted itself over my trembling limbs, my mind cleared as though I was escaping from the grip of an icy fog, and I slowly regained a modicum of composure. As reality replaced fantasy, and the dreamlike images faded from the forefront of my mind, I shuddered with the remembrance of that terrible image, those eyes peering deep into my soul, my eyes! Why should my own eyes have manifested themselves into those of the Ripper? I had killed no-one, had never had a violent thought towards anyone in my life, and yet, there was no denying that as I'd seen that terrible vision of the Ripper the face behind the scarf had been mine

Was it a dream, or could it be that in my own state of disturbance I had started to hallucinate? Was I somehow seeing what the Ripper wanted me to see, feeling things that were being implanted in my mind by a power far beyond my own imagination? That was nonsense, and I knew it! The Ripper had died a hundred years or more ago, and there was no way he could have projected his soul into the twentieth century to terrorise a new generation so long after his demise.

Feeling weak and deeply troubled, I rose from my chair and walked, almost as an old man would, stooped and weary, into the kitchen. I poured myself a large whisky, and virtually fell into the waiting softness of the fireside chair. I sipped the golden liquid slowly, savouring the taste upon my tongue, and the fiery warmth as it hit my throat on its way to my empty stomach. Much as I knew I should, I couldn't bring myself to eat. I felt a strange sensation of detachment, as though I was looking down on myself from another place, seeing the enactment of my struggle to cope with the journal's contents as though watching some grotesque stage play, with myself as the sole cast member. Certainly, the further I'd delved into the infernal journal of the Ripper, I'd begun to feel as though I was someone else, a kind of voyeur peering through a window in time in order to witness the foul deeds of the writer. There was a grim reality about the images which the journal had superimposed upon my usual rational mind, combined with an unnatural feel to everything else that was happening to me, here in the so-called sanctuary of my own home. I remember wishing that I'd never set eyes upon the journal, though it was far too late for such thoughts by then.

As a glimmer of clear thought returned to me, I had a nagging notion that there was something missing from the journal, something of significance in the reported history of the crimes. Had the Ripper omitted to record some detail of note from his writings, and if so what was it? With a new air of determination in my heart I decided to return to the study and delve into my printed notes to try to identify whatever it was that was disturbing me.

An involuntary shiver ran through my body as I re-entered the study, as though the temperature had fallen by about ten degrees just by passing from one room to another. There was a definite air of oppression in the room, and it took quite an effort on my behalf to force myself to approach my desk once more. The journal still lay there, bathed in the wash of the light from my desk lamp, and it seemed to be calling to me, willing me to pick it up, to read the next instalment in its tale of malevolent and insane murder and blood-letting. It took an immense amount of willpower for me to resist its unearthly temptation, but I forced myself not to look directly at its terrible, inviting pages, and instead reached across to take up the pile of notes lying a few inches away from it.

After the entry of 5th October, the Ripper had written no more until the 26th, so I concentrated my search on the dates between those two days. If something significant had occurred while the Ripper was in the hospital, it might help to prove or disprove some of the theories that abounded with relation to the murders. It took me less than five minutes to find what I was looking for. It was the kidney!

On the 16th October 1888, Mr George Lusk, the chairman of the Whitechapel Vigilance Committee had received by post a human kidney in a square cardboard box, which was accompanied by a letter, supposedly from the Ripper, describing it as having belonged to Catherine Eddowes. The letter, which I reproduce here, intimated that the writer had fried and eaten part of the kidney, and, when knowledge of this reached the public, the news hacks of the day almost exhausted themselves with the race to publish in great banner headlines, 'Cannibal in London', 'Jack the Ripper Eats Victim's Kidney', and so on.

Medical opinion of the time was divided in its verdict on the kidney. Despite the fact that Dr Openshaw, curator of the Pathology Museum at London Hospital declared it to be the 'ginny' kidney of a 45-year-old woman afflicted with Bright's

disease, Dr Sedgwick Saunders, the City pathologist stated to
the press that the age and sex of the bearer of a human kidney
could not be determined in the absence of the remainder of the
body, and so the argument went on. From further examination
of the notes, and the opinions of many of the leading doctors of
the time, I tended to agree with the majority that this was not
the kidney of Eddowes, and was more likely a hoax, possibly
perpetrated by a medical student, or someone with a severely
perverse sense of macabre humour.

The letter read as follows:

From hell
Mr Lusk
Sor
I send you half the Kidne I took from one women
prasarved it for you tother piece I fried and ate it
was very
nise I may send you the bloody knif that took it out
if you
only wate a whil longer
signed Catch me when
you can
Mishter Lusk

Surely no-one could have taken this letter seriously. It was such
an obvious fake, and with such a poorly disguised almost 'stage'
Irish accent built into its wording. The letters sent by the writer
of the journal were disguised, yes, but in an intelligent and
calculated fashion. This was just a mish mash of deliberate
misspellings and was quite laughable in its almost childish lack
of sentence construction. The earlier Ripper letters displayed a
calculating and mocking tone towards the reader, this however,

BRIAN L PORTER

was simply the work of a braggart, an attention seeker, and to my mind, a definite hoax! As to the true owner of the kidney, there were many ways in those days for a medical student or anyone employed in a hospital to obtain human organs, and thence to preserve them as this one had been before its mailing to Lusk. I concluded that it had probably come from some poor soul who had died within the walls of a hospital and that the kidney had been removed for examination and then spirited away by the perpetrator of the hoax.

On thing was certain. The writer of the journal, Jack the Ripper, could neither have written the letter, nor mailed the kidney to Lusk. He was in the hospital at the time of its delivery, and therefore unable to have been the sender. What's more, the fact that he made no reference to the kidney in the journal tended to confirm my belief that, at the time of his latest entry, he knew nothing about it, having not had time perhaps to read the newspapers covering his time in hospital, if indeed he was even disposed to do such a thing. More likely he was merely concerned with '*now*' *and* would merely have been satisfied that his name was still on the lips of almost every citizen within the city of London. As he prepared for his next and most gruesome murder to date, I very much doubted that Jack the Ripper would have time to 'catch up on his reading'.

At least now I was satisfied that I had put to sleep the niggling thought in my mind. I knew there'd been something and now I knew what it was. Not only that but I'd solved, to my own satisfaction at least, one of the abiding puzzles associated with the Ripper case. I just wondered, not for the first time, if I would ever be in a position to reveal all that I'd learned, to perhaps be remembered as the man who'd solved the Ripper murders after all these year. Then again, my father and grandfather had had the chance to do the same thing hadn't they? Something, and as yet I didn't know what, had prevented them from doing so. Would I also find that secrecy was the prudent path to follow?

Tiredness was now enveloping me like a dense fog. I felt as though my eyelids were weighed down by rocks, such was the effort involved in trying to keep my eyes open. My arms and legs were leaden, my head too heavy to be supported by my neck, and I felt a strange fluttering in my chest, and a trembling deep inside that spread throughout my entire being. I was exhausted, both mentally, and physically, despite not having exerted myself physically at all apart from a walk to the village and back that day. Although I felt a need to return to the journal, to pry its secrets from within its pages, the need for sleep proved greater in my befuddled mind, and, leaving the lights on, and everything where it was downstairs, I wearily climbed the stairs, almost staggered into the bedroom, and allowed myself to collapse, fully clothed, onto the bed, where I fell asleep in seconds.

THIRTY-ONE
AND SO TO SLEEP, PERCHANCE TO DREAM

As I SLEPT THAT NIGHT, I was again transported to that nightmare world of terrifying images and unspeakable terrors. The face that had haunted me in the study was back, taunting and terrorising me, drifting in and out of focus, a nightmarish caricature made up of part me, part apparition, its black cloak swirling and trailing like a giant bat wing in its wake as it sped towards me from some indistinct fog shrouded horizon. Each time the figure receded it was replaced instantly by the images of the victims, this time appearing as barely corporeal wraith-like figures, floating on an unseen breeze, as though caught in a constant whirlwind, circling in a perpetual spiral, their mouths opening in a cry of silent torture, screaming silently into the wind, and from the place where the diaphanous robes that covered their mutilated bodies ended, a steady shower of fresh, dark red blood dripped towards the unseen ground, until the flow of red from the tortured corpses blotted out the light behind them and the sky slowly darkened from blue to match the redness of the dripping blood. Somewhere amongst these terrible images the face of John

Ross appeared to me, his face a contorted mask of hate, his mouth open in a demonic grin, showing deeply incised canine-like teeth, which also dripped with the blood of his victims, and there behind him, being dragged by a chain held in his right hand, were the two young women so recently slaughtered, writhing in the agonies of violent death, their screams, like those of the Ripper's victims, silent and quickly swept away by the steadily increasing wind that continued to sweep the whole menagerie of death into a continually changing panorama of pain and suffering, as the tormented souls of the murdered and the murderers performed their horrific ballet of death, deep within my quiescent sleeping mind.

The surreal imagery of the nightmare now gave way to a new dreamscape, which, though peaceful by comparison, was equally as terrifying. I now seemed to be floating above the ground myself, slowly traversing an overgrown, deserted cemetery. As the thing that was me hovered ever closer to the ground, the headstones; row upon row of weathered and dilapidated memorials to the dead, came gradually into focus. There, in sharp relief, were the names of Mary Ann Nichols, Annie Chapman, Elizabeth Stride, Catherine Eddowes, and Mary Jane Kelly, and, beneath each of their names, in large letters, the single word, WHORE. As I stared in horror at the despicable and ungodly vista below me, I saw a cloaked and slightly stooped figure approaching the row of graves. He carried a spade, an old-fashioned wooden-handled spade, one of those that appeared to be attached to a broom handle, with no hand grip. The figure moved slowly along the line of graves and then, to my horror, he swung the spade like a weapon and I heard not the clang of metal on stone as it struck the first headstone, but instead there was a dull thud, rather as though the spade had made contact with a human head, and then, to my ultimate horror, the gravestone of Mary Ann Nichols began to bleed!

The trickle of blood from the stone rapidly became a flood, until the grass surrounding the headstone was soon stained red by the river that gushed from the stone. As I watched, detached, yet feeling close enough to reach out and touch the figure in black, he moved along the row of headstones, performing the same act of vandalism on each, with the same result. As the blood from the final headstone joined that of the others, the ground around the graves seemed to open up, and with a terrible sound, like a thousand anguished souls rising up in torment, the twisted, mutilated wreckage of the departed rose from beneath the blood soaked turf, and in a grim and fearful resurrection, each one wailing in resemblance of their final agony, they surrounded me as I floated above the gruesome scene, reaching out, trying to touch me as I tried to twist away in abject terror. I had to escape, for to let them touch me would have tainted me forever, that's how it felt. I kicked out and attempted to manoeuvre myself away from the howling discord of the dead, then, suddenly, I was alone, in a new, quiet part of the cemetery, staring down once more, this time at a single grave, with an unmarked stone. Not a single word adorned that lonely quite singular stone, though, as I floated closer and closer, I saw, at the very bottom of the stone, almost overgrown by the grass that had sprung up around it, a short set of words that, innocent enough in themselves sent a chill through me, even in my dream state. The words read simply, *'Unknown Whore, Edinburgh, 1888'*. Even in the midst of my nightmare, the poor Scottish girl received no recognition, no remembrance. The figure returned, swung the spade once more, and the headstone exploded into a volcano like eruption of blood, this time it spurted upwards in a terrifying arc, until, unable to escape the force of the tide rushing towards me, I was struck by what felt like a tidal wave of warm, sticky, human life-blood, and then, by the greatest of mercies, just before madness overcame me in the midst of that awful nightmarish parody of a graveyard, my body shook and trembled and I was suddenly awake!

I was cold, still fully clothed, and lying on top of the bed, where I'd collapsed into that deep nightmare infested sleep. My head was still filled with the violent and horrific images from which I'd just escaped by virtue of waking up. I looked around me in the darkness, certain that I was still surrounded by those nightmarish apparitions. There was no-one and nothing in the room of course, apart from one trembling and slightly enfeebled specimen of humanity lying in a foetal position on the bed. As my mind retreated further from the horrors induced by the nightmare, and the trembling in my body and the palpitations in my heart slowly dissipated, I looked across at the digital clock on the bedside table. It read 4.15 a.m. How long I'd slept I couldn't say, I had collapsed into bed too exhausted to notice the time, I may have slept for two hours, three, four, I just didn't know. Either way, the exhaustion that had accompanied me up the stairs to the bedroom had only been compounded by the fiendish nightmare I'd just endured, and, far from feeling refreshed from whatever sleep I'd managed to achieve, I felt worse than I had before I'd ascended the stairs.

It was still dark outside, and the wind had gained in intensity as I'd slept. I heard the whispering of the leaves on the trees in the garden, as if the voices of my dream figures had crossed into the real world and were mocking me through the chorus of those rustling, rushing leaves. As I lay unmoving on the bed, the sounds from outside my window were without doubt the saddest sounds I'd ever heard. It was as though nature itself was mourning the souls of those poor wretched women, or was it the sound of the Ripper mocking those souls, delighting in their torment, and whispering his triumph on the wind?

My mind was in turmoil. I knew I had to move, to leave the bedroom, make myself return to a semblance of reality, and leave the nightmare behind me for good. It took an amazing amount of willpower just to move my legs from that safe, tucked-up position. I was like a new born creature struggling from the womb as I slowly stretched my legs, forced myself up on one elbow, and gradually swung myself over the edge of the bed until my feet touched the floor.

Ten minutes later I was in the kitchen, with every light still blazing as I'd left them earlier and was already on my second mug of steaming hot coffee. I'd often wondered how Sarah could drink tea or coffee so hot, laughingly telling her she'd got an asbestos palate, but that night I admit to being able to swallow the hottest coffee I'd ever tasted without feeling the heat at all. I think that was a measure of how numb I'd become, both physically and mentally.

I couldn't go back to the bedroom. I was afraid that if I fell asleep on the bed again the nightmare would return. I could have taken more of Sarah's sleeping tablets of course but decided against it. I wanted to avoid that hung-over feeling they induced, and I knew I had to conclude my study of the journal in the next day or so, before she returned, so I wanted to be as alert as I possibly could, allowing of course for the lack of sleep and stamina sapping mental drain I was beginning to experience.

Instead of the bedroom I opted for the lounge, taking a pot of hot coffee for company. I turned on the gas fire, and felt its warmth begin to suffuse the room, and me with it. I hadn't realised until then quite how cold I'd become, but the fire soon brought a modicum of cheer to my aching bones and befuddled mind. I resisted the urge to turn on the twenty-four-hour news channel on the TV. Judging by the events of the last two days, I wasn't sure what might be revealed had I done so, and I'd had enough for one day!

I pulled up the dralon covered footstool that Sarah usually commandeered to rest her legs on in the evening, eased my feet up and made myself comfortable, and sipped at my coffee. After another two mugs of the reviving brew I felt a little more relaxed and promised myself that I'd try to complete my reading of the journal and great-grandfather's notes during the next twenty-four hours. I think that was the last coherent thought I had before my head lolled to one side against the back of the deep, comfortable armchair, and then, with the gentle hiss of the gas fire for company, and the warmth of its flame casting a comfortable glow towards my weary aching mind and body I fell asleep once more, and this time, there were no dreams.

I woke again at 7.30, more refreshed than I'd perhaps a right to feel. The wind had dropped, the early morning sun was shining through the wide panes of the patio doors, (I hadn't closed the curtains the night before), and the room was beautifully warm, the fire had seen to that. It still gave off that companionable hiss as it radiated it's warmth through the room, and everything looked and felt a little better now that daylight had arrived.

I made my way, first to the bathroom, where the reflection that peered back at me from the mirror shocked me by its appearance. I looked pale, dishevelled, and my eyes looked as thought they'd sunk deep into their sockets. A long, hot soak in the shower, and a good shave soon did something about the way I looked though maybe not about how I felt. Next, it was the kitchen, where a breakfast of toast and marmalade, followed by a couple of boiled eggs and yet more coffee served to deal with the second part of the problem, and, though I admit that my mind still felt as though I were being dragged unwillingly into something I didn't understand in the slightest, I felt better, yes, definitely better. The problem with mental illness of any kind is that it can creep up on the sufferer without them being aware that it's there, and everything can appear normal when in fact it is far from being that.

Perhaps that's why, for the first time in the last three days I felt a little optimistic, maybe at the thought of finishing the journal, completing the journey, maybe finally putting the Ripper and his sad yet murderous story to rest. Of course, that just goes to prove how naïve even a man of my education and so-called intelligence can be. Things were never going to be that simple, were they?

THIRTY-TWO
MILLER'S COURT

AFTER CLEARING AWAY the remains of my breakfast things, I made my way back to my study, filled with my new-found optimism. I admit to feeling a degree of trepidation as I prepared to enter the room, but satisfied myself that everything that had happened over the last two days had been simply a temporary state of mind, probably induced by the recent loss of my father, the loneliness I felt at being separated from Sarah, and an overactive imagination

Even so, I pushed the door open very slowly, and looked around it before entering; as if afraid I might disturb someone, or something, within the room. The room was exactly as I'd left it the night before, at least, I thought it was. As I neared the desk, my sense of well-being quickly evaporated as I noticed the computer screen. I was sure that I'd switched the computer off as I'd left the room, yet the standby light on the monitor was green, and as I touched the mouse the screensaver flashed into life. On the task bar at the bottom of the screen was the Casebook name, and, feeling less and less in control of my emotions, I clicked on the button. The page that flashed into view was not the one I last remembered consulting. This page contained the reports of the murder of Mary Jane Kelly, with some pretty graphic descriptions of her injures included. How on earth had that got there? I definitely couldn't remember having accessed that particular page, and yet there it was. I was mystified, and the equilibrium I'd so carefully regained over the last hour evaporated, as I felt once again that I wasn't as alone as I thought in the house. I knew I needed to get back to the journal. It was as if I was being led inexorably towards its remaining pages, as though it were in some kind of hurry to reveal its final secrets to me, but before then, I wanted to learn more about Mary Jane Kelly. I knew that the Ripper would probably have written his macabre and sinister version of her death, quite possibly on the next page I came to, but first, I wanted to read the facts as recorded at the time.

I couldn't escape the awful feeling that someone was watching me, as though peering over my shoulder, and I spun round as quickly as I could. There was no one there of course; it was just my foolish mind.

As I began to read the sad tale of the death of Mary Kelly I was struck at once by my own stupidity. She had been killed on the night of 9th November, yet the last entry I'd read in the journal had been dated the 26th October. There was still over a week to go in the journal's chronology before he struck again. Why had I thought that the murder would occur within the next couple of days? How could I have so misread the notes on my earlier scan through them? Was this why the computer had somehow led me to the notes again? Was someone, or something, trying to ensure that I followed the story of the murders correctly, and made no error along the way? It was an eerie and uncanny feeling, knowing that the page I was reading had appeared as if by magic, placed there as if by an unseen hand, as though it knew I was drifting away from the true course of events and wanted me to focus my mind once more on the truth of the words on the pages of the insane journal.

The facts surrounding the last canonical victim of the Ripper were as gruesome and horrific as I think a human brain could imagine. As terrible as the poor girl's injuries were, I think it appropriate to record the worst of them here so that you, the reader can perhaps appreciate the severity and wanton destruction of the Ripper's actions on that terrible night.

Mary Jane Kelly's history is shrouded in mystery, her early life recorded purely anecdotally by the stories she herself related to her friends in London during her time there. She appears to have been born in Limerick and moved to Wales as a child when her father obtained work there at an ironworks. She was one of seven or eight children, one a sister, the rest brothers. She married a collier named Davies in 1879, who was reputed to have died in a pit accident two or three years later. She apparently became a prostitute while staying with a cousin in Cardiff, and later moved to London, where she worked for a time in a high-class brothel, not surprisingly due to her youth and apparent good looks. There are unfortunately no records to substantiate any of the above, all of it being simply what Kelly herself related to her acquaintances. At any rate, she eventually ended up in the cess pool of humanity that made up the vast heaving population of London's East End, and lived for a time with a long-term partner, Joseph Barnett, with whom she enjoyed a relatively prosperous existence until he lost his job, and she returned once again to the streets to eke out a living from the sale of her body. As the relationship grew more and more volatile, she and Barnett separated, and she continued to reside in the tiny, one roomed dwelling that bore the address of 13 Miller's Court, Dorset Street, one of the most run down and ill reputed streets in Whitechapel. It was in that small room that her body was discovered on the morning of 9th

November 1888, Mary Kelly having last been seen alive at about 2 a.m.

Doctor Thomas Bond, police surgeon to 'A' Division (Westminster), reported as follows:

Position of body
The body was lying naked in the middle of the bed, the shoulders flat, but the axis of the body inclined to the left side of the bed. The head was turned on the left cheek. The left arm was close to the body with the forearm flexed at a right angle & lying across the abdomen. The right arm was slightly abducted from the body & rested on the mattress, the elbow bent & the forearm supine with the fingers clenched. The legs were wide apart, the left thigh at right angles to the trunk & the right forming an obtuse angle with the pubes.
The whole of the surface of the abdomen & thighs was removed & the abdominal Cavity emptied of its viscera. The breasts were cut off, the arms mutilated by several jagged wounds & the face hacked beyond recognition of the features. The tissues of the neck were severed all round to the bone.
The viscera were found in various parts viz; the uterus & Kidneys with one breast under the head, the other breast by the Rt foot, the Liver between the feet, the intestines by the right side & the spleen by the left side of the body. The flaps removed from the abdomen and thighs were on a table.
The bed clothing at the right corner was saturated with blood, & on the floor beneath was a pool of blood covering about two feet square. The wall by the right side of the bed & in line with the neck was marked by blood which had struck it in a number of separate splashes.
Postmortem examination.
The face was gashed in all directions the nose, cheeks, eyebrows and ears being partly removed. The lips were blanched and cut

by several incisions running obliquely down to the chin. There were also numerous cuts extending irregularly across all the features.

The neck was cut through the skin & other tissues right down to the vertebrae the 5th & 6th being deeply notched. The skin cuts in the front of the neck showed distinct ecchymosis.

The air passage was cut at the lower part of the larynx through the cricoid cartilage.

Both breasts were removed by more or less circular incisions, the muscles down to the ribs being attached to the breasts. The intercostals between the 4th, 5th & 6th ribs were cut through & the contents of the thorax visible through the openings.

The skin & tissues of the abdomen from the costal arch to the pubes were removed in three large flaps. The right thigh was denuded in front to the bone, the flap of skin, including the external organs of generation and part of the right buttock. The left thigh was stripped of skin, fascia and muscles as far as the knee.

The left calf showed a long gash through skin & tissues to the deep muscles & reaching from the knee to 5 inches above the ankle.

Both arms & forearms had extensive and jagged wounds.

The right thumb showed a small superficial incision about 1 inch long, with extravasation of blood in the skin & there were several abrasions on the back of the hand moreover showing the same condition.

On opening the thorax it was found that the right lung was minimally adherent by old firm adhesions. The lower part of the lung was broken and torn away.

The left lung was intact: it was adherent at the apex & there were a few adhesions over the side. In the substances of the lung were several nodules of consolidation.

The pericardium was open below & the Heart absent.

In the abdominal cavity was some partly digested food of fish &
potatoes & similar food was found in the remains of the stomach
attached to the intestines.

So Mary Kelly was not just murdered, she was slaughtered! The poor woman was killed, and then systematically butchered by the Ripper. Though this is the first time in my tale that I have related the full extent of one of the victim's injuries, I have done so in order to establish beyond doubt the extreme depravity of the perpetrator of the horrific series of murders. Also, for the first time in any of the murders, the doctor had identified defensive wounds on the poor girl's hands. Faced with the most vicious killer ever recorded up to that time in London, the Ripper's last known victim had fought to defend herself; she had fought for her life. What had been her last thoughts, I wondered, as she tried in vain to fight off her attacker? She must have been filled with the most appalling dread and fear, and, contrary to the previous murders, this had been no quick kill, no slash of the throat to end the victim's agony swiftly and surely. A further search through my notes revealed that no sign of Kelly's heart had been found. What had the Ripper done with it? Had it become some gruesome trophy, to be displayed in the privacy of his home, to gloat over as a grim reminder of his greatest moment? I shook, both with fear and an anger so strong that I might have been there at the time, a witness to those appalling cruelties, and the utter brutality of the mutilations. It took me a few minutes to regain a little composure and calm myself down, to think rationally again.

I was appalled by the callousness and the barbarity of the slaughter perpetrated on poor Mary Kelly. The desecration of her body was beyond belief and must have taken the Ripper some considerable time. Of course, on this occasion he had had the time, it was his first indoor murder, and he had the opportunity to indulge himself, to provide the world with the perfect example of the extent to which his 'work' could evolve.

No wonder nothing more was heard of Ripper after this appalling crime, I just couldn't conceive of him being able to maintain a grip on the smallest grain of sanity after having committed such an act, and, as though it were intended all along that that was the way I should do it, without thinking I laid down my notes and automatically picked up the journal, turning the page to reveal the next instalment in this infernal tale of one man's damnation.

The next words that came up to greet me from within the journal were not however those of the Ripper. Tucked tightly between the pages written by the hand that had perpetrated such horrific and savage mutilations I saw once again that my great-grandfather had been at work. There was another note there, waiting for me, perhaps to explain in more detail his involvement with the Ripper.

With trembling hands, and with my heart growing heavier with sadness and my brain becoming ever more disturbed by the savage images now forcing their way to the forefront of my mind, I began to read...

THIRTY-THREE
A CONFESSION

I swear in the name of God Almighty that I knew nothing of this dire journal during the time leading up to the murders in Whitechapel, nor indeed until after the murder of Mary Kelly. I place this note here as it seems appropriate in view of what he has written on the following page. At the time I saw him, in his home, he was more or less lucid, though it was evident that all was not well with the man. His fantasies, as I believed them to be at the time, were growing darker and more violent, but I swear I thought them nothing more than the product of his fevered mind. I simply thought him incapable of being the beast that has haunted the streets of our capital for so many weeks. Perhaps my judgement was impaired by my knowledge of his mother, his family, and my own sorry conduct in his story.

You, my son, reading this after my demise, will be shocked to learn of these things, but I must give my conscience free reign before my maker, and throw my memory upon your mercy.

*It was back in the summer of '56 that I was invited
down to the country by a friend and colleague. There I
was invited to the home of a local physician who kept a
house on the outskirts of that beautiful country town. He
had a wife, a beauty by any man's standards, and I, being
not yet married to your mother, felt strangely drawn to
her. She was as beautiful a woman as I had ever set eyes
upon, with her long dark hair, a slim waist, and eyes that
seemed to burn with a hidden fire, a passion for life that
seemed in need of re-awakening, as though she were in a
trance of sorts. There was something of the gipsy about
her looks, a wild, fiery, hidden passion about her
character. Their marriage was not a happy one, so I was
led to believe, though on the surface they seemed devoted
to one another. She was quite taken however, by the
attention I paid to her, in little matters such as bringing
her a flower picked from the garden, or jesting lightly
with her as we walked in the ample gardens of her home,
always of course while her husband was absent. I felt
some guilt in those days, as her husband was a fine man,
and an outstanding local physician, and he had made
me welcome in his home on numerous occasions.
Yet, I could not help myself, and I soon grew enamoured
of the lady. Though she tried hard to avoid the obvious,
and endeavoured to stick hard to her marriage vows,
there came one day when we could no longer control the
hidden passions that burned within both our fragile
bodies, and we succumbed to the carnal desires of the
flesh.*

*Afterwards, shocked by her weakness, and fearful of her
husband's fury should he discover her infidelity, she
forbade me to visit her again, and entreated upon me to*

return to London at my earliest opportunity. I had no choice but to leave the county and returned as she wished to my home and practice in the city.

Some time later, I received a letter from her to say that she was with child and begging me never to visit that town again. I never did, and it was not until recently that the man I now visit, the man who is the writer of these infernal pages, came to my home one day, armed with a letter of introduction from his mother. The letter had been written some years ago, and he had carried it with him until such times as he wished to announce his presence to me. His mother, he told me, had fallen into a deep malaise, and had been confined in an asylum, her mind totally unhinged, until her death. The doctor, who he had always thought of as his father, was dead, and he was alone in the world. He bore me no ill-will, so he said, and wished only to make my acquaintance, as it was obvious to him that his mother had cared for me greatly, and I for her.

I tell you now; just one look at his eyes identified him to me. They were the eyes of his mother, she who I had loved and lost before your poor mother came into my life. I did my best. I introduced him at my club, gave him whatever social assistance I could, and I have fought to keep him on the straight and narrow despite his recent problems. I ask of you, how could I have believed that the son of such a woman, and I am ashamed to say, of mine, could be the monster known throughout the land as Jack the Ripper?

I tell you these things that you may understand the frailty and the folly that have blighted my life and led to such misery and death for others. Though I dare not ask your forgiveness, now that my bones lie bleaching in the earth, I do ask that you try to understand why I have acted as I have, and to try to forgive me for the things I have done in order to keep secret the truth of what has transpired. If you can understand, and can forgive, then I beg you to keep forever this secret between you and my memory, and if you need to confess it, as I have needed to do, then do so only in the manner of this communication. I beg you my son to reveal this dreadful secret only upon death, and even then only to your closest kin, and so to entreat them that they hold this secret in the same way, for all time, for there is nothing that can now be gained from further revelation.

Now, as you read what is to come, I hope that you will grant me that understanding, and I can at least find some semblance of peace in that knowledge, though my tortured soul shall burn forever, of that I sure.

As I said, on this occasion when I visited him, he was quite lucid, hardly deranged at all, and I thought he was improving, that the drugs I had prescribed for him were helping in some way. I hoped that he might have desisted in his use of laudanum, but he said that his headaches had been getting worse, and that the laudanum was the only thing that helped. I knew then that he was addicted to the stuff, and would probably be over-using the opiate. Nevertheless, he conversed quite well for a few minutes, and his education and breeding were quite evident in his whole manner and bearing. I could not help but look at his eyes, those eyes that were so like his mother's, and I expressed my sadness that she had ended in such a way, dying as she had in that place apart from those who cared for her. As I spoke of her, however, his demeanour changed, and his eyes seemed to flare with a baleful and malevolent gaze. I thought he was perhaps in the throes of another brain seizure and was convinced of such when he suddenly announced that Jack the Ripper wasn't finished yet, that he would strike again soon, and that everyone would soon know of his greatest crime to date. I felt that he was being over dramatic and sensationalist, and dismissed this rant as another example of his fevered state, as though he were fixating all his pent up hatred for his sorry state upon the Ripper, identifying with him in his madness, still never for one minute believing that he was indeed that very man. How wrong I was, how very wrong. Would that I could live my life again, and do things differently, but I cannot, and you now know the truth, or, most of it, I am not yet ready to reveal the end to this sorry tale. Perhaps when you have read the rest of his confessional you will understand my torment, and why I did what I did, and why the silence must be total, for all time.

Your father
Burton Cleveland Cavendish

THE NOTE WAS UNDATED, though I knew it must have been written some time after my great-grandfather had read the entire journal, and now I knew, at last! Jack the Ripper *was* a distant relative of mine. He was the illegitimate son of my own great-grandfather, the result of a one-time liaison with a woman whom my ancestor was so obviously infatuated with in his younger days. In fact, from my great-grandfather's words, and from what I'd read in the information provided by the Casebook, I now had a pretty good idea of the identity of the Ripper, though somehow, his name had suddenly become an irrelevance to me. I tried to work it out; if he was the son of my great-grandfather, then he would have been my great uncle, I thought. He must have been, as he would have been my grandfather's half-brother, though grandfather obviously knew nothing of his existence until he'd received this note with the journal so many years ago. I could only imagine his shock and horror at making such a discovery. How, I wondered, had he taken the news that he was so closely related to the killer? More to the point, how had he managed to keep it quiet for so long, only revealing the truth in the form of the journal, left to my father after his death, as it had been bequeathed to me? The answer was straightforward of course. It was there in my great-grandfather's own hand, a plea from the grave, requesting that the secret be kept within the family for all time. Having read his sad and revealing confession to his son, my grandfather, I could understand why.

There was more of course, there had to be. There was something my great-grandfather wasn't revealing, not yet at any rate. I knew it was something terrible, worse perhaps than the revelation of the Ripper's identity, and his involvement with the family. It was a feeling that was growing stronger inside me, a feeling that the final horror of my ancestor's association with Jack the Ripper wasn't quite concluded. I had to go on, complete the journal, and hope to find the truth along the way.

I had been away from the words of The Ripper for too long, it was time to turn another page, to draw ever closer to the night of the murder of Mary Jane Kelly, the night when Jack the Ripper's reign of terror reached its final, bloody crescendo.

THIRTY-FOUR
MARY, MARY, SWEET LITTLE MARY

I was glad that I'd taken the time to study the facts of the Mary Kelly case. I felt that in some way I'd managed to arm myself against whatever the Ripper himself may have subsequently added to the journal. Nothing could be more horrific than the truth, and the words of the doctor who'd carried out the post mortem on the poor girl had been all the more chilling in their cold, professional presentation. My great-grandfather had given enough away in his words to further arm me in my continued journey through what were to be the last few pages of the journal. My own father had always told me to listen to the truth as it presents itself, and that any subsequent lies or exaggerations will therefore cause me no harm. I had done that, as best as I could, and now once again I took hold of the journal and turned from my great-grandfather's note to view once more the handwriting of Jack the Ripper.

As was becoming more and more prevalent by that time, he had missed a number of days between entries, the next one coming some three days after the last.

29th October 1888

Time is running short, the voices are growing louder in my head, the pain so much worse, and the laudanum is failing to relieve me. I take ever more and yet all it does is make me sick, and I am a mask of fever. I must strike again, and soon, the whores are growing too confident, they think I have gone, departed the darkness, but no, I have been sleeping, waiting, resting, and I shall make the streets red once more with whore blood. I've seen her, the one who I shall slice and gut so soon. A pretty thing, could be a ladies maid, but she's not, she is a dirty pestilent whore, and she will die. Have twice spoken with the whore in an ale house on Commercial Street. She has a high opinion of herself this one, and is deserving of my best efforts, I shall slit her well, and leave a sign for all to see.

This short entry proved to me that he was now in the final throws of his insanity. The voices growing louder, the sickness, the fever, all signs of the Ripper's final degeneration. The laudanum, far from bringing relief from his symptoms had now become in itself an additional problem, he was suffering from the cumulative results of opium poisoning, and his body, and indeed his brain, could surely not take much more.

His description of his meetings with Mary Kelly, (for surely it were she he was describing), showed me that in this, his last and most gruesome murder, the Ripper had deliberately stalked his victim, had met her, spoken with her, had spent time with her. From his reference to Commercial Street, and my own check with my notes, I thought he was probably referring to a tavern by the name of the Queen's Head, which was a common haunt of prostitutes on that road. It would have been perfectly reasonable to expect him to have met his victim there. His further comment that 'she thought a lot of herself' further supported my belief that this was Kelly, who was known to be something of a braggart and a weaver of fantasies believing herself to be of a higher social standing than many of the unfortunate women in her profession. There was a stark chill about his final comment to 'slit her well'. Mary Kelly had no idea at the time, yet she had been marked for death well in advance of her actual demise. This final act of the Ripper's had been no random act, but a predetermined calculated attack upon a selected victim. Even now, after all I'd read in the last two days, he had managed to surprise me by the brutally callous selection of the victim of his final and most bloodthirsty murder yet. She was pretty he said, did that make him angry? Was he by then so jealous of those who were unafflicted with the gradual wasting disease such as he suffered that he had selected her because of her good looks? It would be true to remark that none of his previous victims had been either young or particularly well endowed in the beauty stakes, but now here he was, seemingly seeking out and selecting the prettiest prostitute he could find in order to satisfy his latest blood lust. There was a cold-heartedness about his words that filled me with a chill that reached into my soul. Mary Kelly had, at that point in his journal a little over week of life left to her, and the Ripper was counting down the days to the time when he would slake his thirst for blood in the most heinous and horrible example of his work to date. How could she have known that the man she had been drinking with on at least two occasions, by his own admission, was the man being sought by the entire London police force for the murders of her fellow prostitutes, or that she was talking to, perhaps even laughing with the man who would soon bestow upon her the dubious 'honour' of being the last recorded victim of Jack the Ripper?

Another entry was recorded at the bottom of the page, just a short one, but it was all the more damnable for that!

30th October 1888

Mary, Mary, sweet little Mary, I know your name and where you dwell,
Mary, Mary, dirty whore Mary, soon you'll be in Hell.
Hahahaha

He knew her name, he was playing a game in his mind, and the poor girl was being used as the unwitting pawn in his last and most fiendish display of blood curdling viciousness. His mocking verse sent a shudder through me, and I could only imagine the perverse glee that he must have felt as he penned those few words. His mind was by then almost on the verge of collapse, of that I was sure; he was descending ever deeper into the depths of his final insanity, and the unfortunate Mary Kelly was being targeted in the way a cat stalks a bird in the garden, he was watching her, waiting for the moment to strike, while all the time she went about her business as usual, totally unaware of the sudden and brutal end he had planned for her.

I turned the page, and there were more brief, twisted verses lying in wait for me.

31st October 1888

Mary, Mary, whore, whore, whore, soon you'll be dead,
Mary, Mary, whore, whore, whore, I just might cut off your head.

***

1st November 1888

I'll slice and gut the Mary whore,
Till there's nothing left of Mary no more.

***

2nd November 1888

Visited the Queen's Head again. Drank with the whore and gave her money. A shilling to buy drink. She will learn to trust her gentleman friend, and then I'll have my way.

***

3rd November 1888

My head hurts: I cannot wait much longer. The voices will tell me when, but it must be soon. I can feel the need to spill the whore's blood. She must die soon, and I must rest, the work is hard, and I ache with the sickness within me. Cavendish came to see me, poor fool. He still believes me to be hallucinating, wants me to give up the laudanum. He tried to help in a way I suppose. How can I stop now? I tried to tell him, wanted him to understand, him of all people, I needed him to know, to realise the importance of my work. Why won't he believe me? I know I shall go the way of my poor dear Mama, it's started already, so much harder to think, to focus my thoughts on what I must do, and so much pain that I can scarce bear it, I do wish Cavendish could help, but he cannot, will not, for he does not understand, nor believe. I shall visit the park tomorrow. I shall throw crumbs to the ducks on the lake.

So, he plans what was probably the most gruesome and grisly murder known up until that time in London's history, then decides to go and feed the ducks in the park! I felt sure that the Ripper's madness was now complete. This ability to switch from the insane to the mundane in the space of a second's thought convinced me of that. I remember thinking that he probably thought more of those ducks upon the ornamental lake than he did of the lives of those women he so brutally slew. He had at least acknowledged my great-grandfather's attempts to help him, though he'd just as quickly dismissed them, preferring to see his own father as nothing more than a 'poor fool', for not believing his tales of being the Ripper. I tried to imagine how my great-grandfather must have felt when faced with the Ripper's 'confessions'. What father after all would want to freely admit that his own son was the most foul and heinous murderer of his time? Perhaps my ancestor had found it easier to believe, knowing the Ripper's recent history that he was simply confessing to the crimes of another, in an attempt to secure some sort of attention. I know that if I had had a son, I would have done almost anything rather than admit to such a possibility, and I had sympathy for my great-grandfather at that point.

Despite having sat and studied the Kelly case in some detail before applying myself to the journal I still found myself shocked by much of what I was reading. Though I hadn't yet reached the night of her murder in the journal, the entries I was reading were chillingly disturbing to my increasingly fragile mind.

First of all, it had now become abundantly clear that she was not a random victim, as the others had appeared to be, and secondly, the fact that the Ripper had taken the time to form a kind of relationship with her caused me great pain and uneasiness, for it was plain that Mary Kelly had been 'groomed' for murder. The Ripper's self control was slipping away with each and every new entry in the journal, the sick little rhymes, the switch from death to ducks, and the final, most disturbing entry yet as I reached the end of that page.

4th November 1888

I shall kill and gut the whore,
Then Jack shall live for evermore.
For as her blood flows on the floor,
I shall step through history's door.
haha

I was gripped with a terror that, even to this day, I can't properly explain. What did he mean? 'Jack shall live for evermore.' Did he think he was about to be granted some form of immortality? What did he mean by stepping 'through history's door'? Through the door to where? The present? To where I now sat trembling and shaking with the thought, however illogical and impractical that he had somehow found a way to live on beyond the grave, that the killings were some form of rite that had granted him a passage through time and space, giving him the ability to cheat death? I was more than terrified at that point; I was petrified beyond belief. I had the sudden thought that the journal itself might in some way be the doorway he'd written of, a portal, a means of providing him with a window into the future, his future, and enabling him to revisit his crimes in perpetuum from century to century. I quickly tried to tell myself that such thoughts were utter nonsense, nothing more than the rantings of my own mind, brought on by the unsettling nature of the journal and its gory contents. I really did try hard to convince myself of that, but the feeling just wouldn't go away.

With a supreme force of will, I made myself rise from the chair, and walked from the study to head for the kitchen. I needed coffee, tea, something; anything at that moment to take my mind away from those thoughts that were so terrible that no-one on this earth could have imagined for even a moment how I felt just then. As I left the study, I pulled the door closed behind me, and, as I did, I could have sworn that I heard the sound of quiet laughter coming from within the room. I was too afraid to look back, or to open the door, not just yet anyway.

THIRTY-FIVE

DEADLINE

THE KITCHEN FELT warm and inviting after the chill that had fallen over me in the study. Perhaps that was an illusion created by my mind as a result of being surrounded by the ordinariness of kettle, fridge, and the implements of day to day life. As I sat in the fireside chair, hugging a steaming hot cup of coffee, (laced with a shot of whisky), to my chest I tried to rationalise the last few minutes in the study, to bring myself back to a sense of reality, and escape from the surreal and imagined terrors that were taking hold of my conscious mind.

For the umpteenth time I told myself that Jack the Ripper had been dead for around a hundred years, and that it was impossible for his soul, or his spirit, call it what you will, to have survived in some form by investing itself into the pages of a crumpled and weary old journal. Over and over again I repeated that to myself, trying to convince my own mind that I was being totally irrational, and very, very stupid. Why then, despite my so-called logical and intelligent mind did I fail to totally believe myself?

I certainly didn't believe in reincarnation or the spirit world. Ghosts had no part to play in my life. They were the figments of people's overactive imaginations, useful for use by authors and TV executives as a means of producing fictional tales to entertain and terrify the gullible amongst their audiences. So why couldn't I shake off the feeling that something out of the ordinary was happening to me, here in the apparent safety and security of my own home?

My head was aching and every muscle in my body had tensed up, so that I suddenly realised that I was sitting as though I were stiff as a board. I tried to relax, to slow my breathing down. I closed my eyes, hoping to let some of that tension dissipate from my mind. Instead, all I saw in my mind's eye were those terrible images from my nightmares, the wraith like spirits and tortured souls of the Ripper's victims, twisting in their agonies and crying out for help, for release from their eternal torment. I opened my eyes again and rose from the chair. I dragged my weary limbs across to the kitchen sink and splashed copious amounts of cold water on my face, trying to shock myself into the real world, wanting, but not succeeding to force the feelings of dread and foreboding from my mind.

No matter how hard I tried to convince myself otherwise, I couldn't escape the hold that the journal and its writer had exerted over me. It was as though I were trapped in a kind of limbo world, halfway between the reality of my previous life, (it was only a couple of days ago), and the strange half-life that I seemed to be existing in as I trawled through the journal's blood steeped pages. The worrying thought that was growing in my mind was of what would happen to me when I reached the end of the journal? Would I be able to simply put the pages away, and return to the life I'd led before I'd known of its existence, or had I somehow been condemned to live the rest of my life haunted by the knowledge contained within those pages, to live forever in the shadow of the Ripper?

I felt as though a chasm had opened up before me, and that something beyond the boundaries of everyday reality was inexorably pulling me ever closer to its edge. It would take a supreme force of will to retain my grip on what was real and what was not, as the danger grew in my mind that I was slipping into another time, another place. Why else would I be receiving such real and graphic images of the Ripper's victims, his crimes, and why also did I feel as though I were beginning to understand him so well, as if I were peering through a window into his mind?

As these and more disturbing thoughts and emotions filled my head I was pulled back from that dark place by the sudden, shrill, and welcome sound of the telephone ringing. Wanting it to be Sarah, I virtually leaped from the chair and sprang across the room to where the kitchen phone hung on the wall, snatching it from its cradle as though my life or at least my sanity depended upon speaking to my wife. It was Mrs Armitage!

"Robert, are you alright? I spoke to Sarah and she's worried about you, she thinks you're making yourself ill, so I said I'd check on you."

My reply was terse, and perhaps a little unfair, as my neighbour had only my best interests at heart.

"Mrs Armitage, I'm fine, I've told Sarah that, and now I'm telling you the same. Why can't you just leave me alone? I'm terribly busy, now will you please just leave me in peace?"

"Well, alright Robert, if you're sure, but there's no need to be nasty you know. I'm only trying to help."

"Goodbye Mr. Armitage!" I snapped, ungraciously, and hung up on the poor woman. I was instantly sorry if I'd offended her, and contemplated calling her back to apologise, but thought better of it. I knew she must have been horrified to hear the usually mild-mannered Doctor Cavendish speaking to her in such a harsh and perfunctory manner, but I had so wanted it to be Sarah on the phone, and had been intensely disappointed when it turned out to be our neighbour, that I'd literally 'gone off the deep end'. I thought it best to leave her to get over it, which I was sure she would do in no time.

I picked up the phone and dialled my sister-in-law's number. If Sarah wasn't going to call me then I'd call her. Jennifer answered on the second ring, and as soon as I spoke she must have sensed that all wasn't well with her brother-in-law.

"Robert, you sound awful! What are you doing to yourself over there in that house on your own? You sound so tired, and, well, just not yourself. Hang on, I'll get Sarah."

That was just like Jennifer. She'd make her point, and then, without waiting for you to answer, she'd act on it. She'd simply dropped the phone and gone to get her sister, my wife, and she didn't take long. In just a few seconds, Sarah came on the line. It took me ten minutes to convince my wife that I was ok, and to stop her jumping in the car there and then and heading home to be with me. As much as I missed her and needed her I didn't want Sarah anywhere near the house until I'd completed my terrible journey through the Ripper's journal. I just felt that, somehow, it wouldn't be safe for her to be with me until I could re-seal the package and place the journal out of sight of the world once again.

She relented in the end but said that she'd definitely be home the next evening, which left me with just over twenty-four hours to finish the journal, and my great-grandfathers notes along with it. We swapped "I love you's", and I replaced the phone on the wall, made yet another cup of coffee, and with a sense of grim determination, and a desire to try to finish the thing by the next morning if I could, I made my way back to the study.

It was there, right where I'd left it. The journal, the thing that had taken my mind over almost completely in the space of one and a bit days, was waiting for me, waiting to tell me its secrets, and I was drawn to the desk as never before, knowing that my great-uncle was waiting to tell me the rest of his story. I couldn't get away from that fact. He *was* my great uncle, despite his illegitimacy, he had been the son of my great-grandfather, and something of him must therefore exist in me.

That's what was frightening me so much, the fact that the bloodline of my great-grandfather ran as much in the Ripper's veins as it did in mine. OK, his mother and my great-grandmother were different people, but we still had the common factor of my great-grandfather joining us together, and we *were* joined, somehow, in a way I didn't understand. The journal was the link, the thing that had brought us together, and now held us trapped in a strange nether world, not quite of his time, or mine. Somehow I had to break free, escape the journal's hold and place myself firmly back in the reality of the twentieth century, and I knew that I had to do it before Sarah came home. The journal could not be left exposed when she returned, something told me that; a voice in the back of my mind, a warning, and now that I had that deadline to work with, the need to complete my reading of the journal became greater with each passing second.

I walked across the study, my eyes never leaving the journal for a second as I did so, and I sat once more in my comfortable leather office chair, and reached out to the pages, feeling the strange warmth of the worn and weathered paper as my trembling hands closed over them, and I began the final stages of my extraordinary journey through that other time and place, accompanied by the words, the thoughts, and the deeds of Jack the Ripper.

THIRTY-SIX
A MOTIVE FOR THE RIPPER?

TIME WAS RUNNING OUT, for me, the Ripper, and for Mary Jane Kelly. It was strange I know that I felt like that. After all, the Ripper and his victim had both been dead for many years, and there was no reason why I should be thinking about them in real time, as though it were all happening in the present. Something about the journal however had enveloped my senses to the degree that it was impossible to think of what I was reading as a purely historical document. It was definitely having the effect of drawing me into its own macabre world of insanity and violent death.

If I'd been able to view my own situation from the outside, as a doctor viewing a patient I would have been seriously concerned about the state of mind of that patient. As it was of course, I couldn't see what was happening to me, though I was aware of some change taking place in my normal rational way of thinking. All I knew was that Mary Kelly had less than a week of life left to her, and that there was nothing I could do to alter that fact. My great-grandfather had known the Ripper, been witness to his confession of sorts, and had failed to believe him to be the murderer. Something had happened to change his mind, but whatever that was hadn't yet been revealed. I now felt as if I too knew the killer, almost as well as my own ancestor. His name had become an irrelevance, I had a shrewd idea who he was from comparing my great-grandfather's story with the known facts about the suspects in my notes, but it didn't matter any more. There were those of course who would have given almost anything to learn that name, to solve once and for all the mystery of Jack the Ripper's identity, but the more I became pulled into the strange vortex of hypnotic words created in the pages of the journal, the more I realised why my father and grandfather had continued to keep the secret. I'd begun to realise that this was a private, family matter, and that there was more to come, which I felt would confirm their decisions to keep silent as being the correct one to make.

I mentally steeled myself for the next instalment of the Ripper's story, and, as the light outside my window began to fade with the onset of dusk, I began to read once more.

5th November 1888

The pain in my head grows worse by the hour. I am damned by this suffering. The voices scream so loud, but I dare not yet venture out, my eyes are clouded, there is darkness everywhere. The world can wait a little longer, the whore shall die when I am ready, let her think herself safe, clever little whore!

***

6ᵗʰ November 1888

*The newspapers are still full of Jack. They see me
everywhere and nowhere. How many arrests have the
coppers made so far? So many letters they receive, but
they are not mine. They will know soon enough who is
real and who is not. The police are next to useless, they
speak of strange things concerning me, of messages that
I have left, when I have been silent for so long. Are they
so desperate that they invent things about me? Or are
they stupid? Yes they are.*
They cannot lay a hand on me
I'm Jack the Ripper, I'm still running free.
Hehehe

The page ended there, and I could see nothing but a further
degeneration in the mind of the writer. He was slipping into a
world removed from reality, and his words were less lucid, more
staccato, as though he were losing the ability to form full
sentences. His recent use of short rhymes, always in mocking
tones, suggested to me that he was arriving at a point in his
illness where certain of his brain functions were deteriorating,
and he was losing his ability to communicate coherently. The
'screaming voices' in his head were beginning to take over
completely, and he would soon be nothing more than a tool of
his own insanity.

The headaches were worse; he was now suffering from
what may have been quite intolerable pain. Laudanum would
have been of little use to him now, at least not as a means of
deadening the pain. All it would do was fuel his hallucinatory
state, causing him to sweat and shake, and in short, make the
headaches worse.

I turned to the next page, my hands trembling more than
ever. I knew that time was short, not just for me, if I wanted to
complete my strange literary odyssey before Sarah's return, but

also for the Ripper, who was now just a couple of days away from committing his most gruesome and 'memorable' act of violence. How strange to think that, at the time, I felt that the events in the journal were actually happening as I read them, and I was a traveller in time, on a journey over which I had no control. Only by reaching the end could I hope to step off the grim treadmill of death and mutilation perpetrated by my own ancestor, and to which he was giving me, (so I thought), a bizarre and surreal guided tour.

8ᵗʰ November 1888

Yesterday was useless. No food, little sleep, and so much pain. I must strike soon, and this time they will have known nothing like it before. They shall have no excuse to forget my work. As for Cavendish, this time he must believe me, I shall write to him in advance of the deed, and he must, he will believe me, and know that I have succeeded in the quest I have been set.
Today is better, I have my thoughts together again, and the voices are clear as to my course. It will not be long now; I know I am ready to go back to the streets, to set free the river of blood that must flow, to strike terror into the hearts of every damned whore who dares to pollute the streets of London with their filth.

Mary, Mary, little Mary, how red your blood will run Mary, Mary, filthy whore Mary, your time has nearly come.

I shall visit little Mary this very night, though I have no leather aprons left, no matter, I shall not need one, for my plans are well-laid, and I shall work undisturbed in peace this night. Mr Bazalgette's highway shall lead me there, and guide me home, and no-one shall be the wiser of my comings and my goings. Now, a letter to Cavendish, then sleep, for I shall need my energies when darkness falls.

So, the time had come, the 7th November had been dismissed in a few words, the man was ill, too ill to eat or sleep. It was doubtful if he'd ventured out that day, he didn't mention it, and I would have been amazed if he'd dared to show himself in public in such a state as he was in. No, he'd lain low, gathering his strength for this night to come, when he would make a mark so strong on history that his crime would resound not just around London, but, due to the ferocity and severity of the assault on Mary Kelly, around the entire civilised world.

The Ripper had lost none of his cunning and guile however, of that I was sure. That was evidenced by his desire to write to my great-grandfather, his father, and inform him of his intentions. Of course, by sending it on the day before the killing he gave Burton Cavendish no time to prevent him carrying out the murder, but he seemed to have a strange, twisted need for his father to perhaps feel a sense of 'pride' or admiration in his 'work'. After all, he thought he was doing the right thing, he saw no crime in what he was doing, for he was on a mission!

I wondered for a moment if my great-grandfather had placed the letter from the Ripper somewhere within the pages of the journal, as he had his own notes. I would soon find out, there weren't many pages left, and I was growing more and more impatient to reach the end of this strange and terrifying journey into the past. It was imperative that I finish it before my wife came home. I had to remove all traces of the infernal yellowed musty pages, infused as they were with the soul of the murderer, and dripping with the horrors of his deeds, before Sarah walked through the door.

I took a quick break from the task, just long enough to visit the bathroom, where a look in the mirror told me that Sarah would not be pleased to see me in such a state, followed by a visit to the kitchen to prepare a pot of coffee which I took with me as I returned to the study.

As I sat down once again at my desk, I realised that there had been a change in the atmosphere of the room. The afternoon had drawn towards its close, and it was growing darker. Not only that, but I sensed that the sounds of the occasional cars that passed the end of my driveway were muffled, as though their wheels had been fitted with padding of some sort. I looked through the window and saw that a dense bank of fog had descended, bringing that strange, other-worldly stillness to the world outside my house. Everything was still, there were no sounds of birds in the garden, the branches of the trees were dripping with the precipitation caused by the damp air, and in my increasingly fanciful state of mind, I imagined that they were sweating with the dread anticipation of the horrors to come that very night. I knew it, I was doing it again, thinking in terms of the journal being set in real time, I was reading history, not participating in it, and yet...

Having already studied the facts of the Mary Kelly case I felt that I was now prepared as much as I could be for the Ripper's own version of events. I picked up the journal and began where I'd left off.

9th November 1888.

The afternoon is drawing late, darkness falls, and I am tired. I have achieved near perfection. The whore Kelly was fool enough to invite me to her 'home', that hovel in Miller's Court. I charmed her so well she suspected nothing, though she struggled to begin with. I was forced to strangle the dirty bitch before I could cut her. She screamed once, I thought she may have been heard and the game was up, but screams are so common amongst her class no-one came near. I stripped myself and sliced the whore into so many pieces, the blood was everywhere, it was such a sight. I took her filthy body apart, took out her entrails and sliced her dirty little whore's breasts off completely. I spread her out and flensed her well; she looked a pretty picture I should say. The walls ran red with so much blood, oh what a time I had, and the voices screamed and cheered me on as though I were a thoroughbred approaching the finishing line in the Derby. The press have done me proud, I have every headline in London, my, but they found her quick. Now Cavendish will believe me and know who and what I am!

No more Mary, how contrary, you've lost your whoring heart
Mary's dead, where's her heart? Gone in the knacker man's cart.

That was it; all there was to describe the most gruesome murder perpetrated by the Ripper. He had made no attempt to gloat or elaborate in detail on the mutilations he'd inflicted upon the poor girl's body, Compared with the references he'd made to some of the earlier murders this was quite tame, as though the actual act of murder had ceased to excite him as it may have done in the beginning.

Poor Mary Jane Kelly had been enticed by his charm to take her killer back to her own lodgings, where he'd stripped himself to avoid getting too much blood on his clothes before embarking on the appalling mutilations that were to stun and horrify even the most hardened police officers who visited the scene of her murder upon the discovery of her body. Such was the effect of the crime upon them that, in the belief that a victim's eyes might record the last thing they saw, Sir Charles Warren ordered that the girl's eyes be photographed with a special lens in the hope that the image of her killer may have been recorded there. Of course, there was no such image to be found.

As I sat there at my desk, with the darkness of the day closed in around the house, and the fog swirling ever closer to the window, a sudden, chilling thought struck me. Maybe, just maybe, I had stumbled upon the Ripper's motive for the killings. I had already referred to the possibility that he was seeking some sort of recognition from Burton Cavendish. What if it were as simple as that? In his sick and twisted mind, having only recently discovered the truth of his heritage, and with his own mother dead and buried after being declared insane could he actually have believed that he must perform this strange and escalating series of bloody murders in order to gain his father's respect and ensure that he was aware of his illegitimate son's prowess in his chosen 'profession'? In my humble professional opinion, I had to think to myself that it was possible. The whole series of the Jack the Ripper killings could have been nothing more than a cry for attention by an illegitimate child, seeking recognition from his father. In his sick and tormented mind, that could easily have been the case, and his desire to be noticed by his father, to be seen as a person who wielded considerable power and expertise (as my great-grandfather did in his own profession) really could have led him to commit the murders. After all, had he not constantly 'confessed' to my great-grandfather, only to be disbelieved and dismissed as a fantasist, someone trying to attach himself to the Ripper's coat-tails in a desire for attention? Equally, after every rejection of his confessions the severity of his crimes, the degree of mutilation of the victims grew and grew, until his fury exploded like an erupting volcano with the hideous destruction of the person of Mary Jane Kelly. It made sense to me at that point. If my great-grandfather wouldn't believe him, he would go out and do something even more revolting and repugnant in an attempt to shock, or to make 'Cavendish' take notice of him. Eventually he had written a letter, though I had no idea at that time what it contained, informing my great-grandfather of his intentions. I felt that it was all there, in the last line before the silly rhyme, *'Now Cavendish will believe me' That* was what he'd wanted all along, his father's recognition!

As for the rhyme, it was true that Kelly's heart was missing when her body was examined. That mystery was now also explained. There had been many theories at the time, The Ripper had eaten it, or, he'd taken it home and kept it as a trophy, the list went on and on. Instead, he'd cut it out, and at some time during the day I suspected, as opposed to on his way home, as there wouldn't be any horses and carts in the sewers, he'd simply thrown it into a passing knacker-mans cart, along with the remains of any number of dead horses on their way to be burned no doubt. Yes, to me that made sense, he would see it as a fitting end for the heart of a whore, to be burned, so that her heart and soul would be forever engulfed in the flames of Hell.

I felt a sudden terror and a shiver ran through my body as a thought shot to the forefront of my brain. In those last few seconds, as the realisation of his thoughts had come to me I had suddenly felt as though I knew exactly what he'd been thinking when he'd tossed Mary Kelly's heart in that cart; for a few short seconds, I had actually sensed the thoughts that had run through the mind of Jack the Ripper.

That couldn't be true of course could it? At least, that's what I told myself, I was just being fanciful, I was tired, and more than a little disturbed by the effect the journal had exerted upon me these last couple of days, that was all. After all, no-one could sense or feel the thoughts of a dead man, now could they?

I looked up from the desk, it was now almost dark outside, the fog was like an impenetrable cloud, and I realised that I was almost sitting in darkness in the study. I got up, turned the lights on full, and returned to the desk. I couldn't stop now, I had to go on, I just had to.

THIRTY-SEVEN
AN END IN SIGHT

So, now I felt I was close to the conclusion of the terrible saga to which I'd been suddenly introduced by my own dead father. I kept asking myself the same question. Could it really be possible that Jack the Ripper had been born out of one man's insane desire to gain the recognition of the father he'd never known? The more I pondered on the question the more the answer became clearer. It was eminently possible, and I knew, as a psychiatrist, that the sick and diseased mind of an individual can easily take an idea and twist it until putting it into practice becomes totally logical to him or her.

His lack of detail in describing the murder of Mary Kelly, or the scene of utter devastation that he left in the form of her butchered remains convinced me that the murder itself was almost superfluous to his real motive. The gathering severity of each crime now took on a different perspective, as though only by increasing the scale of brutality and mutilation could he hope to 'impress' his father.

In fact the scene that greeted those who witnessed the

aftermath of his 'work' at 13 Millers Court was so horrendous that grown men cried, were physically sick, and many later reported that the sight of her butchered corpse would live forever in their minds. Her clothes had been neatly placed on a chair beside her bed, leaving her naked and exposed. The room itself was like a charnel house, with blood on the walls, the floor, and almost every solid object. Butchery was almost too polite a word for what the Ripper had done to the poor girl's body. As I've described earlier in my report on the post mortem examination, he had literally cut her to pieces. Body parts were strewn around the room, though there was nothing haphazard about their distribution. He had quite carefully placed each piece of dismembered flesh or limb in precise locations, there was certainly no evidence that they'd been thrown in a frenzy or in a random way. Perhaps the thing that caused the most consternation in the minds of the officers attending the scene that morning was the quite appalling mutilation of the girl's face, there was almost nothing left of it, and scarcely enough to positively identify the unfortunate victim, though no-one was in any doubt that it was Mary Jane Kelly. Her upper legs had been almost totally denuded of flesh, and her heart was missing, perhaps the cruellest cut of all.

Why then, did the Ripper choose to mention so little of this in his journal, if not for the fact that it meant so very little to him? I was sure that that was the reason, he just didn't care as such any more, and his voices would probably have told him that he'd done all they'd asked of him in order to justify his self to his father.

Why did I feel as though I knew these things? Once again I felt as though his thoughts had become mine, as if his mind had somehow entered into a parallel existence with my own, allowing me, at a distance of over one hundred years to see with perfect clarity the thoughts and machinations of his sick and deluded mind. Could a mere blood connection between us have caused such a thing to happen? The answer of course was no! I was becoming irrational and anxious myself, of that I was sure, though there seemed little I could do to stop myself from thinking and feeling those terrible thoughts, and I found myself growing increasingly apprehensive as to where the journal would eventually lead me, psychologically speaking. I knew that I would never be quite the same again but hoped that I would be sufficiently recovered from the tortuous task of reading the journal by the time Sarah got home the next evening.

First of course, I had to finish it. I needed to reach the end of the final page and discover whatever dark secrets might still be waiting for me in the words of the Ripper and of my great-grandfather.

Weariness was creeping into every muscle, every sinew, and as much as I wanted to complete my strange expedition into the past sooner rather than later, I knew I needed a break. I left the study and instead of heading for the kitchen, I headed down the hall and opened the front door, intending to refresh myself in the cool night air. Night had by then fallen completely, the darkness compounded by the fog that hung around my house like a shroud. The sound-dampening effect of the fog gave an eerie feel to the night, and as I stood looking out from the threshold of the house, I could have sworn that I could see strange ethereal shapes twisting and moving in the midst of that dark, grey-white cloud. There was a swish in the darkness, as though something had flown silently through the bank of fog, then I realised it was just the sound-deadened drone of an expensive and quiet car engine as a vehicle passed the entrance to the drive. The fog had brought an intense cold to the night, and I stood there shivering for a good five minutes as I attempted to gather my thoughts before returning to the study. I realised that my clothes were becoming damp and my shirt was clinging to my back, and decided to leave the fog, the night, and whatever sounds and apparitions they might wish to conjure, to themselves. I shut the door, and leaned against the oak panels, not moving until I began to feel a modicum of warmth returning to my body.

I told myself I should eat, and actually entered the kitchen with that intention before deciding that I was past the point of needing food, for this night anyway. I poured myself a large whisky and carried the bottle and my glass with me as I returned to my chair in the study, my window upon the world of the Ripper. Not wishing to starve myself completely, I also tucked under my arm a large packet of cheese biscuits, just in case the need to eat returned at some point in the night. So it was that I made myself comfortable once more and looked forward with a mixture of trepidation and anticipation to my third night in the company of Jack the Ripper. Would it provide me with satisfactory answers to the questions in my mind? Only time would tell, and time of course was a commodity that was beginning to run in short supply, after tonight, I had less than twenty four hours before Sarah returned, and I needed to be finished by then, my very own inner voice was telling me that, loud and clear.

I admit that I wasn't quite sure why, what effect it would have on her if she knew the truth about the journal, or even of its existence, but I did know that *under no circumstances* must Sarah ever see or know of the journal. It would place her at terrible risk, and again, I had no idea why, *I just knew.* What would I do with the journal when I'd finished it? Should I destroy it? Should I reseal it and lock it away in a safe, or lodge it with a solicitor as my father had done? Sarah and I had no children, so who would I leave it to if I kept it intact, and decided to maintain the family secret and tradition? As soon as I asked myself the question I knew the answer, and as much as it saddened me to burden a future generation with the thing that lay on my desk in front of me, I knew exactly what I had to do.

Deciding that to hesitate any longer would be futile, I made up my mind to plough on and try to disseminate the last few pages of the journal as quickly as I could. I poured another whisky and was quickly warmed by the amber liquid as it slipped easily down my throat. I stretched my arms out as far as they would go, and flexed my feet to try to maintain a decent level of blood circulation, as I intended to stay in my chair until I'd completed the task I'd set myself.

The sad and at the same time monstrous tale of the life of Jack the Ripper had been almost forced upon me by the hand of my dead father, placing me in a situation where I could do nothing other than sit and read the self-confessions of the long dead progeny of my great-grandfather. Now, I intended to read the journal to its conclusion, to read through the night if necessary, and finally to lay the ghost that appeared to have haunted every generation of my family from Victorian times to the present day. If the soul of Jack the Ripper were indeed somehow locked within the pages of his infamous and ghastly journal, imprinted by the words written with his own murderous hand, then I was determined to be the one who finally put an end to the journal's influence over my family. A new determination rose within me, a sense of boldness and bravado that I could outwit the evil soul of my illegitimate ancestor and ensure that his influence over our family was forever buried along with his own black heart, wherever that might be. Had I been able to see what was written on the concluding pages of the journal I might not have been so sure of myself, but such of course, is the folly of mere mortal man.

My hands reached out once more to lift the infernal journal of Jack the Ripper, and as I felt the strange and unearthly warmth of its pages once again, without warning, every light in the room went out and I was plunged into the ultimate psychological horror of total darkness!

THIRTY-EIGHT
A SINGLE VOICE, CRYING IN THE NIGHT

THE SUDDEN DESCENT into darkness played havoc with my increasingly fragile state of mind. I felt a surge of panic, and twisted in my seat, fully expecting to see some glowing spectral figure hovering in the doorway, ready to whisk me off to the spirit world, or worse. I was like a child who wakes in the night, filled with dread from a nightmare, imaging monsters to be hiding under the bed, or snakes creeping from out of the walls, but of course, Dr Robert Cavendish didn't believe in monsters, did I?

I sat rooted to the spot, unable to raise myself from the chair for at least a minute, until the trembling in my frame began to subside, and rationality took over my mind. Logic dictated that one of two things had happened. Either a power cut had occurred, or a fuse had blown, taking the lights with it. I fumbled around in the dark until I managed to open the bottom drawer of my desk where I kept a small penlight torch, as I was always losing things behind the desk, and especially behind the computer hard drive. The little torch had proved its worth many times in the past, and at last my groping fingers made contact with its familiar shape amongst the drawer's contents.

With a sense of relief it burst into life at the flick of the 'on' switch, and at least I had a sliver of light by which to negotiate my way to the fuse box under the stairs. I was still slightly apprehensive as I set off, half-expecting to be waylaid by that spectral figure that lingered in the back of my mind, but I made it safely to the door under the stairs and quickly saw the cause of the problem. Something, a short circuit perhaps, had caused the main fuse to blow, and the circuit breaker had tripped and sent me plummeting into that surprisingly frightening darkness. As I pushed the switch on the circuit breaker back to its rightful position I was rewarded with a flood of light from the kitchen doorway opposite my position, and relief washed over me like a tidal wave.

Feeling quite foolish at having allowed myself to become so spooked by a simple thing like a blown fuse I made my way sheepishly into the kitchen, in need of coffee, and its stimulating properties. I switched on the radio as the kettle boiled and as I sat at the table with the hot steaming mug in my hand the late evening news was being reported by the local radio station. In a grim voice the newscaster was announcing that the suspect in case of the two local murders, John Trevor Ross, had been found hanging in his cell that afternoon. He had been declared dead on arrival at the hospital. In a further revelation it appeared that Ross's family had been connected by marriage to the family of one of the original suspects in the Jack the Ripper case over a hundred years earlier, though the police refused to release the family name connected with the case.

I felt as though I'd been struck by a thunderbolt. I didn't hear another word as the newscaster continued with the bulletin. All I could think of was the fact that John Ross, like me, had some link with the Ripper, though admittedly the newscaster had only said that he was distantly related to one of the suspects, and hadn't been able to reveal which one. I was in no doubt however that it was true. Somewhere, along the course of history's time line, both John Ross and I had been touched by the curse of the Ripper, and he had perhaps taken the only way out he knew in order to escape that curse, to prevent himself descending further into the insane madness that had suddenly and overwhelmingly taken hold of him. The coincidence of his having been brought to me as patient was further proof, at least to my own way of thinking, that the Ripper had reached out across the years to take a hold on the lives of his distant, if only loosely related descendants. Perhaps, like my great-grandfather I had been given a chance to help John Ross, to save him from the awful illness that had taken hold of him and led him to commit such brutal murder. If that was the case, then, like my great-grandfather, I appeared to have failed. The only help I'd given him had been to prescribe drugs to control what I thought was a mild paranoia, and eventually to advise him to co-operate with the police, when perhaps he might have benefited from a more sympathetic approach.

Reality seemed a million miles away as I made my way, with leaden feet back to the study, chiding myself all the way to my chair. I had entered a world that was so far removed from the safe sane one I usually inhabited that I wondered if I'd blundered into a nightmare of my own making, allowing myself to have become so affected by the words of the Ripper as contained in the musty yellow pages which, even now, were drawing me like a magnet towards them once more. But no, it was more than that. I was sure there was definitely something out of the ordinary taking place, and, though I wasn't sure what it was or where it was leading me, I was now more determined than ever to see the whole thing through to the end. John Trevor Ross may himself have had some tenuous relationship to me, or the Ripper, or even my great-grandfather, and through him, to me; I just didn't know, but I was sure as hell not going to give up now! I made myself a mental promise to contact his mother in the next couple of days, make sure she was ok, though of course she couldn't possibly be. She'd just lost her son, bad enough that he'd been diagnosed as suffering from a mental illness, but he'd gone on to commit two murders, he'd taken the lives of two innocent women, and probably destroyed the futures of their husbands and families. It was as if, even after all this time, the evil that was Jack the Ripper was still at work, and along with the two most recent victims, John Trevor Ross himself had fallen victim to the hands of the killer and become yet another gruesome addition to the list of those whose lives had been torn apart by the Whitechapel Murderer.

With a weary sigh, I switched on and re-booted the computer, in case I needed to refer to the Casebook website again and reclined into the comfort of the leather chair. I had a feeling it was going to be a long night, and that it would be some time before I managed to lay my head down to sleep.

As I lifted the journal from my desk, I was once again subjected to the strange feeling that came from handling its strangely warm and sticky pages. I still couldn't get away from the thought that somehow it was infused or imprinted with the essence of the Ripper's evil, and that to merely touch it brought me in direct with the soul of the killer. Despite, or perhaps because of that feeling, I was impatient to read whatever came next in his horrendous memoir, and to see if my great-grandfather would cast any further light on whatever other terrible secret he seemed to have previously hinted at.

14th November 1888

I have languished these last days in a terrible state. Why hasn't Cavendish come? He must have received my letter; he must know by now that I have told him the truth. My head is in such ferment, such pain. I have done all that the voices have asked of me, and now they have deserted me, I am alone. They have not spoken one word to me since I put that whore Kelly to sleep. Have I displeased them? They do not even whisper in my head any longer. Shall I spill more blood, was it not enough that I sliced and gutted the whore until I could scarce stand up, so weary did the work make me? And so deep did it run upon the floor that her blood fair made me slip upon it as I tried to stand still to complete the task. Two days I say, two days it took to finally wash the whore's blood from my self, and even though I removed and covered up my clothes still there was so much of the stuff that her blood stained even my shirt and my socks, so much so that I have burned them.
I called out in the night, but they will not come, my voices are so silent. Where are they? Why have they left me alone? Where is Cavendish? He must come; he is the only one who knows. He will tell me what to do.

***

20th November 1888

I am losing track of time and days. I can no longer work, and they will surely not let me back now. I have heard nothing from Cavendish, yet the whole of London is

*ablaze with news of the Ripper, of me, of what I have
done to rid the city of the whores. Every newspaper, on
every street corner screams out of my prowess, and the
police still blunder forth in fruitless search for Jack, and
I am here all the time, but where is Cavendish?*

I found something almost pitiful about the latest entries in the
journal of Jack the Ripper. He had become almost childlike in
his cries for help. His voices were gone, as if in perpetrating the
final and most hideous murder of his career to date his own
mind, that which in reality had created his voices, had switched
off that part of itself, perhaps in a sort of self-defence
mechanism, as though deep down, in the most secretive and
complex depths of his mind, even Jack the Ripper had become
appalled and revolted at the scale of his crime. He was crying in
the night, crying for help that would not come, and he was
certainly desperate for my great-grandfather to attend upon
him. After all, over a week had now passed since the terrible
night of Mary Kelly's death, and he would have expected some
response from my great-grandfather by that time, assuming of
course that he'd received the Ripper's letter.

I was intrigued by his mention of losing his job. This at
least confirmed that up until some point at least, he was
engaged in gainful employment. I thought, having formed my
own opinion of his identity that I knew exactly where he
worked and in what capacity, and in some ways this admission
in the journal further confirmed my thoughts of his identity.
This fitted well with the facts I had ascertained from my notes.

There were now so few pages left in the journal, and I was
confident that I would be able to complete my reading of it by

277

my own self-imposed deadline. I just wished, like the Ripper, that I could understand why my great-grandfather hadn't responded to the letter, to his advance warning of the murder of Mary Kelly. The answer to that question was soon to be revealed to me and was almost as intriguing as anything I had read over the previous three days!

THIRTY-NINE
A QUESTION OF ETHICS?

As I TURNED YET another page in the grim story that was unfolding before me, the words of my great-grandfather were once again lying in wait for me, as before, tucked tightly between the pages of the Ripper's journal. The explanation for his not having responded to the Rippers letter was staring at me as I began to read incredulously his latest addition to the journal.

My son,

It is well after the fact that I sit and write this note, which I hereby append to the awful tale you are now reading. As you know, events in London took a terrible turn in the weeks of Autumn, 1888, and, after my dear friend Sir William was spoken to at length and on various occasions, it was of course my turn. As you know, the police interviewed me, in addition to any

number of eminent (and not so eminent) members of my
profession, it having been widely suggested by many so-
called experts that Jack the Ripper was a doctor. I
cannot for the life of me conceive that anyone would
seriously suggest such a thing, yet the official police force
seemed to have granted the theory some degree of
credibility. The inspector, whose name was Abberline,
was quite polite, but seemed to carry out the interview
with no great conviction, as though he deemed me
irrelevant to the case, and was merely questioning me on
the orders of some superior.

I am grateful to you for having received me so graciously
after the ordeal of spending so many hours in the
company of those worthy officers of the law, who I
managed to satisfy as to my personal innocence. I
cannot thank you enough for your warm hospitality and
for allowing me to spend those few days in the comfort
and sanctuary of your home.
You can imagine my disbelief, and my shock then, when,
on returning home, I found there, lying in wait for me, a
letter of the most heinous kind, and by it's contents I was
perplexed and at the same time damned by my previous
inability to grasp the truth and to act upon it.

I insert this note at this point in the journal as it is to my
mind the relevant location for it. Why did I not believe
his earlier attempts to confess his guilt to me? I can
never answer that, though now I will surely be damned
for all time. He wrote to me in advance of the killing of
the poor woman Mary Jane Kelly, and detailed for me
the injuries and mutilations he fully intended to carry
out upon the person of that poor unfortunate. Had I not

*been ensconced first of all with the officers of Scotland
Yard, and thereafter a guest in your home, I would have
found the letter the day after the crime. As it was, it had
fallen to me to discover the awful truth too late, and my
heart and mind were fearful and undecided as to the
correct course of action to pursue.*

*Had I disclosed the information I am now privy to it
would not only have destroyed the good name of our
family, but would doubtless lead to the arrest, trial, and
probable execution of the man who was after all, your
half-brother, my own son. Despite the fact that he was
most seriously ill with the most foul disease of the mind,
I knew that the cries for retribution would have led to
his being denied the defence of insanity, the public
needed revenge, and I am sure it would have swift and
terminal. I wished to spare him, and his mother's
memory that disgrace. Though I do not expect you to
have any thought or feeling for the man, who you have
never, and will never meet, please think of the quandary
that so beset my mind. If I turned in evidence against
him, and my own shortcomings in the case were
revealed, not only would my professional reputation be
visibly and most publicly brought into disrepute, but
think also of the effect that such a revelation would have
had on your poor mother. She of course knows nothing of
his existence, and I intend that she never will.*

*I had to decide what best to do, for I could not of course
allow him to continue to kill and mutilate his fellow
beings; that goes without saying. His employer, a man of
great compassion and forbearance would appear to be
losing patience with his continued absences caused by*

his 'illness'. How he has continued to even attempt to carry on with his daily routine of life is beyond my ken. He has duped not only me, but the entire world around him. How could he have perpetrated such fiendish crimes and continued to live a normal life in the face of such damnable acts? Time was running out, for me and for him, I had to act, to put an end to the killing, and to prevent a scandal that would destroy your mother, you, and everyone connected with the family.

Read the conclusion of the journal my son, and then let my actions be judged by you alone, for it is with your future in mind that I have done the things I have done. When you have read what is yet to be revealed I beg of you to forgive me, and, if it possible, somewhere in your heart, forgive the man who was your brother, for he was incapable of preventing the fate that destroyed his life.

Your father, Burton Cleveland Cavendish

A sense of fear and helplessness was beginning to envelop me as I placed the journal down lightly on the desk. My own great-grandfather had himself been interviewed and questioned by the police, and by Frederick Abberline himself, famous as one of the leading detectives in the hunt for Jack the Ripper. My great-grandfather had missed receiving the Ripper's letter because he had gone to stay with my grandfather, Merlin Cavendish after his discharge from the police station. He'd spent a number of days there; that much was plain by his words and in so doing had perhaps made his own position harder to sustain when he eventually did receive the letter. The police may have wished to know why he had delayed in passing on the information supplied by the Ripper and may not have immediately believed his story of having stayed with my grandfather without having returned to his own home first.

Not only that, but I understood how he must have felt, finally realising that his own bastard son had been telling him the truth all along. He really was Jack the Ripper, and my great-grandfather could, as he had said in his original letter at the beginning of the journal, have done something to stop him! I could only begin to imagine the turmoil he must have felt. How does one admit, and then decide what to do when faced with the fact that one's own son is the most hated and evil murderer in living memory, with all of London holding its breath as they followed the police investigation, waiting and hoping for the arrest of the monster they lived in fear of?

A greater fear had gripped me however, the fear that a far greater secret was hidden just around the corner, that my great-grandfather was still holding something back. Now that his connection to the Ripper had been most firmly established in my mind, I needed to know what had happened to both of these antecedents of mine after the conclusion of the murders. I knew of course, roughly, what had happened to my great-grandfather. Burton Cleveland Cavendish had retired in 1889, (I think), and had left the city of London, settling with my great-grandmother and his son, (my grandfather) not too far from where I live today. Of course it would have been far more 'countrified' in those days, and they would in all probability have lived a fairly comfortable, almost idyllic life. He had died at home peacefully not long before the outbreak of The Great War, soon after my great-grandmother, (it was said by my father that he had died of a broken heart, unable to go on without the love of his life). No major events in his life had been recorded or passed down in the family history, and until now, I had never had reason to think of him as being any different from any other respectable Victorian medical professional. That of course left me with the one, burning question. What had happened to the Ripper after the murder of Mary Jane Kelly? The thought suddenly struck me that the journal or my great-grandfather's notes may not be completely comprehensive on the matter, and that thought terrified me more than I can possibly relate in words.

I *had* to know what had happened to him! It had become the single most important requirement of my life. As I sat there in my study, with the house enshrouded in fog, cut off from the real world by thoughts real and imagined, and all manner of demons playing within my mind, I knew that my own future, like that of my grandfather's, would depend on discovering the fate of the killer of Mary Kelly and the other poor unfortunates who suffered at his hands. Such would be the mental turmoil were I to be left in the dark about the conclusion of my great-grandfather's involvement with the Ripper, and the subsequent actions taken by both of them, that I knew that my own sanity was also very much on the line. In less than three whole days, my world had been turned upside-down, my mind taken on a journey into a strange and terrifying world where the realities of time and space had appeared to be suspended, at least within the confines of my study. I was now on the verge of discovering the conclusion of this strange and compelling sojourn into the world of the surreal, and I had to be able to dispel the irrational thoughts that threatened to take hold of my psyche. I needed to be able to dismiss the Ripper and his insanity from my world, and return it, and him to the pages of history where he belonged.

The hands on the clock seemed to be in a hurry to reach midnight as I prepared myself for the concluding pages of the journal. The pile of pages was now thin, and there couldn't be much left. I just had to hope that what I needed to know would be waiting for me as I turned a page once again, and saw the handwriting of the Ripper reaching out to me from another faded yellow, yet still warm and sticky leaf of the incredible journal of Jack the Ripper.

FORTY
A TIME OF DECISION

The date is uncertain. My last few days have passed in a haze, and I have not dared to venture out. I am in such pain; such turmoil and I know that I am becoming worse. My voices have deserted me, they are silent, and I am alone, though perhaps not quite. Cavendish at last came to see me. He was much affected by my appearance and demeanour, and was I think quite sympathetic toward me though he exhibited such horror at his belief in my pronunciations at last. He knows the truth now, and I am sure he will not turn against me, the fruit of his loins. Ha! He has advised that I stay within the walls of my home and has promised to visit each day and to care for my ills and ailments. He has prescribed for me, and the effects of the drug are quite debilitating. I can scarce move from my chair but must from time to time to eat and drink. He has assured me that all will be well, and that he will ensure I am well provided for. I must not continue in my work, he has made that clear, though I admit I have no desire to slit another whore.

The smell of the blood of the last slut is still heavy in my nostrils, and the sight of the meat that I sliced from her body is engrained upon my eyes. I can do no more, for now at least. I have showed Cavendish this journal, so that he is in no doubt of my claims. He read a portion, no more, and his shock was amusing. What a good man he is!

THIS ENTRY, undated by the writer revealed his rapid descent into a sort of fugue, he was becoming lost. Perhaps he was becoming more and more detached from reality, the world outside having less meaning for him as time went by. He talked of my great-grandfather visiting him, and he appeared quite content that Burton Cavendish at last believed that he was Jack the Ripper. He showed no remorse for his crimes, simply a lack of desire to commit any further atrocities, at least for the moment. I assumed from his words that my great-grandfather had prescribed some form of sedation for him; in order perhaps to prevent him from becoming enraged enough to venture out into the streets once again in his desire for yet more bloodletting. Whether my great-grandfather was truly sympathetic towards him, or just trying to placate the man whist deciding on his next course of action I was yet to discern.

The answer to that question lay just around the corner, or should I say over the page, as I turned to the next leaf in the journal to find great-grandfather's words awaiting me once more.

Burton Cleveland Cavendish M.D. 30th November 1888,

My heart is heavy, my soul troubled. Though I would

not wish to admit it to a single living soul, I now know
the truth about the child I sired in such unfortunate
circumstances. For whatever reason, he has lost his mind
to the madness of insanity, and is the monster sought by
the police and the whole of the respectable population of
the land. How do you tell anyone that your own progeny
is none other than the murderer known to everyone as
'Jack the Ripper'? Knowing what happened to his poor
dear mother I should perhaps not be so surprised at his
state of health, but, even so, it saddens me that he has
sunk to this. I know that my duty lies in giving him over
to the constabulary, and yet, I cannot escape the fact that
he is not entirely responsible for his crimes, for he cannot
help the illness that has taken over his mind. I am sure
though, that no-one would believe that to be entirely true
and that the world would not be happy unless he were to
end his days swinging at the end of a rope. I can not
wish that gruesome end upon him, as much as his crimes
may demand brutal retribution. But, I am left with the
quandary of what I should do next. I have given him
medication, and that should keep him housebound for a
while, (as long as he takes it every day). If he stops, and
goes on to repeat his crimes, I should have no alternative
other than to give him up to the forces of the law.
My son, if you are reading this I must beg that you try
hard to understand the troubles of my mind. Would I be
less than sympathetic to your plight my son if it had
been you in such a troubled state of mind? Of course not,
and you would expect no less would you not?

Still, I have hard decisions to make. I cannot let him
simply go free to kill again, and if I were to admit him to
a hospital, his rantings and ravings would soon attract

*the wrong kind of attention, and my failure to act sooner
on his protestations of involvement in the killings would
have serious repercussions both for my career, and, I
fear, for the good name of our family, not to mention
breaking your poor mother's heart.*

*I have decided for the time being to visit him each and
every day, to try to keep him sufficiently sedated with
large doses of opiates until I know for certain the actions
I shall finally take to resolve the matter. I think I know
in my heart that there can be only one way to end this
once and for all, and to ensure that his name, and that of
the family remains unsullied. He must not be brought to
trial, and only I can prevent him from perpetrating more
atrocities. I must reconcile my heart and soul with God
and do what must be done.*

BCC.

The words of my great-grandfather chilled me through and
through, for I had no doubt as to his intended actions. He had
tried, I'm sure, to do everything he could for his illegitimate
offspring, but, on finding him to be the killer of those poor
unfortunate women, he had been placed in a virtually
impossible situation. How could he reveal the truth, without
shaming and exposing his own family to the slurs that would
surely be directed at them? Certainly, his professional
reputation would have been severely damaged by his
confessions of omission, his failure to act, based purely, (as it
would be seen), on his fatherly connection to the killer.

The sound of the clock on the wall suddenly intruded into

my thoughts, its constant ticking seeing to grow louder by the second. My head was filled with the sound, though in reality it must have been as quiet as it always was. The thud, thud, thud, of the second hand as it continued its journey around the clock face was becoming an incessant clamouring dissonance in my brain, and my head felt as though it were about to explode. Outside, the fog lay in a thick cloud around the house, and the dark starless night cast its pall upon my suddenly shrinking world. I was being gripped by a fever of panic, a fear that was threatening to engulf me and drag me into a strange world of half-remembered images and reminiscences, as though I were ready to lose myself in the thoughts and the deeds of those who had lived and died so long ago. Not for the first time since picking up the journal I was in danger of being lost to its incredible power, its strange stranglehold on me growing tighter by the second, and then, without conscious thought my mind broke free, and I threw the infernal thing from my hands, and as it crashed with a thud into the opposite wall of the study I was snapped back into the real world, my shaking hands slowly returning to normal, and my brain, my mind, regaining their grip on reality, long enough for me to gain my composure, and take long, deep breaths, until the pounding in my head had ceased, and I was once more left sitting quietly and alone in the chair, with the journal and its hideous contents lying in the corner of the room, against the wall where it had fallen.

I sat there for ten minutes without once trying to move from the chair. I simply sat staring at the journal, wondering how it could exert such an influence over me, how it could possibly engender such fear, such terrible thoughts within me, and most of all, how it could have brought me in so short a time to the brink of breaking point, to the edge of sanity and reason.

There was only one way to find out, one way to finally answer whatever questions about the Ripper remained in my mind. Finally, with a great effort, both mentally and physically, for my limbs seemed numb, I rose from the chair and moved to pick up the journal from where it lay. As I did so, I could have sworn I heard a sigh, low and weary from somewhere close to hand, but of course there was no-one there. It could only be my imagination.

With a deep sigh of resignation I seated myself once more and turned to the next page. I was shocked to see that it was blank, as was the next, and the next! I was struck by a rising tide of panic and terrible foreboding. Being only a few pages left in the journal it wasn't hard to see that the Ripper had made no further entries in his journal of terror. What had happened? Why had he suddenly stopped writing? Surely his ego, his sense of self aggrandizement and his need to justify himself, even in the privacy of his journal would not have made him give up making his entries. With a rising sense of panic, fearing that the answers to all the questions I still needed resolved would be denied to me, I flicked over page after page, and finally turned to the last two pages of the book, and there, between them, as had happened so often, was another note from my great-grandfather.

FORTY-ONE
THE LAST CONFESSION

WITH SHAKING HANDS, and with a grim sense of inevitability about what was about to come, I settled myself as comfortably as I could for what I assumed would be the conclusion of the tragedy that had befallen my family so many years ago. Barely able to contain my feelings of impatience and fascination, I began to read my great-grandfather's final entry in the hideous secret journal of Jack the Ripper.

January 1889

*Jack the Ripper is dead! There will be no more killing,
no more butchery of the innocent, though in putting an
end to the beast who stalked the streets of our city I have
sullied myself for all time, and only God in Heaven can
be my judge. I could no longer bear the torment of seeing
him in the state to which he had been reduced, both by
his illness, and by my own ministrations of increasing
doses of morphine, with which I hoped to sedate and*

*control him in those latter days. With each subsequent
visit he appeared to grow worse, though he confessed to
having missed taking various doses of the drug due to the
adverse effect it was having upon him. He had even gone
so far as to venture into the outside world once again,
and I feared not only for him, but for others if he should
relapse into his murderous state once more, especially as
he spoke quite vociferously of the continuing newspaper
exposure of the hunt for the Ripper. It was clear to me
that he could never be free of the demons that had
invaded his brain, the madness that had enveloped his
nature to the exclusion of any good that may have been
within his soul.*

*I had no choice, my dear son, you must believe that, for I
laboured long and hard, and gave thought to all manner
of means of helping him, while at the same time
protecting him and the world from his terrible curse, but
alas, could think of no other way. Upon each visit I read
more of the infernal and damnable words contained
within these pages, and gradually became more and
more convinced of the need to terminate the reign of
terror he had imposed upon the fair city of London. I
made note of the fact that he referred in the early pages
to a man he identified solely as 'T' and convinced him to
tell me the man's true name. It transpired that he had
been visiting a doctor for some time in relation to the
syphilitic infection, and I made a point of visiting the
man at his surgery. Without revealing my familial
connection to his patient, I was able through our
professional brotherhood to convince him to divulge
certain of his own thoughts. He assured me that
although he has always done his best for his patient, he*

had grave doubts as to the overall sanity of the man, and had actually entertained thoughts that he may have been connected to the Ripper case, though he never had any proof on which to base his assumption. I of course gave no credence to his ideas and left him after simply assuring him that I was nothing more than a concerned friend to the man. He accepted this without question, and we parted amicably.

As to end of the Ripper, I gradually increased the dosage of morphine until he was quite compliant. It would have been impossible to carry out what I intended from his own home, so, in the dead of night, I returned to his abode, and convinced him to come with me in my carriage, which I had driven myself, suitably attired as a nondescript cab driver, having first convinced him to write a note alluding to his desire to end his life, an easy matter in his heavily drugged condition. He allowed me to help him into the coach, where he soon fell into a deep sleep. Believe me my son, I had little stomach for that night's work, but knew that I had no choice if I were to protect the family, and his own, from the scandal and approbation that would surely have come our way if he were revealed as the Ripper. I drove to a quiet area near the great river Thames, where I assisted him from the carriage. He was totally unaware of where he was, and it was all he could do to walk, even aided by my helpful arm. He was no longer the feared and dastardly figure sought by all good-minded people, the sight of him in that state was of a pathetic, sad, and already dying man. Knowing that to be true gave me the strength to do what I had to do, and there, on the banks of the river, I administered his final dose of morphine, ensuring that

*he would feel no further pain. His collapse into
unconsciousness was rapid, and as soon as he slumped
upon the ground, I took a number of rocks from the
interior of the carriage, which I had brought specifically
for the purpose, and placed them in the pockets of his
coat, along with the note he had written. It was a simple
task to then force his inert body over the low wall, and
with a muffled splash, he tumbled into the dark waters of
the Thames.*

*I watched him sink below the surface, and I admit that
my eyes were awash with tears as he disappeared silently
from my sight for the last time. He was after all the fruit
of my loins, my blood flowed in his veins, and, had it not
been for the tainted side of his otherwise brilliant mind,
he might have been a most noble and excellent fellow.
Sadly, such was not the case, and his madness had now
brought me to this. Though I knew that I was now little
better than he, a murderer of a fellow human being, I felt
a great weight lift from me as he sank forever into the
murk of the filthy water. I comforted myself with the
knowledge that Jack the Ripper would never again stalk
the streets of Whitechapel, and that the stain of character
which had afflicted him would never be allowed to
reproduce itself in the form of his offspring.*

*I was in a sombre mood as I returned to my home that
night, and over the following days the newspapers
continued to shout for action by the constabulary in
apprehending the killer. The thought rose in my mind
that at some future date some poor innocent could be
arrested and charged with the crimes of the Ripper, and
I made a promise to myself that if that were to happen,
and an innocent man were to be found guilty, I would*

have no choice other than to reveal the existence of the journal, and place myself at the mercy of the judiciary. It is my fervent hope that such an eventuality never takes place, for then all I have done to protect those involved would have been in vain.

His body was discovered some days ago, floating near the Torpedo Works in Chiswick, though I had hoped it would remain immersed and undiscovered. It is to be hoped that the note is intact, and that he is believed to have been a suicide case. There will of course be an inquest, and I must make an effort to attend, as much as it will be difficult for me. I did after all attend upon him on occasions in the hospital, and it will not appear suspicious that I attend to discover the cause of the death of someone I knew. I just hope that I am not asked to give evidence, as it would be difficult for me to tell untruths under the oath.

It has been such a trial; you must try to understand my son. Had I allowed him to remain among us the danger to everyone would have been immense. Even to see him in an asylum with the possibility that someone might believe his rantings would have placed us all at risk. I had no choice. You must see that. It is better this way, for him, for us all. His name, and that of his family, and ours will not be sullied by the knowledge that he was the most vile killer to walk the streets of London, and, after all, there will be no more killing. His murderous reign is over, and peace will now fall upon the streets of Whitechapel once more. Given time, I am sure that the name of Jack the Ripper will fade from the people's memory, and the series of unsolved murders will fall

*into the category of a historical footnote. After all,
terrible though the crimes were, the victims were not of a
social class to command attention for any length of time,
and, were it not for the horrendous mutilations carried
out upon them, the murders would not have attracted
such attention as they have.*

*It is for me to live with my actions, and one day, when I
am face to face with He who is my maker, only then
shall I face true retribution for what I have done, though
rest assured my son, that it was not done lightly, or
without a sense of conscience. I shall be forever haunted,
not only by my own actions in ridding the world of he
who was the Ripper, but by the sight of his face, trusting
me to the last, as I administered that final, fatal dose of
the drug to him, and of the sound of his body as it
splashed into the waters of the Thames, and the
complete lack of recognition by him of what was finally
befalling him as he sank to his end.*

*These things will live with me until my own inevitable
demise, and I must conceal from all, even you my son,
all that I know of the facts of my involvement with the
case. Only after my own death will these pages, and my
notes be passed into your hands, and you will know the
whole sorry truth.*
*I shall make no further reference on this matter; my
confession is known unto God, and now, as you read
this, to you also. Judge me not too harshly, I beg you, and
my sole wish is that you keep this secret within your
heart for as long as you shall live, and, if you are blessed
with a son, let him find this in the way you have, so that
he may know, and be warned, that the blood of Jack the*

Ripper is mine, and yours, and will live forever in the veins of those who come after us, for I cannot blame his mother entirely, he was as much mine as hers, and I must bear some responsibility, he was of my seed.

I hope and pray that you are never placed in a position such as I have been, that you never have to fight your own conscience, never have to take the awful actions that have blighted what years I have left to me, but, if you do find the awful truth of my bloodline raising its head in any way, you will know why, and you alone must decide what must be done.

Tears were streaming down my face as I read this last, and most terrifying and revealing entry in the journal. These were not the words of Jack the Ripper; this was the final and most terribly moving confession of my great-grandfather, who, driven to despair by his conscience and his desire to 'do the right thing', to prevent further atrocities being committed had taken the most terrible and difficult decision to end the life of his own illegitimate son, to finally bring down the curtain on the tortured life of Jack the Ripper. There was so much that was tragic about his words, and so much that was erroneous in the light of history

I could almost see him, visiting the Ripper in those final days, keeping him drugged and compliant whilst he decided upon the course of action he would take. He must have exhibited great sympathy, earned the total trust of his patient, his son, the man who might have been a credit to his family but who was prevented from being so by fearful illness of the mind and body. It must have caused him such agonies of the mind to finally decide to end the life of one whom he had caused to be born into the world. I could even understand him believing that it was his responsibility and no-one else's to bring the Ripper to his final retribution on Earth. Yet, in the midst of such anguish, my great-grandfather had got something wrong. He thought that the Ripper would be forgotten, nothing more than a footnote in history. How wrong could he have been? Then there was the reference to the lack of importance of the victims. Burton Cleveland Cavendish was, after all a product of the society and the times into which he'd been born. To him, the deaths of a few prostitutes would have been appalling, but not so as to cause any significant ripples in the social order of the day, so it was perhaps natural for him to suppose as he did. If only he'd known how wrong he was!

Then again, I thought that even had he been able to see into the future, he would have acted exactly as he did, for in his mind he was protecting the family name, and to a man of his standing, that would of course have been paramount. Could I understand him? Of course. Did I agree with his actions? I wasn't sure then, and I'm still unsure. Could I, or perhaps you have taken the awful step of killing your own offspring in order to prevent them killing again, and to keep the secret of that shame within the family? I've asked myself that question so many times since those awful few days, and I still can't answer it honestly, even to myself.

As I sat in my study, with the fears and tribulations of the last three days at the forefront of my mind, I had to face that final point in my great-grandfather's last entry, was it possible that something in his genes had been imprinted on the male members of our family? Could I be carrying the same genetic defect of the mind in my own psychological make-up? Was I another Jack the Ripper in the making? I thought of John Ross. He was not of my great-grandfather's seed, yet he had displayed those same Ripper-like tendencies as the man who had written the terrible journal I'd just read. It was obvious to me that the defective gene (if one existed), must have come from the Ripper's mother, or at least have been passed through her. My great-grandfather wasn't privy to the kind of genetic information we have available to us today, so it would have been natural for him to think himself responsible for planting the 'demon seed' in his offspring.

I had to think that the genetic 'fault' lay with the Ripper's mother's side of the family and had somehow been passed to the unfortunate Ross. My own grandfather and father had never shown any such tendencies, and I certainly hadn't, so I was sure that I was safe from such a fate.

It was becoming late, the fog still lay like a shroud, and Sarah was coming home the next day. I had stayed up until the early hours of the morning and had completed my journey through the journal of Jack the Ripper ahead of the deadline I'd set myself earlier. Though I was still shaking from the emotional turmoil created by the words that almost seemed to breathe as they met my eyes from the surface of every page, I felt as if the worst were over. The trail had led to an almost inevitable conclusion, and there was little if anything left for me to fear. My great-grandfather had confessed to the murder of Jack the Ripper, yet I couldn't bring myself to condemn him, for he had possibly saved the lives of a number of other women by doing so. That the Ripper was my relative, albeit a distant one, would live with me for ever, as would my great-grandfather's words, but, despite all the unsettling and nerve-jangling episodes of the last three days and nights I now felt safe, as though there were nothing left in the journal that could harm me, or Sarah, or cause any further disturbance to my life.

I closed the book, the back-page rustling as it closed over the preceding pages, and the journal seemed to sigh with resignation as though its work were done. As I rose from the chair and made my weary way up to bed to grab a few precious hours of sleep, intending to be as fresh as I could be for Sarah's return the next night, I could have sworn, just for a moment, that a second faint shadow was keeping mine company as I trod the stairs to bed. But then, that couldn't have been, could it? I was safe, the journal was ended, the Ripper dead and buried, and the truth of my great-grandfather's involvement explained in full.

The warm feelings of safety and of mental equilibrium wrapped themselves around me as I climbed under the duvet and fell into a deep sleep. It would soon be morning, and I knew in my heart that the nightmare was over, and of course it *was* over, wasn't it?

FORTY-TWO
NOTHING IS EVER QUITE AS IT SEEMS

THE DOUBLE STRIKE of the blade into my chest literally took my breath away, as both lungs were punctured in rapid succession. I felt the blood begin to rise in my throat and tried to scream, but the scream was strangled at birth as the gleaming blade slashed viciously across my throat, severing the carotid artery, and my precious life-blood spurted like a horizontal shower from the resulting gash. My eyes clouded over, and I looked up to see the hideous grinning figure of the Ripper staring down at me with a look of intense satisfaction, and grim fascination on his face, as though he were savouring every second of my pain and confusion.

As I felt the last dregs of life draining from my almost lifeless body I tried to form the one word, 'Why?' but of course it wouldn't come. My voice was nothing more than a hissing gurgle as I felt my life ebbing away, becoming nothing, floating, joining with the writhing figures that seemed to materialize from the air around me, wrapping themselves around me, gathering me up, and lifting me above myself until I looked down and saw below me the lifeless corpse of what had once been me, with the haunting and hideous figure of the Ripper still hunched over the body. The killer looked up as though seeing the tableau being enacted above him and his lips peeled back in a grim rictus of a smile, and he laughed, a gruesome and hideous cacophonous laugh that felt as though it encompassed all the evil in the world, bringing it all to this one point in time and space, and the walls around the room shook as the laugh trailed away to nothing, and he looked up once more, and melted away into nothingness.

The things that were the spirits of the Ripper's victims welcomed me with an outpouring of screams and wailing, their agonies still tormenting them after over a century of death, for they were not at peace. They pulled at me, drawing me nearer and nearer to the ceiling, and I saw a vast portal begin to open where the ceiling should have been. Once through that doorway I knew that there'd be no turning back, and I would be trapped forever in the nether-world of the damned and restless souls, doomed to wander forever in the ether that surrounds the living world, forbidden the right to enjoy eternal rest.

As the formless shapes pulled harder and harder at the remnants of my soul, I fought back with everything I had, resolutely refusing to give myself up to sharing their fate. One of the things came so close to me that I could smell its fetid breath as it opened its mouth in front of me and the mouth became a huge maw that threatened to engulf me and carry me away into the void. I struggled against the thing that was pulling me into itself, and suddenly, as though I were being reborn into the world a loud scream escaped from my lips, the things surrounding me disappeared as quickly as they'd appeared and I was enveloped once again by the silent darkness of the night.

I was awake, though not awake, a sensation I'd felt before during the last few days, nothing seemed real, I didn't know what was real or what wasn't any more, and then, through the darkness I heard a familiar voice calling to me, softly at first, then louder, and louder, the intensity of the voice imploring me to return to the land of reality, to live again, to be whole.

"Robert, Robert my darling, can you hear me? Doctor, his eyelids are moving, I think he can hear me!"

It was Sarah, it was her voice, but it couldn't be, she wasn't due home until the next night, and what did she mean 'Doctor?' What doctor? This didn't make sense.

I felt as though someone was trying to peel my eyelids back, and then a piercing light flickered across my line of sight.

"You're right Mrs Cavendish," a voice said in what seemed to be the distance. "I do believe he's coming round."

"Oh, Robert, please, open your eyes my love, just let me know that you can hear me, anything, please, just give me a sign."

I felt Sarah take my hand in hers, and without really realising I was doing it, I squeezed her hand gently.

"Oh, thank God," I heard her say, and with a superhuman effort I slowly forced my eyes to open. Sure enough Sarah was sitting by the side of the bed, but it wasn't our bed. It was one of the all too familiar purely functional beds beloved of the National Health Service. I was in a hospital! But how? Why? I was confused, and it took more than a little effort to ask the simple question,

"What am I doing here?"

"Oh, my poor Robert," Sarah replied, "you've been here for two weeks, you were in a motor accident with your poor father.

You've been in a coma, and I've been here with you all the time my love."

I was more than confused by then, and I must have looked it, as Sarah continued.

"You must have been having some terrible dreams Robert, you've been screaming and shouting all manner of strange things, and you've even thought that Jack the Ripper was in the room with us."

I was about to say "But he was", when I suddenly realised that I must have been badly injured in the crash, and somehow in my delirium after whatever they'd done to put me back together, I'd hallucinated the whole thing. There was no journal, no great-uncle Jack the Ripper, and no curse upon the family. My great-grandfather had had nothing to do with the case, and I'd dreamed the whole thing in my own drug induced state.

As the days wore on I grew stronger, and Sarah, who loves me more than I have a right to expect from any person was a constant strength to me, never leaving my side, always there to hold my hand, to talk to me, even being the one to break the news that although I'd survived the crash, my father hadn't been so lucky. He was dead, as I'd known all along from my dream. The funeral had been held as I'd languished in the hospital; my brother having decided that to be the best course of action, as no-one knew if or when I'd come round.

Two weeks after waking in the hospital, and with most of my injuries reasonably healed, I was deemed well enough to leave the hospital. The doctors made me promise to spend at least a month resting at home before even thinking of returning to work, and I was still weak enough to readily agree to their request. Sarah drove us home, and I was elated at the prospect of sleeping in our own bed once more, of being able to hold her in my arms properly, and just being able to relax and begin to enjoy life once again. It was strange, but all my grieving for the loss of my father seemed to have been wrapped up in the dream state I'd lived through in the hospital. I reasoned that in a semi-conscious moment shortly after my admission I'd probably heard someone say that my father hadn't made it, and that perhaps that had been the trigger for the strange set of circumstances that had taken over my brain as I languished in that bed.

On the way home Sarah told me that her sister Jennifer had given birth to a beautiful baby boy, whom she and her husband had called Jack, and again I presumed that I had overheard that information as Sarah mentioned it to someone in the hospital, perhaps even to me, as she'd said that she'd spent many hours at my bedside simply holding my hand and talking to me as I'd lain asleep in a comatose state.

That first night at home was sheer bliss, Sarah held me close to her in bed, and with her arms around me I fell asleep in no time, and this time, there were no dreams, no nightmares, no visions or spirits to disturb my sleep. The next morning I awoke feeling bright and refreshed and ate the best breakfast I could remember eating for years. Sarah insisted that I sit and relax afterwards. She had nothing to do that day and would happily sit and keep me company.

She went to the bookcase and selected a novel for me, a Clive Cussler, she knew he was one of my favourites, and that I'd bought that particular book just before the accident, and therefore hadn't read it yet. She made sure I was comfortable with my feet up and a cup of coffee and seated herself in the chair opposite with a book of her own, and the morning began to pass in idyllic tranquillity.

At about eleven-thirty the telephone rang, and Sarah

quickly held her hand up to me in a signal that she'd get it. She rose and walked across the lounge to pick up the phone. I took little notice; it was probably her sister with news of little Jack. A minute or so later Sarah called to me from across the room.

"Robert, my darling, its David, your father's solicitor. Apparently your father left a strange package of incredibly old papers in his care to be passed to you after his funeral. He wants to know when you'll be well enough to go and pick it up......?"

EPILOGUE

Robert Cavendish died in 1998, aged just forty-two, and just two years after the car accident that claimed the life of his father. Though his wife Sarah devoted herself to his care after the accident he was never well enough to return to work, and his health, both physical and mental slowly deteriorated as time went by. She told her sister Jennifer that Robert was never quite the same again after receiving a package of his father's papers from his solicitor, but he would never talk about it. It still came as a surprise to his wife however when he was diagnosed with a brain tumour just six months before his death. It was inoperable, and spread rapidly, and Robert eventually died peacefully with Sarah at his side. As he lay in bed, his life slowly ebbing away, Sarah swears that Robert suddenly opened his eyes wide, look upwards towards the ceiling, and a strange look came over his face, followed by his last words, "They're here."

They'd discussed the aftermath of his death in detail upon his terminal illness being diagnosed. Sarah followed Roberts's last wishes to the letter, and he was buried near his father, with just family present. In accordance with his firm instructions Sarah emptied the safe in his study and lodged a sealed package she found there with Robert's solicitors, with instructions that it be passed to his nephew Jack upon his reaching the age of twenty-one. She had no idea what was in the package and Robert had expressly stated that she must never open it. She continues to live in the house she shared with Robert, though she has often remarked to her neighbour Mrs Armitage that she can sense a presence in the house, as though Robert is watching over her.

Robert's nephew Jack Thomas Reid is now ten years old, and the apple of his parent's eyes. He is a good-looking boy, and in many ways bears a striking resemblance to his uncle Robert. In the last twelve months however, the boy has begun to suffer from some strange behavioural problems and is fixated with the sight and smell of blood. His parents hope he will grow out of this odd characteristic, and Jack is currently undergoing therapy with a specialist child psychiatrist.

AUTHOR'S FOOTNOTE

Students of the Jack the Ripper phenomenon will doubtless form their own conclusions as to the identity of the Ripper, as depicted in this story, based on clues provided in this book. I would ask those who have studied the case for many years and who may have their own solution in mind to remember that this tale is nothing more than a fiction, rather than an attempt to throw new light on an old subject. The suspect I have used as my model for the Ripper may or may not have been the infamous Whitechapel murderer, and the tale related in these pages is simply the product of an author's imagination. Or....... is it?

ABOUT THE AUTHOR

Brian L Porter is a multiple award-winning, Amazon International bestselling author and poet with over twenty bestsellers to his name. He's best known for his successful Mersey Mystery series and his true life, bestselling Family of Rescue Dogs Series.

He also writes children's books as Harry Porter and romantic poetry as Juan Pablo Jalisco, (Of Aztecs and Conquistadors), another bestseller.

He is a grandfather, a former member of the Royal Air Force, is married to Juliet and together they live in the North of England, sharing their home with their canine family of nine rescued dogs.

To learn more about Brian L Porter and discover more Next Chapter authors, visit our website at www.nextchapter.pub.

Printed in Great Britain
by Amazon

17212099R00189